PETER PAN

PETER PAN

I dedicate this edition
of PETER PAN to
my daughter Laura,
with love.

PETER PAN

Illustrated by
GREG HILDEBRANDT
Story by J.M. Barrie

The Unicorn Publishing House
New Jersey

◆ ◆ ◆ ◆ ◆

Special thanks to Yoh Jinno, Joe Scrocco, Bill McGuire, Kathy Pizar, Bob Rebach, and the entire Unicorn staff

◆ ◆ ◆ ◆ ◆

Printing History 15 14 13 12 11 10 9 8 7 6 5 4 3 2

◆ ◆ ◆ ◆ ◆

Library of Congress Cataloging-in-Publication Data
Barrie, J.M. (James Matthew), 1860-1937.
Peter Pan.
Summary: The adventures of the three Darling children in Never-Never Land with Peter Pan, the boy who would not grow up.
(1. Fantasy) I. Hildebrandt, Greg, ill. II. Title.
PZ7.B27539Pd   1987c   (Fic)   87-10785

CAST OF CHARACTERS

Matthew McCann - Peter Pan
Jean L. Scrocco - Tinkerbell
Janeen Love - Mrs. Darling
John Enteman, Esq. - George Darling
Jessica Bystrak - Wendy Darling
Daniel Zugale - John Darling
Michael Lee Corso Jr. - Michael Darling
Vincent Colandrea - Captain James Hook
Russell A. Corso - Smee
Dennis Flynn - Cecco, Great Big Little Panther
Greg Hildebrandt - Alf Mason
Carl Drozdowicz - Robt. Mullins
Gene O'Brien - Gentleman Starkey
Brian McGee - Tootles
Robbie McCann - Curly
Matthew Zugale - Nibs
Alan Braun - Slightly
Justin Swigart - The Twins
Heidi Corso - Tiger Lily
Bill McGuire - Lean Wolf; Fairy
Krista Wetherill - Fairy
Dean Hansen - Fairy; Mermaid
Carol Colandrea - Mermaid
Mary Hildebrandt - Mermaid
Laura Hildebrandt - Mermaid
Judy McCann - Mermaid; Wendy, grown-up

Nana - Compliments of:
Gene and Lynne Sheninger

LIST OF ILLUSTRATIONS

CONTENTS

CHAPTER I

PETER BREAKS THROUGH

ll children, except one, grow up. They soon know that they will grow up, and the way Wendy knew was this. One day when she was two years old she was playing in a garden, and she plucked another flower and ran with it to her mother. I suppose she must have looked rather delightful, for Mrs. Darling put her hand to her heart and cried, "Oh, why can't you remain like this for ever!" This was all that passed between them on the subject, but henceforth Wendy knew that she must grow up. You always know after you are two. Two is the beginning of the end.

Of course they lived at 14, and until Wendy came her mother was the chief one. She was a lovely lady, with a romantic mind and such a sweet mocking mouth. Her romantic mind was like the tiny boxes, one within the other, that come from the puzzling East, however many you discover there is always one more; and her sweet mocking mouth had one kiss on it that Wendy could never get, though there it was, perfectly conspicuous in the right-hand corner.

The way Mr. Darling won her was this: the many gentlemen who had been boys when she was a girl discovered simultaneously that they loved her, and they all ran to her house to propose to her except Mr. Darling, who took a cab and nipped in first, and so he got her. He got all of her, except the innermost box and the kiss. He never knew about the box, and in time he gave up trying for the kiss. Wendy thought Napoleon could have got it, but I can picture him trying, and then going off in a passion, slamming the door.

Mr. Darling used to boast to Wendy that her mother not only loved him but respected him. He was one of those deep ones who know about stocks and shares. Of course no one really knows, but he quite seemed to know, and he often said stocks were up and shares were down in a way that would have made any woman respect him.

Mrs. Darling was married in white, and at first she kept the books perfectly, almost gleefully, as if it were a game, not so much as a Brussels sprout was missing; but by and by whole cauliflowers dropped out, and instead of them there were pictures of babies without faces. She drew them when she should have been totting up. They were Mrs. Darling's guesses.

Wendy came first, then John, then Michael.

For a week or two after Wendy came it was doubtful whether they would be able to keep her, as she was another mouth to feed. Mr. Darling was frightfully proud of her, but he was very honourable, and he sat on the edge of Mrs. Darling's bed, holding her hand and calculating expenses, while she looked at him imploringly. She wanted to risk it, come what might, but that was not his way; his way was with a pencil and a piece of paper, and if she confused him with suggestions he had to begin at the beginning again.

"Now don't interrupt," he would beg of her.

"I have one pound seventeen here, and two and six at the office; I can cut off my coffee at the office, say ten shillings, making two nine and six, with your eighteen and three makes three nine seven, with five naught naught in my cheque-book makes eight nine seven, — who is that moving? — eight nine seven, dot and carry seven — don't speak, my own — and the pound you lent to that man who came to the door — quiet, child — dot and carry child — there, you've done it! — did I say nine nine seven? yes, I said nine nine seven; the question is, can we try it for a year on nine nine seven?"

"Of course we can, George," she cried. But she was prejudiced in Wendy's favour, and he was really the grander character of the two.

"Remember mumps," he warned her almost threateningly, and off he went again. "Mumps one pound, that is what I have put down, but I daresay it will be more like thirty shillings — don't speak — measles one five, German measles half a guinea, makes two fifteen six — don't waggle your finger — whooping-cough, say fifteen shillings" — and so on it went, and it added up differently each time, but at last Wendy just got through, with mumps reduced to twelve six, and the two kinds of measles treated as one.

There was the same excitement over John, and Michael had even a narrower squeak; but both were kept, and soon, you might have seen the three of them going in a row to Miss Fulsom's Kindergarten school, accompanied by their nurse.

Mrs. Darling loved to have everything just so, and Mr. Darling had a passion for being exactly like his neighbours; so, of course, they had a nurse. As they were poor, owing to the amount of milk the children drank, this nurse was a prim Newfoundland dog, called Nana, who had belonged to no one in particular until the Darlings engaged her. She had always thought children important, however, and the Darlings had become acquainted with her in Kensington Gardens, where she spent most of her spare time peeping into perambulators, and was much hated by careless nursemaids, whom she followed to their homes and complained of to their mistresses. She proved to be quite a treasure of a nurse. How thorough she was at bath-time, and up at any moment of the night if one of her charges made the slightest cry. Of course her kennel was in the nursery. She had a genius for knowing when a cough is a thing to have no patience with and when it needs stocking round your throat. She believed to her last day in old-fashioned remedies like rhubarb leaf, and made sounds of contempt over all this new-fangled talk about germs, and so on. It was a lesson in propriety to see her escorting the children to school, walking sedately by their side when they were well behaved, and butting them back into line if they strayed. On John's footer days she never once forgot his sweater, and she usually carried an umbrella in her mouth in case of rain. There is a room in the basement of Miss Fulsom's school where the nurses wait. They sat on forms, while Nana lay on the floor, but that was the only difference. They affected to ignore her as of an inferior social status to themselves, and she despised their light talk. She resented visits to the nursery from Mrs. Darling's friends, but if they did come she first whipped off Michael's pinafore and put him into the one with blue braiding, and smoothed out Wendy and made a dash at John's hair.

No nursery could possibly have been conducted more correctly, and Mr. Darling knew it, yet he sometimes wondered uneasily whether the neighbours talked.

He had his position in the city to consider.

Nana also troubled him in another way. He had sometimes a feeling that she did not admire him. "I know she admires you tremendously, George," Mrs. Darling would assure him, and then she would sign to the children to be specially nice to father. Lovely dances followed, in which the only other servant, Liza, was sometimes allowed to join. Such a midget she looked in her long skirt and maid's cap, though she had sworn, when engaged, that she would never see ten again. The gaiety of those romps! And gayest of all was Mrs. Darling, who would pirouette so wildly that all you could see of her was the kiss, and then if you had dashed at her you might have got it. There never was a simpler happier family until the coming of Peter Pan.

Mrs. Darling first heard of Peter when she was tidying up her children's minds. It is the nightly custom of every good mother after her children are asleep to rummage in their minds and put things straight for next morning, repacking into their proper places the many articles that have wandered during the day. If you could keep awake (but of course you can't) you would see your own mother doing this, and you would find it very interesting to watch her. It is quite like tidying up drawers. You would see her on her knees, I expect, lingering humorously over some of your contents, wondering where on earth you had picked this thing up, making discoveries sweet and not so sweet, pressing this to her cheek as if it were as nice as a kitten, and hurriedly stowing that out of sight. When you wake in the morning, the naughtinesses and evil passions with which you went to bed have been folded up small and placed at the bottom of your mind, and on the top, beautifully aired, are spread out your prettier thoughts, ready for you to put on.

I don't know whether you have ever seen a map of a person's mind. Doctors sometimes draw maps of other parts of you, and your own map can become intensely interesting, but catch them trying to draw a map of a child's mind, which is not only confused, but keeps going round all the time. There are zigzag lines on it, just like your temperature on a card, and these are probably roads in the island, for the Neverland is always more or less an island, with astonishing splashes of colour here and there, and coral reefs and rakish-looking craft in the offing, and savages and lonely lairs, and gnomes who are mostly tailors, and caves through which a river runs, and princes with six elder brothers, and a hut fast going to decay, and one very small old lady with a hooked nose. It would be an easy map if that were all, but there is also first day at school, religion, fathers, the round pond, needle-work, murders, hangings, verbs that take the dative, chocolate pudding day, getting into braces, say ninety-nine, threepence for pulling out your tooth yourself, and so on, and either these are part of the island or they are another map showing through, and it is all rather confusing, especially as nothing will stand still.

Of course the Neverlands vary a good deal. John's, for instance, had a lagoon with flamingoes flying over it at which John was shooting, while Michael, who was very small, had a flamingo with lagoons flying over it. John lived in a boat turned upside down on the sands, Michael in a wigwam, Wendy in a house of leaves deftly sewn together. John had no friends, Michael had friends at night, Wendy had a pet wolf forsaken by its parents. But on the whole the Neverlands have a family resemblance, and if they stood still in a row you could say of them that they have each other's nose, and so forth. On these magic shores children at play are for ever beaching their coracles. We too have been there; we can still hear the sound of the surf, though we shall land no more.

Of all delectable islands the Neverland is the snuggest and most compact, not large and sprawly, you know, with tedious distances between one adventure and another, but nicely crammed. When you play at it by day with the chairs and tablecloth, it is not in the least alarming, but in the two minutes before you go to sleep it becomes very nearly real. That is why there are night-lights.

Occasionally in her travels through her children's minds Mrs. Darling found things she could not understand, and of these quite the most perplexing was the word Peter. She knew of no Peter, and yet he was here and there in John and Michael's minds, while Wendy's began to be scrawled all over with him. The name stood out in bolder letters than any of the other words, and as Mrs. Darling gazed she felt that it had an oddly cocky appearance.

"Yes, he is rather cocky," Wendy admitted with regret. Her mother had been questioning her.

"But who is he, my pet?"

"He is Peter Pan, you know, mother."

At first Mrs. Darling did not know, but after thinking back into her childhood she just remembered a Peter Pan who was said to live with the fairies. There were odd stories about him, as that when children died he went part of the way with them, so that they should not be frightened. She had believed in him at the time, but now that she was married and full of sense she quite doubted whether there was any such person.

"Besides," she said to Wendy, "he would be grown up by this time."

"Oh no, he isn't grown up," Wendy assured her confidently, "and he is just my size." She meant that he was her size in both mind and body; she didn't know how she knew it, she just knew it.

Mrs. Darling consulted Mr. Darling, but he smiled pooh-pooh. "Mark my words," he said, "it is some nonsense Nana has been putting into their heads; just the sort of idea a dog would have. Leave it alone, and it will blow over."

But it would not blow over, and soon the troublesome boy gave Mrs. Darling quite a shock.

Children have the strangest adventures without being troubled by them. For instance, they may remember to mention, a week after the event happened, that when they were in the wood they met their dead father and had a game with him. It was in this casual way that Wendy one morning made a disquieting revelation. Some leaves of a tree had been found on the nursery floor, which certainly were not there when the children went to bed, and Mrs. Darling was puzzling over them when Wendy said with a tolerant smile:

"I do believe it is that Peter again!"

"Whatever do you mean, Wendy?"

"It is so naughty of him not to wipe," Wendy said, sighing. She was a tidy child.

She explained in quite a matter-of-fact way that she thought Peter sometimes came to the nursery in the night and sat on the foot of her bed and played on his pipes to her. Unfortunately she never woke, so she didn't know how she knew, she just knew.

"What nonsense you talk, precious! No one can get into the house without knocking."

"I think he comes in by the window," she said.

"My love, it is three floors up."

"Weren't the leaves at the foot of the window, mother?"

It was quite true; the leaves had been found very near the window.

Mrs. Darling did not know what to think, for it all seemed so natural to Wendy that you could not dismiss it by saying she had been dreaming.

"My child," the mother cried, "why did you not tell me of this before?"

"I forgot," said Wendy lightly. She was in a hurry to get her breakfast.

Oh, surely she must have been dreaming.

But, on the other hand, there were the leaves. Mrs. Darling examined them carefully; they were skeleton leaves, but she was sure they did not come from any tree that grew in England. She crawled about the floor, peering at it with a candle for marks of a strange foot. She rattled the poker up the chimney and tapped the walls. She let down a tape from the window to the pavement, and it was a sheer drop of thirty feet, without so much as a spout to climb up by.

Certainly Wendy had been dreaming.

But Wendy had not been dreaming, as the very next night showed, the night on which the extraordinary adventures of these children may be said to have begun.

On the night we speak of all the children were once more in bed. It happened to be Nana's evening off, and Mrs. Darling had bathed them and sung to them till one by one they had let go her hand and slid away into the land of sleep.

All were looking so safe and cosy that she smiled at her fears now and sat down tranquilly by the fire to sew.

It was something for Michael, who on his birthday was getting into shirts. The fire was warm, however, and the nursery dimly lit by three night-lights, and presently the sewing lay on Mrs. Darling's lap. Then her head nodded, oh, so gracefully. She was asleep. Look at the four of them, Wendy and Michael over there, John here, and Mrs. Darling by the fire. There should have been a fourth night-light.

While she slept she had a dream. She dreamt that the Neverland had come too near and that a strange boy had broken through from it. He did not alarm her, for she thought she had seen him before in the faces of many women who have no children. Perhaps he is to be found in the faces of some mothers also. But in her dream he had rent the film that obscures the Neverland, and she saw Wendy and John and Michael peeping through the gap.

The dream by itself would have been a trifle, but while she was dreaming the window of the nursery blew open, and a boy did drop on the floor. He was accompanied by a strange light, no bigger than your fist, which darted about the room like a living thing, and I think it must have been this light that wakened Mrs. Darling.

She started up with a cry, and saw the boy, and somehow she knew at once that he was Peter Pan. If you or I or Wendy had been there we should have seen that he was very like Mrs. Darling's kiss. He was a lovely boy, clad in skeleton leaves and the juices that ooze out of trees, but the most entrancing thing about him was that he had all his first teeth. When he saw she was a grown-up, he gnashed the little pearls at her.

CHAPTER II

THE SHADOW

rs. Darling screamed, and, as if in answer to a bell, the door opened, and Nana entered, returned from her evening out. She growled and sprang at the boy, who leapt lightly through the window. Again Mrs. Darling screamed, this time in distress for him, for she thought he was killed, and she ran down into the street to look for his little body, but it was not there; and she looked up, and in the black night she could see nothing but what she thought was a shooting star.

She returned to the nursery, and found Nana with something in her mouth, which proved to be the boy's shadow. As he leapt at the window Nana had closed it quickly, too late to catch him, but his shadow had not had time to get out; slam went the window and snapped it off.

You may be sure Mrs. Darling examined the shadow carefully, but it was quite the ordinary kind.

Nana had no doubt of what was the best thing to do with this shadow. She hung it out at the window, meaning "He is sure to come back for it; let us put it where he can get it easily without disturbing the children."

But unfortunately Mrs. Darling could not leave it hanging out at the window, it looked so like the washing and lowered the whole tone of the house. She thought of showing it to Mr. Darling, but he was totting up winter great-coats for John and Michael, with a wet towel round his head to keep his brain clear, and it seemed a shame to trouble him; besides, she knew exactly what he would say: "It all comes of having a dog for a nurse."

She decided to roll the shadow up and put it away carefully in a drawer, until a fitting opportunity came for telling her husband. Ah me!

The opportunity came a week later, on that never-to-be-forgotten Friday. Of course it was a Friday.

"I ought to have been specially careful on a Friday," she used to say afterwards to her husband, while perhaps Nana was on the other side of her, holding her hand.

"No, no," Mr. Darling always said, "I am responsible for it all. I, George Darling, did it. *Mea culpa, mea culpa.*" He had had a classical education.

They sat thus night after night recalling that fatal Friday, till every detail of it was stamped on their brains and came through on the other side like the faces on a bad coinage.

"If only I had not accepted that invitation to dine at 27," Mrs. Darling said.

"If only I had not poured my medicine into Nana's bowl," said Mr. Darling.

"If only I had pretended to like the medicine," was what Nana's wet eyes said.

"My liking for parties, George."

"My fatal gift of humour, dearest."

"My touchiness about trifles, dear master and mistress."

Then one or more of them would break down altogether; Nana at the thought, "It's true, it's true, they ought not to have had a dog for a nurse." Many a time it was Mr. Darling who put the handkerchief to Nana's eyes.

"That fiend!" Mr. Darling would cry, and Nana's bark was the echo of it, but Mrs. Darling never upbraided Peter; there was something in the right-hand corner of her mouth that wanted her not to call Peter names.

They would sit there in the empty nursery, recalling fondly every smallest detail of that dreadful evening. It had begun so uneventfully, so precisely like a hundred other evenings, with Nana putting on the water for Michael's bath and carrying him to it on her back.

"I won't go to bed," he had shouted, like one who still believed that he had the last word on the subject, "I won't, I won't. Nana, it isn't six o'clock yet. Oh dear, oh dear, I shan't love you any more, Nana. I tell you I won't be bathed, I won't, I won't!"

Then Mrs. Darling had come in, wearing her white evening-gown. She had dressed early because Wendy so loved to see her in her evening-gown, with the necklace George had given her. She was wearing Wendy's bracelet on her arm; she had asked for the loan of it. Wendy so loved to lend her bracelet to her mother.

She had found her two older children playing at being herself and father on the occasion of Wendy's birth, and John was saying:

"I am happy to inform you, Mrs. Darling, that you are now a mother," in just such a tone as Mr. Darling himself may have used on the real occasion.

Wendy had danced with joy, just as the real Mrs. Darling must have done.

Then John was born, with the extra pomp that he conceived due to the birth of a male, and Michael came from his bath to ask to be born also, but John said brutally that they did not want any more.

Michael had nearly cried. "Nobody wants me," he said, and of course the lady in evening-dress could not stand that.

"I do," she said, "I so want a third child."

"Boy or girl?" asked Michael, not too hopefully.

"Boy."

Then he had leapt into her arms. Such a little thing for Mr. and Mrs. Darling and Nana to recall now, but not so little if that was to be Michael's last night in the nursery.

They go on with their recollections.

"It was then that I rushed in like a tornado, wasn't it?" Mr. Darling would say, scorning himself; and indeed he had been like a tornado.

Perhaps there was some excuse for him. He, too, had been dressing for the party, and all had gone well with him until he came to his tie. It is an astounding thing to have to tell, but this man, though he knew about stocks and shares, had no real mastery of his tie. Sometimes the thing yielded to him without a contest, but there were occasions when it would have been better for the house if he had swallowed his pride and used a made-up tie.

This was such an occasion. He came rushing into the nursery with the crumpled little brute of a tie in his hand.

"Why, what is the matter, father dear?"

"Matter!" he yelled; he really yelled. "This tie, it will not tie." He became dangerously sarcastic. "Not round my neck! Round the bed-post! Oh yes, twenty times have I made it up round the bed-post, but round my neck, no! Oh dear no! begs to be excused!"

He thought Mrs. Darling was not sufficiently impressed, and he went on sternly, "I warn you of this, mother, that unless this tie is round my neck we don't go out to dinner to-night, and if I don't go out to dinner to-night, I never go to the office again, and if I don't go to the office again, you and I starve, and our children will be flung into the streets."

Even then Mrs. Darling was placid. "Let me try, dear," she said, and indeed that was what he had come to ask her to do, and with her nice cool hands she tied his tie for him, while the children stood around to see their fate decided. Some men would have resented her being able to do it so easily, but Mr. Darling was far too fine a nature for that; he thanked her carelessly, at once forgot his rage, and in another moment was dancing round the room with Michael on his back.

"How wildly we romped!" says Mrs. Darling now, recalling it.

"Our last romp!" Mr. Darling groaned.

"O George, do you remember Michael suddenly said to me, 'How did you get to know me, mother?' "

"I remember!"

"They were rather sweet, don't you think, George?"

"And they were ours, ours! and now they are gone."

The romp had ended with the appearance of Nana, and most unluckily Mr. Darling collided against her, covering his trousers with hairs. They were not only new trousers, but they were the first he had ever had with braid on them, and he had to bite his lip to prevent the tears coming. Of course Mrs. Darling brushed him, but he began to talk again about its being a mistake to have a dog for a nurse.

"George, Nana is a treasure."

"No doubt, but I have an uneasy feeling at times that she looks upon the children as puppies."

"Oh no, dear one, I feel sure she knows they have souls."

"I wonder," Mr. Darling said thoughtfully, "I wonder." It was an opportunity, his wife felt, for telling him about the boy. At first he pooh-poohed the story, but he became thoughtful when she showed him the shadow.

"It is nobody I know," he said, examining it carefully, "but he does look a scoundrel."

"We were still discussing it, you remember," says Mr. Darling, "when Nana came in with Michael's medicine. You will never carry the bottle in your mouth again, Nana, and it is all my fault."

Strong man though he was, there is no doubt that he had behaved rather foolishly over the medicine. If he had a weakness, it was for thinking that all his life he had taken medicine boldly, and so now, when

Michael dodged the spoon in Nana's mouth, he had said reprovingly, "Be a man, Michael."

"Won't; won't!" Michael cried naughtily. Mrs. Darling left the room to get a chocolate for him, and Mr. Darling thought this showed want of firmness.

"Mother, don't pamper him," he called after her. "Michael, when I was your age I took medicine without a murmur. I said 'Thank you, kind parents, for giving me bottles to make me well.' "

He really thought this was true, and Wendy, who was now in her night-gown, believed it also, and she said, to encourage Michael, "That medicine you sometimes take, father, is much nastier, isn't it?"

"Ever so much nastier," Mr. Darling said bravely, "and I would take it now as an example to you, Michael, if I hadn't lost the bottle."

He had not exactly lost it; he had climbed in the dead of night to the top of the wardrobe and hidden it there. What he did not know was that the faithful Liza had found it, and put it back on his wash-stand.

"I know where it is, father," Wendy cried, always glad to be of service. "I'll bring it," and she was off before he could stop her. Immediately his spirits sank in the strangest way.

"John," he said, shuddering, "it's most beastly stuff. It's that nasty, sticky, sweet kind."

"It will soon be over, father," John said cheerily, and then in rushed Wendy with the medicine in a glass.

"I have been as quick as I could," she panted.

"You have been wonderfully quick," her father retorted, with a vindictive politeness that was quite thrown away upon her. "Michael first," he said doggedly.

"Father first," said Michael, who was of a suspicious nature.

"I shall be sick, you know," Mr. Darling said threateningly.

"Come on, father," said John.

"Hold your tongue, John," his father rapped out.

Wendy was quite puzzled. "I thought you took it quite easily, father."

"That is not the point," he retorted. "The point is, that there is more in my glass than in Michael's spoon." His proud heart was nearly bursting. "And it isn't fair; I would say it though it were with my last breath; it isn't fair."

"Father, I am waiting," said Michael coldly.

"It's all very well to say you are waiting; so am I waiting."

"Father's a cowardy custard."

"So are you a cowardy custard."

"I'm not frightened."

"Neither am I frightened."

"Well, then, take it."

"Well, then, you take it."

Wendy had a splendid idea. "Why not both take it at the same time?"

"Certainly," said Mr. Darling. "Are you ready, Michael?"

Wendy gave the words, one, two, three, and Michael took his medicine, but Mr. Darling slipped his behind his back.

There was a yell of rage from Michael, and "O father!" Wendy exclaimed.

"What do you mean by 'O father'?" Mr. Darling demanded. "Stop that row, Michael. I meant to take mine, but I — I missed it."

It was dreadful the way all the three were looking at him, just as if they did not admire him. "Look here, all of you," he said entreatingly, as soon as Nana had gone into the bathroom, "I have just thought of a splendid joke. I shall pour my medicine into Nana's bowl, and she will drink it, thinking it is milk!"

It was the colour of milk; but the children did not have their father's sense of humour, and they looked at him reproachfully as he poured the medicine into Nana's bowl. "What fun!" he said doubtfully, and they did not dare expose him when Mrs. Darling and Nana returned.

"Nana, good dog," he said, patting her, "I have put a little milk into your bowl, Nana."

Nana wagged her tail, ran to the medicine, and began lapping it. Then she gave Mr. Darling such a look, not an angry look: she showed him the great red tear that makes us so sorry for noble dogs, and crept into her kennel.

Mr. Darling was frightfully ashamed of himself, but he would not give in. In a horrid silence Mrs. Darling smelt the bowl. "O George," she said, "it's your medicine!"

"It was only a joke," he roared, while she comforted her boys, and Wendy hugged Nana. "Much good," he said bitterly, "my wearing myself to the bone trying to be funny in this house."

And still Wendy hugged Nana. "That's right," he shouted. "Coddle her! Nobody coddles me. Oh dear no! I am only the breadwinner, why should I be coddled — why, why, why!"

"George," Mrs. Darling entreated him, "not so loud; the servants will hear you." Somehow they had got into the way of calling Liza the servants.

"Let them!" he answered recklessly. "Bring in the whole world. But I refuse to allow that dog to lord it in my nursery for an hour longer."

The children wept, and Nana ran to him beseechingly, but he waved her back. He felt he was a strong man again. "In vain, in vain," he cried; "the proper place for you is the yard, and there you go to be tied up this instant."

"George, George," Mrs. Darling whispered, "remember what I told you about that boy."

Alas, he would not listen. He was determined to show who was master in that house, and when commands would not draw Nana from the kennel, he lured her out of it with honeyed words, and seizing her roughly, dragged her from the nursery. He was ashamed of himself, and yet he did it. It was all owing to his too affectionate nature, which craved for admiration. When he had tied her up in the back-yard, the wretched father went and sat in the passage, with his knuckles to his eyes.

In the meantime Mrs. Darling had put the children to bed in unwonted silence and lit their night-lights. They could hear Nana barking, and John whimpered, "It is because he is chaining her up in the yard," but Wendy was wiser.

"That is not Nana's unhappy bark," she said, little guessing what was about to happen; "that is her bark when she smells danger."

Danger!

"Are you sure, Wendy?"

"Oh yes."

Mrs. Darling quivered and went to the window. It was securely fastened. She looked out, and the night was peppered with stars. They were crowding round the house, as if curious to see what was to take place there, but she did not notice this, nor that one or two of the smaller ones winked at her. Yet a nameless fear clutched at her heart and made her cry, "Oh, how I wish that I wasn't going to a party to-night!"

Even Michael, already half asleep, knew that she was perturbed, and he asked, "Can anything harm us, mother, after the night-lights are lit?"

"Nothing, precious," she said; "they are the eyes a mother leaves behind her to guard her children."

She went from bed to bed singing enchantments over them, and little Michael flung his arms round her. "Mother," he cried, "I'm glad of you." They were the last words she was to hear from him for a long time.

No. 27 was only a few yards distant, but there had been a slight fall of snow, and Father and Mother Darling picked their way over it deftly not to soil their shoes. They were already the only persons in the street, and all the stars were watching them. Stars are beautiful, but they may not take an active part in anything, they must just look on forever. It is a punishment put on them for something they did so long ago that no star now knows what it was. So the older ones have become glassy-eyed and seldom speak (winking is the star language), but the little ones still wonder. They are not really friendly to Peter, who has a mischievous way of stealing up behind them and trying to blow them out; but they are so fond of fun that they were on his side to-night, and anxious to get the grown-ups out of the way. So as soon as the door of 27 closed on Mr. and Mrs. Darling there was a commotion in the firmament, and the smallest of all the stars in the Milky Way screamed out:

"Now, Peter!"

CHAPTER III

COME AWAY, COME AWAY!

or a moment after Mr. and Mrs. Darling left the house the night-lights by the beds of the three children continued to burn clearly. They were awfully nice little night-lights, and one cannot help wishing that they could have kept awake to see Peter; but Wendy's light blinked and gave such a yawn that the other two yawned also, and before they could close their mouths all the three went out.

There was another light in the room now, a thousand times brighter than the night-lights, and in the time we have taken to say this, it has been in all the drawers in the nursery, looking for Peter's shadow, rummaged the wardrobe and turned every pocket inside out. It was not really a light; it made this light by flashing about so quickly, but when it came to rest for a second you saw it was a fairy, no longer than your hand, but still growing. It was a girl called Tinker Bell exquisitely gowned in a skeleton leaf, cut low and square, through which her figure could be seen to the best advantage. She was slightly inclined to *embonpoint.*

A moment after the fairy's entrance the window was blown open by the breathing of the little stars, and Peter dropped in. He had carried Tinker Bell part of the way, and his hand was still messy with the fairy dust.

"Tinker Bell," he called softly, after making sure that the children were asleep. "Tink, where are you?" She was in a jug for the moment, and liking it extremely; she had never been in a jug before.

"Oh, do come out of that jug, and tell me, do you know where they put my shadow?"

The loveliest tinkle as of golden bells answered him. It is the fairy

language. You ordinary children can never hear it, but if you were to hear it you would know that you had heard it once before.

Tink said that the shadow was in the big box. She meant the chest of drawers, and Peter jumped at the drawers, scattering their contents to the floor with both hands, as kings toss ha'pence to the crowd. In a moment he had recovered his shadow, and in his delight he forgot that he had shut Tinker Bell up in the drawer.

If he thought at all, but I don't believe he ever thought, it was that he and his shadow, when brought near each other, would join like drops of water, and when they did not he was appalled. He tried to stick it on with soap from the bathroom, but that also failed. A shudder passed through Peter, and he sat on the floor and cried.

His sobs woke Wendy, and she sat up in bed. She was not alarmed to see a stranger crying on the nursery floor; she was only pleasantly interested.

"Boy," she said courteously, "why are you crying?"

Peter could be exceedingly polite also, having learned the grand manner at fairy ceremonies, and he rose and bowed to her beautifully. She was much pleased, and bowed beautifully to him from the bed.

"What's your name?" he asked.

"Wendy Moira Angela Darling," she replied with some satisfaction. "What's your name?"

"Peter Pan."

She was already sure that he must be Peter, but it did seem a comparatively short name.

"Is that all?"

"Yes," he said rather sharply. He felt for the first time that it was a shortish name.

"I'm so sorry," said Wendy Moira Angela.

"It doesn't matter," Peter gulped.

She asked where he lived.

"Second to the right," said Peter, "and then straight on till morning."

"What a funny address!"

Peter had a sinking. For the first time he felt that perhaps it was a funny address.

"No, it isn't," he said.

"I mean," Wendy said nicely, remembering that she was hostess, "is that what they put on the letters?"

He wished she had not mentioned letters.

"Don't get any letters," he said contemptuously.

"But your mother gets letters?"

"Don't have a mother," he said. Not only had he no mother, but he had not the slightest desire to have one. He thought them very over-rated persons. Wendy, however, felt at once that she was in the presence of a tragedy.

"O Peter, no wonder you were crying," she said, and got out of bed and ran to him.

"I wasn't crying about mothers," he said rather indignantly. "I was crying because I can't get my shadow to stick on. Besides, I wasn't crying."

"It has come off?"

"Yes."

Then Wendy saw the shadow on the floor, looking so draggled, and she was frightfully sorry for Peter. "How awful!" she said, but she could not help smiling when she saw that he had been trying to stick it on with soap. How exactly like a boy!

Fortunately she knew at once what to do. "It must be sewn on," she said, just a little patronisingly.

"What's sewn?" he asked.

"You're dreadfully ignorant."

"No, I'm not."

But she was exulting in his ignorance. "I shall sew it on for you, my little man," she said, though he was as tall as herself, and she got out her house-wife, and sewed the shadow on to Peter's foot.

"I daresay it will hurt a little," she warned him.

"Oh, I shan't cry," said Peter, who was already of opinion that he had never cried in his life. And he clenched his teeth and did not cry, and soon his shadow was behaving properly, though still a little creased.

"Perhaps I should have ironed it," Wendy said thoughtfully, but Peter, boylike, was indifferent to appearances, and he was now jumping about in the wildest glee. Alas, he had already forgotten that he owed his bliss to Wendy. He thought he had attached the shadow himself. "How clever I am!" he crowed rapturously, "oh, the cleverness of me!"

It is humiliating to have to confess that this conceit of Peter was one of his most fascinating qualities. To put it with brutal frankness, there never was a cockier boy.

But for the moment Wendy was shocked. "You conceit," she exclaimed, with frightful sarcasm; "of course I did nothing!"

"You did a little," Peter said carelessly, and continued to dance.

"A little!" she replied with hauteur. "If I am no use I can at least withdraw," and she sprang in the most dignified way into bed and covered her face with the blankets.

To induce her to look up he pretended to be going away, and when this failed he sat on the end of the bed and tapped her gently with his foot. "Wendy," he said, "don't withdraw. I can't help crowing, Wendy, when I'm pleased with myself." Still she would not look up, though she was listening eagerly. "Wendy," he continued, in a voice that no woman has ever yet been able to resist, "Wendy, one girl is more use than twenty boys."

Now Wendy was every inch a woman, though there were not very many inches, and she peeped out of the bed-clothes.

"Do you really think so, Peter?"

"Yes, I do."

"I think it's perfectly sweet of you," she declared, "and I'll get up again," and she sat with him on the side of the bed. She also said she would give him a kiss if he liked, but Peter did not know what she meant, and he held out his hand expectantly.

"Surely you know what a kiss is?" she asked, aghast.

"I shall know when you give it to me," he replied stiffly, and not to hurt his feelings she gave him a thimble.

"Now," said he, "shall I give you a kiss?" and she replied with a slight primness, "If you please." She made herself rather cheap by inclining her face toward him, but he merely dropped an acorn button into her hand, so she slowly returned her face to where it had been before, and said nicely that she would wear his kiss on the chain round her neck. It was lucky that she did put it on that chain, for it was afterwards to save her life.

When people in our set are introduced, it is customary for them to ask each other's age, and so Wendy, who always liked to do the correct thing, asked Peter how old he was. It was not really a happy question to ask him; it was like an examination paper that asks grammar, when what you want to be asked is Kings of England.

"I don't know," he replied uneasily, "but I am quite young." He really knew nothing about it, he had merely suspicions, but he said at a venture, "Wendy, I ran away the day I was born."

Wendy was quite surprised, but interested; and she indicated in the charming drawing-room manner, by a touch on her night-gown, that he could sit nearer her.

"It was because I heard father and mother," he explained in a low voice, "talking about what I was to be when I became a man." He was extraordinarily agitated now. "I don't want ever to be a man," he said with passion. "I want always to be a little boy and to have fun. So I ran away to Kensington Gardens and lived a long long time among the fairies."

She gave him a look of the most intense admiration, and he thought it was because he had run away, but it was really because he knew fairies. Wendy had lived such a home life that to know fairies struck her as quite delightful. She poured out questions about them, to his surprise, for they were rather a nuisance to him, getting in his way and so on, and indeed he sometimes had to give them a hiding. Still, he liked them on the whole, and he told her about the beginning of fairies.

"You see, Wendy, when the first baby laughed for the first time, its laugh broke into a thousand pieces, and they all went skipping about, and that was the beginning of fairies."

Tedious talk this, but being a stay-at-home she liked it.

"And so," he went on good-naturedly, "there ought to be one fairy for every boy and girl."

"Ought to be? Isn't there?"

"No. You see children know such a lot now, they soon don't believe in fairies, and every time a child says, 'I don't believe in fairies,' there is a fairy somewhere that falls down dead."

Really, he thought they had now talked enough about fairies, and it struck him that Tinker Bell was keeping very quiet. "I can't think where she has gone to," he said, rising, and he called Tink by name. Wendy's heart went flutter with a sudden thrill.

"Peter," she cried, clutching him, "you don't mean to tell me that there is a fairy in this room!"

"She was here just now," he said a little impatiently. "You don't hear her, do you?" and they both listened.

"The only sound I hear," said Wendy, "is like a tinkle of bells."

"Well, that's Tink, that's the fairy language. I think I hear her too."

The sound came from the chest of drawers, and Peter made a merry face. No one could ever look quite so merry as Peter, and the loveliest of gurgles was his laugh. He had his first laugh still.

"Wendy," he whispered gleefully, "I do believe I shut her up in the drawer!"

He let poor Tink out of the drawer, and she flew about the nursery screaming with fury. "You shouldn't say such things," Peter retorted. "Of course I'm very sorry, but how could I know you were in the drawer?"

Wendy was not listening to him. "O Peter," she cried, "if she would only stand still and let me see her!"

"They hardly ever stand still," he said, but for one moment Wendy saw the romantic figure come to rest on the cuckoo clock. "O the lovely!" she cried, though Tink's face was still distorted with passion.

"Tink," said Peter amiably, "this lady says she wishes you were her fairy."

Tinker Bell answered insolently.

"What does she say, Peter?"

He had to translate. "She is not very polite. She says you are a great ugly girl, and that she is my fairy."

He tried to argue with Tink. "You know you can't be my fairy, Tink, because I am a gentleman and you are a lady."

To this Tink replied in these words, "You silly ass," and disappeared into the bathroom. "She is quite a common fairy," Peter explained apologetically, "she is called Tinker Bell because she mends the pots and kettles."

They were together in the armchair by this time, and Wendy plied him with more questions.

"If you don't live in Kensington Gardens now ——— "

"Sometimes I do still."

"But where do you live mostly now?"

"With the lost boys."

"Who are they?"

"They are the children who fall out of their perambulators when the nurse is looking the other way. If they are not claimed in seven days they are sent far away to the Neverland to defray expenses. I'm captain."

"What fun it must be!"

"Yes," said cunning Peter, "but we are rather lonely. You see we have no female companionship."

"Are none of the others girls?"

"Oh no; girls, you know, are much too clever to fall out of their prams."

This flattered Wendy immensely. "I think," she said, "it is perfectly lovely the way you talk about girls; John there just despises us."

For reply Peter rose and kicked John out of bed, blankets and all; one kick. This seemed to Wendy rather forward for a first meeting, and

she told him with spirit that he was not captain in her house. However, John continued to sleep so placidly on the floor that she allowed him to remain there. "And I know you meant to be kind," she said, relenting, "so you may give me a kiss."

For the moment she had forgotten his ignorance about kisses. "I thought you would want it back," he said a little bitterly, and offered to return her thimble.

"Oh dear," said the nice Wendy, "I don't mean a kiss, I mean a thimble."

"What's that?"

"It's like this." She kissed him.

"Funny!" said Peter gravely. "Now shall I give you a thimble?"

"If you wish to," said Wendy, keeping her head erect this time.

Peter thimbled her, and almost immediately she screeched. "What is it, Wendy?"

"It was exactly as if some one were pulling my hair."

"That must have been Tink. I never knew her so naughty before."

And indeed Tink was darting about again, using offensive language.

"She says she will do that to you, Wendy, every time I give you a thimble."

"But why?"

"Why, Tink?"

Again Tink replied, "You silly ass." Peter could not understand why, but Wendy understood, and she was just slightly disappointed when he admitted that he came to the nursery window not to see her but to listen to stories.

"You see I don't know any stories. None of the lost boys know any stories."

"How perfectly awful," Wendy said.

"Do you know," Peter asked, "why swallows build in the eaves of houses? It is to listen to the stories. O Wendy, your mother was tellng you such a lovely story."

"Which story was it?"

"About the prince who couldn't find the lady who wore the glass slipper."

"Peter," said Wendy excitedly, "that was Cinderella, and he found her, and they lived happy ever after."

Peter was so glad that he rose from the floor, where they had been sitting, and hurried to the window. "Where are you going?" she cried with misgiving.

"To tell the other boys."

"Don't go Peter," she entreated, "I know such lots of stories."

Those were her precise words, so there can be no denying that it was she who first tempted him.

He came back, and there was a greedy look in his eyes now which ought to have alarmed her, but did not.

"Oh, the stories I could tell to the boys!" she cried, and then Peter gripped her and began to draw her toward the window.

"Let me go!" she ordered him.

"Wendy, do come with me and tell the other boys."

Of course she was very pleased to be asked, but she said, "Oh dear, I can't. Think of mummy! Besides, I can't fly."

"I'll teach you."

"Oh, how lovely to fly."

"I'll teach you how to jump on the wind's back, and then away we go."

"Oo!" she exclaimed rapturously.

"Wendy, Wendy, when you are sleeping in your silly bed you might be flying about with me saying funny things to the stars."

"Oo!"

"And, Wendy, there are mermaids."

"Mermaids! With tails?"

"Such long tails."

"Oh," cried Wendy, "to see a mermaid!"

He had become frightfully cunning. "Wendy," he said, "how we should all respect you."

She was wriggling her body in distress. It was quite as if she were trying to remain on the nursery floor.

But he had no pity for her.

"Wendy," he said, the sly one, "you could tuck us in at night."

"Oo!"

"None of us has ever been tucked in at night."

"Oo," and her arms went out to him.

"And you could darn our clothes, and make pockets for us. None of us has any pockets."

How could she resist. "Of course it's awfully fascinating!" she cried. "Peter, would you teach John and Michael to fly too?"

"If you like," he said indifferently, and she ran to John and Michael and shook them. "Wake up," she cried, "Peter Pan has come and he is to teach us to fly."

John rubbed his eyes. "Then I shall get up," he said. Of course he was on the floor already. "Hallo," he said, "I am up!"

Michael was up by this time also, looking as sharp as a knife with six blades and a saw, but Peter suddenly signed silence. Their faces assumed the awful craftiness of children listening for sounds from the grown-up world. All was as still as salt. Then everything was right. No, stop! Everything was wrong. Nana, who had been barking distressfully all the evening, was quiet now. It was her silence they had heard!

"Out with the light! Hide! Quick!" cried John, taking command for the only time throughout the whole adventure. And thus when Liza entered, holding Nana, the nursery seemed quite its old self, very dark, and you could have sworn you heard its three wicked inmates breathing angelically as they slept. They were really doing it artfully from behind the window curtains.

Liza was in a bad temper, for she was mixing the Christmas puddings in the kitchen, and had been drawn away from them, with a raisin still on her cheek, by Nana's absurd suspicions. She thought the best way of getting a little quiet was to take Nana to the nursery for a moment, but in custody of course.

"There, you suspicious brute," she said, not sorry that Nana was in disgrace. "They are perfectly safe, aren't they? Every one of the little angels sound asleep in bed. Listen to their gentle breathing."

Here Michael, encouraged by his success, breathed so loudly that they were nearly detected. Nana knew that kind of breathing, and she tried to drag herself out of Liza's clutches.

But Liza was dense. "No more of it, Nana," she said sternly, pulling her out of the room. "I warn you if you bark again I shall go straight for master and missus and bring them home from the party, and then, oh, won't master whip you, just."

She tied the unhappy dog up again, but do you think Nana ceased to bark? Bring master and missus home from the party? Why, that was just what she wanted. Do you think she cared whether she was whipped so long as her charges were safe? Unfortunately Liza returned to her puddings, and Nana, seeing that no help would come from her, strained and strained at the chain until at last she broke it. In another moment she had burst into the dining-room of 27 and flung up her paws to heaven, her most expressive way of making a communication. Mr. and Mrs. Darling knew at once that something terrible was happening in their nursery, and without a good-bye to their hostess they rushed into the street.

But it was now ten minutes since three scoundrels had been breathing behind the curtains, and Peter Pan can do a great deal in ten minutes.

We now return to the nursery.

"It's all right," John announced, emerging from his hiding-place. "I say, Peter, can you really fly?"

Instead of troubling to answer him Peter flew round the room, taking the mantelpiece on the way.

"How topping!" said John and Michael.

"How sweet!" cried Wendy.

"Yes, I'm sweet, oh, I am sweet!" said Peter, forgetting his manners again.

It looked delightfully easy, and they tried it first from the floor and then from the beds, but they always went down instead of up.

"I say, how do you do it?" asked John, rubbing his knee. He was quite a practical boy.

"You just think lovely wonderful thoughts," Peter explained, "and they lift you up in the air."

He showed them again.

"You're so nippy at it," John said, "couldn't you do it very slowly once?"

Peter did it both slowly and quickly. "I've got it now, Wendy!" cried John, but soon he found he had not. Not one of them could fly an inch, though even Michael was in words of two syllables, and Peter did not know A from Z.

Of course Peter had been trifling with them, for no one can fly unless the fairy dust has been blown on him. Fortunately, as we have mentioned, one of his hands was messy with it, and he blew some on each of them, with the most superb results.

"Now just wriggle your shoulders this way," he said, "and let go."

They were all on their beds, and gallant Michael let go first. He did not quite mean to let go, but he did it, and immediately he was borne across the room.

"I flewed!" he screamed while still in mid-air. John let go and met Wendy near the bathroom.

"Oh, lovely!"

"Oh, ripping!"

"Look at me!"

"Look at me!"

"Look at me!"

They were not nearly so elegant as Peter, they could not help kicking a little, but their heads were bobbing against the ceiling, and there is almost nothing so delicious as that. Peter gave Wendy a hand at first, but had to desist, Tink was so indignant.

Up and down they went, and round and round. Heavenly was Wendy's word.

"I say," cried John, "why shouldn't we all go out!"

Of course it was to this that Peter had been luring them.

Michael was ready: he wanted to see how long it took him to do a billion miles. But Wendy hesitated.

"Mermaids!" said Peter again.

"Oo!"

"And there are pirates."

"Pirates," cried John, seizing his Sunday hat, "let us go at once!"

It was just at this moment that Mr. and Mrs. Darling hurried with Nana out of 27. They ran into the middle of the street to look up at the nursery window; and, yes, it was still shut, but the room was ablaze with light, and most heart-gripping sight of all, they could see in shadow on the curtain three little figures in night attire circling round and round, not on the floor but in the air.

Not three figures, four!

In a tremble they opened the street door. Mr. Darling would have rushed upstairs, but Mrs. Darling signed to him to go softly. She even tried to make her heart go softly.

Will they reach the nursery in time? If so, how delightful for them, and we shall all breathe a sigh of relief, but there will be no story. On the other hand, if they are not in time, I solemnly promise that it will all come right in the end.

They would have reached the nursery in time had it not been that the little stars were watching them. Once again the stars blew the window open, and that smallest star of all called out:

"Cave, Peter!"

Peter knew that there was not a moment to lose. "Come," he cried imperiously, and soared out at once into the night, followed by John and Michael and Wendy.

Mr. and Mrs. Darling and Nana rushed into the nursery too late. The birds were flown.

CHAPTER IV

THE FLIGHT

"Second to the right, and straight on till morning."

That, Peter had told Wendy, was the way to the Neverland; but even birds, carrying maps and consulting them at windy corners, could not have sighted it with these instructions. Peter, you see, just said anything that came into his head.

At first his companions trusted him implicitly, and so great were the delights of flying that they wasted time circling round church spires or any other tall objects on the way that took their fancy.

John and Michael raced, Michael getting a start.

They recalled with contempt that not so long ago they had thought themselves fine fellows for being able to fly round a room.

Not so long ago. But how long ago? They were flying over the sea before this thought began to disturb Wendy seriously. John thought it was their second sea and their third night.

Sometimes it was dark and sometimes light, and now they were very cold and again too warm. Did they really feel hungry at times, or were they merely pretending, because Peter had such a jolly new way of feeding them? His way was to pursue birds who had food in their mouths suitable for humans and snatch it from them; then the birds would follow and snatch it back; and they would all go chasing each other gaily for miles, parting at last with mutual expressions of good-will. But Wendy noticed with gentle concern that Peter did not seem to know that this was rather an odd way of getting your bread and butter, nor even that there are other ways.

Certainly they did not pretend to be sleepy, they were sleepy; and that was a danger, for the moment they popped off, down they fell. The awful thing was that Peter thought this funny.

"There he goes again!" he would cry gleefully, as Michael suddenly dropped like a stone.

"Save him, save him!" cried Wendy, looking with horror at the cruel sea far below. Eventually Peter would dive through the air, and catch Michael just before he could strike the sea, and it was lovely the way he did it; but he always waited till the last moment, and you felt it was his cleverness that interested him and not the saving of human life. Also he was fond of variety, and the sport that engrossed him one moment would suddenly cease to engage him, so there was always the possibility that the next time you fell he would let you go.

He could sleep in the air without falling, by merely lying on his back and floating, but this was, partly at least, because he was so light that if you got behind him and blew he went faster.

"Do be more polite to him," Wendy whispered to John, when they were playing "Follow my Leader."

"Then tell him to stop showing off," said John.

When playing Follow my Leader, Peter would fly close to the water and touch each shark's tail in passing, just as in the street you may run your finger along an iron railing. They could not follow him in this with much success, so perhaps it was rather like showing off, especially as he kept looking behind to see how many tails they missed.

"You must be nice to him," Wendy impressed on her brothers. "What could we do if he were to leave us!"

"We could go back," Michael said.

"Well, then, we could go on," said John.

"That is the awful thing, John. We should have to go on, for we don't know how to stop."

This was true, Peter had forgotten to show them how to stop.

John said that if the worst came to the worst, all they had to do was to go straight on, for the world was round, and so in time they must come back to their own window.

"And who is to get food for us, John?"

"I nipped a bit out of that eagle's mouth pretty neatly, Wendy."

"After the twentieth try," Wendy reminded him. "And even though we became good at picking up food, see how we bump against clouds and things if he is not near to give us a hand."

Indeed they were constantly bumping. They could now fly strongly, though they still kicked far too much; but if they saw a cloud in front of them, the more they tried to avoid it, the more certainly did they bump into it. If Nana had been with them, she would have had a bandage round Michael's forehead by this time.

Peter was not with them for the moment, and they felt rather lonely up there by themselves. He could go so much faster than they that he would suddenly shoot out of sight, to have some adventure in which they had no share. He would come down laughing over something fearfully funny he had been saying to a star, but he had already forgotten what it was, or he would come up with mermaid scales still sticking to him, and yet not be able to say for certain what had been happening. It was really rather irritating to children who had never seen a mermaid.

"And if he forgets them so quickly," Wendy argued, "how can we expect that he will go on remembering us?"

Indeed, sometimes when he returned he did not remember them, at least not well. Wendy was sure of it. She saw recognition come into his eyes as he was about to pass them the time of day and go on; once even she had to call him by name.

"I'm Wendy," she said agitatedly.

He was very sorry. "I say, Wendy," he whispered to her, "always if you see me forgetting you, just keep on saying 'I'm Wendy,' and then I'll remember."

Of course this was rather unsatisfactory. However, to make amends he showed them how to lie out flat on a strong wind that was going their way, and this was such a pleasant change that they tried it several times and found they could sleep thus with security. Indeed they would have slept longer, but Peter tired quickly of sleeping, and soon he would cry in his captain voice, "We get off here." So with occasional tiffs, but on the whole rollicking, they drew near the Neverland; for after many moons they did reach it, and, what is more, they had been going pretty straight all the time, not perhaps so much owing to the guidance of Peter or Tink as because the island was out looking for them. It is only thus that any one may sight those magic shores.

"There it is," said Peter calmly.

"Where, where?"

"Where all the arrows are pointing."

Indeed a million golden arrows were pointing it out to the children, all directed by their friend the sun, who wanted them to be sure of their way before leaving them for the night.

Wendy and John and Michael stood on tip-toe in the air to get their first sight of the island. Strange to say, they all recognised it at once, and until fear fell upon them they hailed it, not as something long dreamt of and seen at last, but as a familiar friend to whom they were returning home for the holidays.

"John, there's the lagoon!"

"Wendy, look at the turtles burying their eggs in the sand."

"I say, John, I see your flamingo with the broken leg!"

"Look, Michael, there's your cave!"

"John, what's that in the brushwood?"

"It's a wolf with her whelps. Wendy, I do believe that's your little whelp!"

"There's my boat, John, with her sides stove in!"

"No, it isn't! Why, we burned your boat."

"That's her, at any rate. I say, John, I see the smoke of the redskin camp!"

"Where? Show me, and I'll tell you by the way the smoke curls whether they are on the war-path."

"There, just across the Mysterious River."

"I see now. Yes, they are on the war-path right enough."

Peter was a little annoyed with them for knowing so much, but if he wanted to lord it over them his triumph was at hand, for have I not told you that anon fear fell upon them?

It came as the arrows went, leaving the island in gloom.

In the old days at home the Neverland had always begun to look a little dark and threatening by bedtime. Then unexplored patches arose in it and spread, black shadows moved about in them, the roar of the beasts of prey was quite different now, and above all, you lost the certainty that you would win. You were quite glad that the night-lights were in. You even liked Nana to say that this was just the mantelpiece over here, and that the Neverland was all make-believe.

Of course the Neverland had been make-believe in those days, but it was real now, and there were no night-lights, and it was getting darker every moment, and where was Nana?

They had been flying apart, but they huddled close to Peter now. His careless manner had gone at last, his eyes were sparkling, and a tingle went through them every time they touched his body. They were now over the fearsome island, flying so low that sometimes a tree grazed their feet. Nothing horrid was visible in the air, yet their progress had become slow and laboured, exactly as if they were pushing their way through hostile forces. Sometimes they hung in the air until Peter had beaten on it with his fists.

"They don't want us to land," he explained.

"Who are they?" Wendy whispered, shuddering.

But he could not or would not say. Tinker Bell had been asleep on his shoulder, but now he wakened her and sent her on in front.

Sometimes he poised himself in the air, listening intently, with his hand to his ear, and again he would stare down with eyes so bright that they seemed to bore two holes to earth. Having done these things, he went on again.

His courage was almost appalling. "Would you like an adventure now," he said casually to John, "or would you like to have your tea first?"

Wendy said "tea first" quickly, and Michael pressed her hand in gratitude, but the braver John hesitated.

"What kind of adventure?" he asked cautiously.

"There's a pirate asleep in the pampas just beneath us," Peter told him. "If you like, we'll go down and kill him."

"I don't see him," John said after a long pause.

"I do."

"Suppose," John said, a little huskily, "he were to wake up."

Peter spoke indignantly. "You don't think I would kill him while he was sleeping! I would wake him first, and then kill him. That's the way I always do."

"I say! Do you kill many?"

"Tons."

John said "how ripping," but decided to have tea first. He asked if there were many pirates on the island just now, and Peter said he had never known so many.

"Who is captain now?"

"Hook," answered Peter, and his face became very stern as he said that hated word.

"Jas. Hook?"

"Ay."

Then indeed Michael began to cry, and even John could speak in gulps only, for they knew Hook's reputation.

"He was Blackbeard's bo'sun," John whispered huskily. "He is the worst of them all. He is the only man of whom Barbecue was afraid."

"That's him," said Peter.

"What is he like? Is he big?"

"He is not so big as he was."

"How do you mean?"

"I cut off a bit of him."

"You!"

"Yes, me," said Peter sharply.

"I wasn't meaning to be disrespectful."

"Oh, all right."

"But, I say, what bit?"

"His right hand."

"Then he can't fight now?"

"Oh, can't he just!"

"Left-hander?"

"He has an iron hook instead of a right hand, and he claws with it."

"Claws!"

"I say, John," said Peter.

"Yes."

"Say, 'Ay, ay, sir.' "

"Ay, ay, sir."

"There is one thing," Peter continued, "that every boy who serves under me has to promise, and so must you."

John paled.

"It is this, if we meet Hook in open fight, you must leave him to me."

"I promise," John said loyally.

For the moment they were feeling less eerie, because Tink was flying with them, and in her light they could distinguish each other. Unfortunately she could not fly so slowly as they, and so she had to go round and round them in a circle in which they moved as in a halo. Wendy quite liked it, until Peter pointed out the drawback.

"She tells me," he said, "that the pirates sighted us before the darkness came, and got Long Tom out."

"The big gun?"

"Yes. And of course they must see her light, and if they guess we are near it they are sure to let fly."

"Wendy!"

"John!"

"Michael!"

"Tell her to go away at once, Peter," the three cried simultaneously, but he refused.

"She thinks we have lost the way," he replied stiffly, "and she is rather frightened. You don't think I would send her away all by herself when she is frightened!"

For a moment the circle of light was broken, and something gave Peter a loving little pinch.

"Then tell her," Wendy begged, "to put out her light."

"She can't put it out. That is about the only thing fairies can't do. It just goes out of itself when she falls asleep, same as the stars."

"Then tell her to sleep at once," John almost ordered.

"She can't sleep except when she's sleepy. It's the only other thing fairies can't do."

"Seems to me," growled John, "these are the only two things worth doing."

Here he got a pinch, but not a loving one.

"If only one of us had a pocket," Peter said, "we could carry her in it." However, they had set off in such a hurry that there was not a pocket between the four of them.

He had a happy idea. John's hat!

Tink agreed to travel by hat if it was carried in the hand. John carried it, though she had hoped to be carried by Peter. Presently Wendy took the hat, because John said it struck against his knee as he flew; and this, as we shall see, led to mischief, for Tinker Bell hated to be under an obligation to Wendy.

In the black topper the light was completely hidden, and they flew on in silence. It was the stillest silence they had ever known, broken once by a distant lapping, which Peter explained was the wild beasts drinking at the ford, and again by a rasping sound that might have been the branches of trees rubbing together, but he said it was the redskins sharpening their knives.

Even these noises ceased. To Michael the loneliness was dreadful. "If only something would make a sound!" he cried.

As if in answer to his request, the air was rent by the most tremendous crash he had ever heard. The pirates had fired Long Tom at them.

The roar of it echoed through the mountains, and the echoes seemed to cry savagely, "Where are they, where are they, where are they?"

Thus sharply did the terrified three learn the difference between an island of make-believe and the same island come true.

When at last the heavens were steady again, John and Michael found themselves alone in the darkness. John was treading the air mechanically, and Michael without knowing how to float was floating.

"Are you shot?" John whispered tremulously.

"I haven't tried yet," Michael whispered back.

We know now that no one had been hit. Peter, however, had been carried by the wind of the shot far out to sea, while Wendy was blown upwards with no companion but Tinker Bell.

It would have been well for Wendy if at that moment she had dropped the hat.

I don't know whether the idea came suddenly to Tink, or whether she had planned it on the way, but she at once popped out of the hat and began to lure Wendy to her destruction.

Tink was not all bad: or, rather, she was all bad just now, but, on the other hand, sometimes she was all good. Fairies have to be one thing or the other, because being so small they unfortunately have room for one feeling only at a time. They are, however, allowed to change, only it must be a complete change. At present she was full of jealousy of Wendy. What she said in her lovely tinkle Wendy could not of course understand, and I believe some of it was bad words, but it sounded kind, and she flew back and forward, plainly meaning "Follow me, and all will be well."

What else could poor Wendy do? She called to Peter and John and Michael, and got only mocking echoes in reply. She did not yet know that Tink hated her with the fierce hatred of a very woman. And so, bewildered, and now staggering in her flight, she followed Tink to her doom.

CHAPTER V

THE ISLAND COME TRUE

eeling that Peter was on his way back, the Neverland had again woke into life. We ought to use the pluperfect and say wakened, but woke is better and was always used by Peter.

In his absence things are usually quiet on the island. The fairies take an hour longer in the morning, the beasts attend to their young, the redskins feed heavily for six days and nights, and when pirates and lost boys meet they merely bite their thumbs at each other. But with the coming of Peter, who hates lethargy, they are all under way again: if you put your ear to the ground now, you would hear the whole island seething with life.

On this evening the chief forces of the island were disposed as follows. The lost boys were out looking for Peter, the pirates were out looking for the lost boys, the redskins were out looking for the pirates, and the beasts were out looking for the redskins. They were going round and round the island, but they did not meet because all were going at the same rate.

All wanted blood except the boys, who liked it as a rule, but to-night were out to greet their captain. The boys on the island vary, of course, in numbers, according as they get killed and so on; and when they seem to be growing up, which is against the rules, Peter thins them out; but at this time there were six of them, counting the twins as two. Let us pretend to lie here among the sugarcane and watch them as they steal by in single file, each with his hand on his dagger.

They are forbidden by Peter to look in the least like him, and they wear the skins of bears slain by themselves, in which they are so round and furry that when they fall they roll. They have therefore become very sure-footed.

The first to pass is Tootles, not the least brave but the most unfortunate of all that gallant band. He had been in fewer adventures than any of them, because the big things constantly happened just when he had stepped round the corner; all would be quiet, he would take the opportunity of going off to gather a few sticks for firewood, and then when he returned the others would be sweeping up the blood. This ill-luck had given a gentle melancholy to his countenance, but instead of souring his nature had sweetened it, so that he was quite the humblest of the boys. Poor kind Tootles, there is danger in the air for you to-night. Take care lest an adventure is now offered you, which, if accepted, will plunge you in deepest woe. Tootles, the fairy Tink who is bent on mischief this night is looking for a tool, and she thinks you the most easily tricked of the boys. 'Ware Tinker Bell.

Would that he could hear us, but we are not really on the island, and he passes by, biting his knuckles.

Next comes Nibs, the gay and debonair, followed by Slightly, who cuts whistles out of the trees and dances ecstatically to his own tunes. Slightly is the most conceited of the boys. He thinks he remembers the days before he was lost, with their manners and customs, and this has given his nose an offensive tilt. Curly is fourth; he is a pickle, and so often has he had to deliver up his person when Peter said sternly, "Stand forth the one who did this thing," that now at the command he stands forth automatically whether he has done it or no. Last come the Twins, who cannot be described because we should be sure to be describing the wrong one. Peter never quite knew what twins were, and his band were not allowed to know anything he did not know, so these two were always vague about themselves, and did their best to give satisfaction by keeping close together in an apologetic sort of way.

The boys vanish in the gloom, and after a pause, but not a long pause, for things go briskly on the island, come the pirates on their track. We hear them before they are seen, and it is always the same dreadful song:

"Avast belay, yo ho, heave to,
A-pirating we go,
And if we're parted by a shot
We're sure to meet below!"

A more villainous-looking lot never hung in a row on Execution dock. Here, a little in advance, ever and again with his head to the ground listening, his great arms bare, pieces of eight in his ears as ornaments, is the handsome Italian Cecco, who cut his name in letters of blood on the back of the governor of the prison at Gao. That gigantic black behind him has had many names since he dropped the one with which dusky mothers still terrify their children on the banks of the Guadjomo. Here is Bill Jukes, every inch of him tattooed, the same Bill Jukes who got six dozen on the *Walrus* from Flint before he would drop the bag of moidores; and Cookson, said to be Black Murphy's brother (but this was never proved), and Gentleman Starkey, once an usher in a public school and still dainty in his ways of killing; and Skylights (Morgan's Skylights); and the Irish bo'sun Smee, an oddly genial man who stabbed, so to speak, without offence, and was the only Non-conformist in Hook's crew; and Noodler, whose hands were fixed on backwards; and Robt. Mullins and Alf Mason and many another ruffian long known and feared on the Spanish Main.

In the midst of them, the blackest and largest jewel in that dark setting, reclined James Hook, or as he wrote himself, Jas. Hook, of whom it is said he was the only man that the Sea-Cook feared. He lay at his ease in a rough chariot drawn and propelled by his men, and instead of a right hand he had the iron hook with which ever and anon he encouraged them to increase their pace. As dogs this terrible man treated and addressed them, and as dogs they obeyed him. In person he was cadaverous and blackavized, and his hair was dressed in long curls, which at a little distance looked like black candles, and gave a singularly threatening expression to his handsome countenance. His eyes were of the blue of the forget-me-not, and of a profound melancholy, save when he was plunging his hook into you, at which time two red spots appeared in them and lit them up horribly. In manner, something of the grand seigneur still clung to him, so that he even ripped you up with an air, and I have been told that he was a *raconteur* of repute. He was never more sinister than when he was most polite, which is probably the truest test of breeding; and the elegance of his diction, even when he was swearing, no less than the distinction of his demeanour, showed him one of a different caste from his crew. A man of indomitable courage, it was said of him that the only thing he shied at was the sight of his own blood, which was thick and of an unusual colour. In dress he somewhat aped the attire associated with the name of Charles II, having heard it said in some earlier period of his career that he bore a strange resemblance to the ill-fated Stuarts; and in his mouth he had a holder of his own contrivance which enabled him to smoke two cigars at once. But undoubtedly the grimmest part of him was his iron claw.

Let us now kill a pirate, to show Hook's method. Skylights will do. As they pass, Skylights lurches clumsily against him, ruffling his lace collar; the hook shoots forth, there is a tearing sound and one screech, then the body is kicked aside, and the pirates pass on. He has not even taken the cigars from his mouth.

Such is the terrible man against whom Peter Pan is pitted. Which will win?

On the trail of the pirates, stealing noiselessly down the war-path, which is not visible to inexperienced eyes, come the redskins, every one of them with his eyes peeled. They carry tomahawks and knives, and their naked bodies gleam with paint and oil. Strung around them are scalps, of boys as well as of pirates, for these are the Piccaninny tribe, and not to be confused with the softer-hearted Delawares or the Hurons. In the van, on all fours, is Great Big Little Panther, a brave of so many scalps that in his present position they somewhat impede his progress. Bringing up the rear, the place of greatest danger, comes Tiger Lily, proudly erect, a princess in her own right. She is the most beautiful of dusky Dianas and the belle of the Piccaninnies, coquettish, cold and amorous by turns; there is not a brave who would not have the wayward thing to wife, but she staves off the altar with a hatchet. Observe how they pass over fallen twigs without making the slightest noise. The only sound to be heard is their somewhat heavy breathing. The fact is that they are all a little fat just now after the heavy gorging, but in time they will work this off. For the moment, however, it constitutes their chief danger.

The redskins disappear as they have come like shadows, and soon their place is taken by the beasts, a great and motley procession: lions, tigers, bears, and the innumerable smaller savage things that flee from them, for every kind of beast, and, more particularly, all the man-eaters, live cheek by jowl on the favoured island. Their tongues are hanging out, they are hungry to-night.

When they have passed, comes the last figure of all, a gigantic crocodile. We shall see for whom she is looking presently.

The crocodile passes, but soon the boys appear again, for the procession must continue indefinitely until one of the parties stops or changes its pace. Then quickly they will be on top of each other.

All are keeping a sharp look-out in front, but none suspects that the danger may be creeping up from behind. This shows how real the island was.

The first to fall out of the moving circle was the boys. They flung themselves down on the sward, close to their underground home.

"I do wish Peter would come back," every one of them said nervously, though in height and still more in breadth they were all larger than their captain.

"I am the only one who is not afraid of the pirates," Slightly said, in the tone that prevented his being a general favourite, but perhaps some distant sound disturbed him, for he added hastily, "but I wish he would come back, and tell us whether he has heard anything more about Cinderella."

They talked of Cinderella, and Tootles was confident that his mother must have been very like her.

It was only in Peter's absence that they could speak of mothers, the subject being forbidden by him as silly.

"All I remember about my mother," Nibs told them, "is that she often said to father, 'Oh, how I wish I had a cheque-book of my own!' I don't know what a cheque-book is, but I should just love to give my mother one."

While they talked they heard a distant sound. You or I, not being wild things of the woods, would have heard nothing, but they heard it, and it was the grim song:

"Yo ho, yo ho, the pirate life,
The flag o' skull and bones,
A merry hour, a hempen rope,
And hey for Davy Jones."

At once the lost boys — but where are they? They are no longer there. Rabbits could not have disappeared more quickly.

I will tell you where they are. With the exception of Nibs, who has darted away to reconnoitre, they are already in their home under the ground, a very delightful residence of which we shall see a good deal presently. But how have they reached it? for there is no entrance to be seen, not so much as a large stone, which if rolled away would disclose the mouth of a cave. Look closely, however, and you may note that there are here seven large trees, each with a hole in its hollow trunk as large as a boy. These are the seven entrances to the home under the ground, for which Hook has been searching in vain these many moons. Will he find it to-night?

As the pirates advanced, the quick eye of Starkey sighted Nibs disappearing through the wood, and at once his pistol flashed out. But an iron claw gripped his shoulder.

"Captain, let go!" he cried, writhing.

Now for the first time we hear the voice of Hook. It was a black voice. "Put back that pistol first," it said threateningly.

"It was one of those boys you hate. I could have shot him dead."

"Ay, and the sound would have brought Tiger Lily's redskins upon us. Do you want to lose your scalp?"

"Shall I after him, captain," asked pathetic Smee, "and tickle him with Johnny Corkscrew?" Smee had pleasant names for everything, and his cutlass was Johnny Corkscrew, because he wriggled it in the wound. One could mention many lovable traits in Smee. For instance, after killing, it was his spectacles he wiped instead of his weapon.

"Johnny's a silent fellow," he reminded Hook.

"Not now, Smee," Hook said darkly. "He is only one, and I want to mischief all the seven. Scatter and look for them."

The pirates disappeared among the trees, and in a moment their captain and Smee were alone. Hook heaved a heavy sigh, and I know not why it was, perhaps it was because of the soft beauty of the evening, but there came over him a desire to confide to his faithful bo'sun the story of his life. He spoke long and earnestly, but what it was all about Smee, who was rather stupid, did not know in the least.

Anon he caught the word Peter.

"Most of all," Hook was saying passionately, "I want their captain, Peter Pan. 'Twas he cut off my arm." He brandished the hook threateningly. "I've waited long to shake his hand with this. Oh, I'll tear him!"

"And yet," said Smee, "I have often heard you say that hook was worth a score of hands, for combing the hair and other homely uses."

"Ay," the captain answered, "if I was a mother I would pray to have my children born with this instead of that," and he cast a look of pride upon his iron hand and one of scorn upon the other. Then again he frowned.

"Peter flung my arm," he said, wincing, "to a crocodile that happened to be passing by."

"I have often," said Smee, "noticed your strange dread of crocodiles."

"Not of crocodiles," Hook corrected him, "but of that one crocodile." He lowered his voice. "It liked my arm so much, Smee, that it has followed me ever since, from sea to sea and from land to land, licking its lips for the rest of me."

"In a way," said Smee, "it's a sort of compliment."

"I want no such compliments," Hook barked petulantly. "I want Peter Pan, who first gave the brute its taste for me."

He sat down on a large mushroom, and now there was a quiver in his voice. "Smee," he said huskily, "that crocodile would have had me before this, but by a lucky chance it swallowed a clock which goes tick tick inside it, and so before it can reach me I hear the tick and bolt." He laughed, but in a hollow way.

"Some day," said Smee, "the clock will run down, and then he'll get you."

Hook wetted his dry lips. "Ay," he said, "that's the fear that haunts me."

Since sitting down he had felt curiously warm. "Smee," he said, "this seat is hot." He jumped up. "Odds bobs, hammer and tongs, I'm burning."

They examined the mushroom, which was of a size and solidity unknown on the mainland; they tried to pull it up, and it came away at once in their hands, for it had no root. Stranger still, smoke began at once to ascend. The pirates looked at each other. "A chimney!" they both exclaimed.

They had indeed discovered the chimney of the home under the ground. It was the custom of the boys to stop it with a mushroom when enemies were in the neighbourhood.

Not only smoke came out of it. There came also children's voices, for so safe did the boys feel in their hiding-place that they were gaily chattering. The pirates listened grimly, and then replaced the mushroom. They looked around them and noted the holes in the seven trees.

"Did you hear them say Peter Pan's from home?" Smee whispered, fidgeting with Johnny Corkscrew.

Hook nodded. He stood for a long time lost in thought, and at last a curdling smile lit up his swarthy face. Smee had been waiting for it. "Unrip your plan, captain," he cried eagerly.

"To return to the ship," Hook replied slowly through his teeth, "and cook a large rich cake of a jolly thickness with green sugar on it. There can be but one room below, for there is but one chimney. The silly moles had not the sense to see that they did not need a door apiece. That shows they have no mother. We will leave the cake on the shore of the Mermaids' Lagoon. These boys are always swimming about there, playing with the mermaids. They will find the cake and they will gobble it up, because, having no mother, they don't know how dangerous 'tis to eat rich damp cake." He burst into laughter, not hollow laughter now, but honest laughter. "Aha, they will die!"

Smee had listened with growing admiration.

"It's the wickedest, prettiest policy ever I heard of!" he cried, and in their exultation they danced and sang:

> "Avast, belay, when I appear,
> By fear they're overtook,
> Nought's left upon your bones when you
> Have shaken claws with Cook."

They began the verse, but they never finished it, for another sound broke in and stilled them. It was at first such a tiny sound that a leaf might have fallen on it and smothered it, but as it came nearer it was more distinct.

Tick tick tick tick!

Hook stood shuddering, one foot in the air.

"The crocodile!" he gasped, and bounded away, followed by his bo'sun.

It was indeed the crocodile. It had passed the redskins, who were now on the trail of the other pirates. It oozed on after Hook.

Once more the boys emerged into the open; but the dangers of the night were not yet over, for presently Nibs rushed breathless into their midst, pursued by a pack of wolves. The tongues of the pursuers were hanging out; the baying of them was horrible.

"Save me, save me!" cried Nibs, falling on the ground.

"But what can we do, what can we do?"

It was a high compliment to Peter that at that dire moment their thoughts turned to him.

"What would Peter do?" they cried simultaneously.

Almost in the same breath they cried, "Peter would look at them through his legs."

And then, "Let us do what Peter would do."

It is quite the most successful way of defying wolves, and as one boy

they bent and looked through their legs. The next moment is the long one, but victory came quickly, for as the boys advanced upon them in this terrible attitude, the wolves dropped their tails and fled.

Now Nibs rose from the ground, and the others thought that his staring eyes still saw the wolves. But it was not wolves he saw.

"I have seen a wonderfuller thing," he cried, as they gathered round him eagerly. "A great white bird. It is flying this way."

"What kind of a bird, do you think?"

"I don't know," Nibs said, awestruck, "but it looks so weary, and as it flies it moans, 'Poor Wendy.' "

"Poor Wendy?"

"I remember," said Slightly instantly, "there are birds called Wendies."

"See, it comes!" cried Curly, pointing to Wendy in the heavens.

Wendy was now almost overhead, and they could hear her plaintive cry. But more distinct came the shrill voice of Tinker Bell. The jealous fairy had now cast off all disguise of friendship, and was darting at her victim from every direction, pinching savagely each time she touched.

"Hullo, Tink," cried the wondering boys.

Tink's reply rang out: "Peter wants you to shoot the Wendy."

It was not in their nature to question when Peter ordered. "Let us do what Peter wishes," cried the simple boys. "Quick, bows and arrows!"

All but Tootles popped down their trees. He had a bow and arrow with him, and Tink noted it, and rubbed her little hands.

"Quick, Tootles, quick," she screamed. "Peter will be so pleased."

Tootles excitedly fitted the arrow to his bow. "Out of the way, Tink," he shouted, and then he fired, and Wendy fluttered to the ground with an arrow in her breast.

CHAPTER VI

THE LITTLE HOUSE

oolish Tootles was standing like a conqueror over Wendy's body when the other boys sprang, armed, from their trees.

"You are too late," he cried proudly, "I have shot the Wendy. Peter will be so pleased with me."

Overhead Tinker Bell shouted "Silly ass!" and darted into hiding. The others did not hear her.

They had crowded round Wendy, and as they looked a terrible silence fell upon the wood. If Wendy's heart had been beating they would all have heard it.

Slightly was the first to speak. "This is no bird," he said in a scared voice. "I think it must be a lady."

"A lady?" said Tootles, and fell a-trembling.

"And we have killed her," Nibs said hoarsely.

They all whipped off their caps.

"Now I see," Curly said; "Peter was bringing her to us." He threw himself sorrowfully on the ground.

"A lady to take care of us at last," said one of the twins, "and you have killed her!"

They were sorry for him, but sorrier for themselves, and when he took a step nearer them they turned from him.

Tootles' face was very white, but there was a dignity about him now that had never been there before.

"I did it," he said, reflecting. "When ladies used to come to me in dreams, I said, 'Pretty mother, pretty mother.' But when at last she really came, I shot her."

He moved slowly away.

"Don't go," they called in pity.

"I must," he answered, shaking; "I am so afraid of Peter."

It was at this tragic moment that they heard a sound which made the heart of every one of them rise to his mouth. They heard Peter crow.

"Peter!" they cried, for it was always thus that he signalled his return.

"Hide her," they whispered, and gathered hastily around Wendy. But Tootles stood aloof.

Again came that ringing crow, and Peter dropped in front of them. "Greeting, boys," he cried, and mechanically they saluted, and then again was silence.

He frowned.

"I am back," he said hotly, "why do you not cheer?"

They opened their mouths, but the cheers would not come. He overlooked it in his haste to tell the glorious tidings.

"Great news, boys," he cried, "I have brought at last a mother for you all."

Still no sound, except a little thud from Tootles as he dropped on his knees.

"Have you not seen her?" asked Peter, becoming troubled. "She flew this way."

"Ah me!" one voice said, and another said, "Oh, mournful day."

Tootles rose. "Peter," he said quietly, "I will show her to you," and when the others would still have hidden her he said, "Back, twins, let Peter see."

So they all stood back, and let him see, and after he had looked for a little time he did not know what to do next.

"She is dead," he said uncomfortably. "Perhaps she is frightened at being dead."

He thought of hopping off in a comic sort of way till he was out of sight of her, and then never going near the spot any more. They would all have been glad to follow if he had done this.

But there was the arrow. He took it from her heart and faced his band.

"Whose arrow?" he demanded sternly.

"Mine, Peter," said Tootles on his knees.

"Oh, dastard hand," Peter said, and he raised the arrow to use it as a dagger.

Tootles did not flinch. He bared his breast. "Strike, Peter," he said firmly, "strike true."

Twice did Peter raise the arrow, and twice did his hand fall. "I cannot strike," he said with awe, "there is something stays my hand."

All looked at him in wonder, save Nibs, who fortunately looked at Wendy.

"It is she," he cried, "the Wendy lady, see, her arm!"

Wonderful to relate, Wendy had raised her arm. Nibs bent over her and listened reverently. "I think she said 'Poor Tootles,' " he whispered.

"She lives," Peter said briefly.

Slightly cried instantly, "The Wendy lady lives."

Then Peter knelt beside her and found his button. You remember she had put it on a chain that she wore round her neck.

"See," he said, "the arrow struck against this. It is the kiss I gave her. It has saved her life."

"I remember kisses," Slightly interposed quickly, "let me see it. Ay, that's a kiss."

Peter did not hear him. He was begging Wendy to get better quickly, so that he could show her the mermaids. Of course she could not answer yet, being still in a frightful faint; but from overhead came a wailing note.

"Listen to Tink," said Curly, "she is crying because the Wendy lives."

Then they had to tell Peter of Tink's crime, and almost never had they seen him look so stern.

"Listen, Tinker Bell," he cried, "I am your friend no more. Begone from me forever."

She flew on to his shoulder and pleaded, but he brushed her off. Not until Wendy again raised her arm did he relent sufficiently to say, "Well, not forever, but for a whole week."

Do you think Tinker Bell was grateful to Wendy for raising her arm? Oh dear no, never wanted to pinch her so much. Fairies indeed are strange, and Peter, who understood them best, often cuffed them.

But what to do with Wendy in her present delicate state of health?

"Let us carry her down into the house," Curly suggested.

"Ay," said Slightly, "that is what one does with ladies."

"No, no," Peter said, "you must not touch her. It would not be suffi-ciently respectful."

"That," said Slightly, "is what I was thinking."

"But if she lies there," Tootles said, "she will die."

"Ay, she will die," Slightly admitted, "but there is no way out."

"Yes, there is," cried Peter. "Let us build a little house round her."

They were all delighted. "Quick," he ordered them, "bring me each of you the best of what we have. Gut our house. Be sharp."

In a moment they were as busy as tailors the night before a wedding. They skurried this way and that, down for bedding, up for firewood, and while they were at it, who should appear but John and Michael. As they dragged along the ground they fell asleep standing, stopped, woke up, moved another step and slept again.

"John, John," Michael would cry, "wake up! Where is Nana, John, and mother?"

And then John would rub his eyes and mutter, "It is true, we did fly."

You may be sure they were very relieved to find Peter.

"Hullo, Peter," they said.

"Hullo," replied Peter amicably, though he had quite forgotten them. He was very busy at the moment measuring Wendy with his feet to see how large a house she would need. Of course he meant to leave room for chairs and a table. John and Michael watched him.

"Is Wendy asleep?" they asked.

"Yes."

"John," Michael proposed, "let us wake her and get her to make supper for us," and as he said it some of the other boys rushed on carrying branches for the building of the house. "Look at them!" he cried.

"Curly," said Peter in his most captain voice, "see that these boys help in the building of the house."

"Ay, ay, sir."

"Build a house?" exclaimed John.

"For the Wendy," said Curly.

"For Wendy?" John said, aghast. "Why, she is only a girl!"

"That," explained Curly, "is why we are her servants."

"You? Wendy's servants!"

"Yes," said Peter, "and you also. Away with them."

The astounded brothers were dragged away to hack and hew and carry. "Chairs and a fender first," Peter ordered. "Then we shall build the house round them."

"Ay," said Slightly, "that is how a house is built; it all comes back to me."

Peter thought of everything. "Slightly," he cried, "fetch a doctor."

"Ay, ay," said Slightly at once, and disappeared, scratching his head. But he knew Peter must be obeyed, and he returned in a moment, wearing John's hat and looking solemn.

"Please, sir," said Peter, going to him, "are you a doctor?"

The difference between him and the other boys at such a time was that they knew it was make-believe, while to him make-believe and true were exactly the same thing. This sometimes troubled them, as when they had to make-believe that they had had their dinners.

If they broke down in their make-believe he rapped them on the knuckles.

"Yes, my little man," anxiously replied Slightly, who had chapped knuckles.

"Please, sir," Peter explained, "a lady lies very ill."

She was lying at their feet, but Slightly had the sense not to see her.

"Tut, tut, tut," he said, "where does she lie?"

"In yonder glade."

"I will put a glass thing in her mouth," said Slightly, and he made-believe to do it, while Peter waited. It was an anxious moment when the glass thing was withdrawn.

"How is she?" inquired Peter.

"Tut, tut, tut," said Slightly, "this has cured her."

"I am glad!" Peter cried.

"I will call again in the evening," Slightly said; "give her beef tea out of a cup with a spout to it"; but after he had returned the hat to John he blew big breaths, which was his habit on escaping from a difficulty.

In the meantime the wood had been alive with the sound of axes; almost everything needed for a cosy dwelling already lay at Wendy's feet.

"If only we knew," said one, "the kind of house she likes best."

"Peter," shouted another, "she is moving in her sleep."

"Her mouth opens," cried a third, looking respectfully into it. "Oh, lovely!"

"Perhaps she is going to sing in her sleep," said Peter. "Wendy, sing the kind of house you would like to have."

Immediately, without opening her eyes, Wendy began to sing:

> "I wish I had a pretty house,
> The littlest ever seen,
> With funny little red walls
> And roof of mossy green."

They gurgled with joy at this, for by the greatest good luck the branches they had brought were sticky with red sap, and all the ground was carpeted with moss. As they rattled up the little house they broke into song themselves:

> "We've built the little walls and roof
> And made a lovely door,
> So tell us, mother Wendy,
> What are you wanting more?"

To this she answered rather greedily:

> "Oh, really next I think I'll have
> Gay windows all about,
> With roses peeping in, you know,
> And babies peeping out."

With a blow of their fists they made windows, and large yellow leaves were the blinds. But roses — ?

"Roses!" cried Peter sternly.

Quickly they made-believe to grow the loveliest roses up the walls. Babies?

To prevent Peter ordering babies they hurried into song again:

> "We've made the roses peeping out,
> The babes are at the door,
> We cannot make ourselves, you know,
> 'Cos we've been made before."

Peter, seeing this to be a good idea, at once pretended that it was his own. The house was quite beautiful, and no doubt Wendy was very cosy within, though, of course, they could no longer see her. Peter strode up and down, ordering finishing touches. Nothing escaped his eagle eye. Just when it seemed absolutely finished,

"There's no knocker on the door," he said.

They were very ashamed, but Tootles gave the sole of his shoe, and it made an excellent knocker.

Absolutely finished now, they thought.

Not a bit of it. "There's no chimney," Peter said; "we must have a chimney."

"It certainly does need a chimney," said John importantly. This gave Peter an idea. He snatched the hat off John's head, knocked out the bot-

tom, and put the hat on the roof. The little house was so pleased to have such a capital chimney that, as if to say thank you, smoke immediately began to come out of the hat.

Now really and truly it was finished. Nothing remained to do but to knock.

"All look your best," Peter warned them; "first impressions are awfully important."

He was glad no one asked him what first impressions are; they were all too busy looking their best.

He knocked politely, and now the wood was as still as the children, not a sound to be heard except from Tinker Bell, who was watching from a branch and openly sneering.

What the boys were wondering was, would anyone answer the knock? If a lady, what would she be like?

The door opened and a lady came out. It was Wendy. They all whipped off their hats.

She looked properly surprised, and this was just how they had hoped she would look.

"Where am I?" she said.

Of course Slightly was the first to get his word in. "Wendy lady," he said rapidly, "for you we built this house."

"Oh, say you're pleased," cried Nibs.

"Lovely, darling house," Wendy said, and they were the very words they had hoped she would say.

"And we are your children," cried the twins.

Then all went on their knees, and holding out their arms cried, "O Wendy lady, be our mother."

"Ought I?" Wendy said, all shining. "Of course it's frightfully fascinating, but you see I am only a little girl. I have no real experience."

"That doesn't matter," said Peter, as if he were the only person present who knew all about it, though he was really the one who knew least. "What we need is just a nice motherly person."

"Oh dear!" Wendy said, "you see I feel that is exactly what I am."

"It is, it is," they all cried; "we saw it at once."

"Very well," she said, "I will do my best. Come inside at once, you naughty children; I am sure your feet are damp. And before I put you to bed I have just time to finish the story of Cinderella."

In they went; I don't know how there was room for them, but you can squeeze very tight in the Neverland. And that was the first of the many

joyous evenings they had with Wendy. By and by she tucked them up in the great bed in the home under the trees, but she herself slept that night in the little house, and Peter kept watch outside with drawn sword, for the pirates could be heard carousing far away and the wolves were on the prowl. The little house looked so cosy and safe in the darkness, with a bright light showing through its blinds, and the chimney smoking beautifully, and Peter standing on guard. After a time he fell asleep, and some unsteady fairies had to climb over him on their way home from an orgy. Any of the other boys obstructing the fairy path at night they would have mischiefed, but they just tweaked Peter's nose and passed on.

CHAPTER VII

THE HOME
UNDER THE GROUND

One of the first things Peter did next day was to measure Wendy and John and Michael for hollow trees. Hook, you remember, had sneered at the boys for thinking they needed a tree apiece, but this was ignorance, for unless your tree fitted you it was difficult to go up and down, and no two of the boys were quite the same size. Once you fitted, you drew in your breath at the top, and down you went at exactly the right speed, while to ascend you drew in and let out alternately, and so wriggled up. Of course, when you have mastered the action you are able to do these things without thinking of them, and then nothing can be more graceful.

But you simply must fit, and Peter measures you for your tree as carefully as for a suit of clothes: the only difference being that the clothes are made to fit you, while you have to be made to fit the tree. Usually it is done quite easily, as by your wearing too many garments or too few, but if you are bumpy in awkward places or the only available tree is an odd shape, Peter does some things to you, and after that you fit. Once you fit, great care must be taken to go on fitting, and this, as Wendy was to discover to her delight, keeps a whole family in perfect condition.

Wendy and Michael fitted their trees at the first try, but John had to be altered a little.

After a few days' practice they could go up and down as gaily as buckets in a well. And how ardently they grew to love their home under the ground; especially Wendy! It consisted of one large room, as all houses should do, with a floor in which you could dig if you wanted to go fishing, and in this floor grew stout mushrooms of a charming colour, which were used as stools. A Never tree tried hard to grow in the centre of the room, but every morning they sawed the trunk through, level with the floor. By tea-time it was always about two feet high, and then they put a door on top of it, the whole thus becoming a table; as soon as they cleared away, they sawed off the trunk again, and thus there was more room to play. There was an enormous fireplace which was in almost any part of the room where you cared to light it, and across this Wendy stretched strings, made of fibre, from which she suspended her washing. The bed was tilted against the wall by day, and let down at 6:30, when it filled nearly half the room; and all the boys slept in it, except Michael, lying like sardines in a tin. There was a strict rule against turning round until one gave the signal, when all turned at once. Michael should have used it also, but Wendy would have a baby, and he was the littlest, and you know what women are, and the short and the long of it is that he was hung up in a basket.

It was rough and simple, and not unlike what baby bears would have made of an underground house in the same circumstances. But there was one recess in the wall, no larger than a bird-cage, which was the private apartment of Tinker Bell. It could be shut off from the rest of the home by a tiny curtain, which Tink, who was most fastidious, always kept drawn when dressing or undressing. No woman, however large, could have had a more exquisite boudoir and bed-chamber combined. The couch, as she always called it, was a genuine Queen Mab, with club legs; and she varied the bedspreads according to what fruit-blossom was in season. Her mirror was a Puss-in-boots, of which there are now only three, unchipped, known to the fairy dealers; the wash-stand was Pie-crust and reversible, the chest of drawers an authentic Charming the Sixth, and the carpet and rugs of the best (the early) period of Margery and Robin. There was a chandelier from Tiddlywinks for the look of the thing, but of course she lit the residence herself. Tink was very contemptuous of the rest of the house, as indeed was perhaps inevitable, and her chamber, though beautiful, looked rather conceited, having the appearance of a nose permanently turned up.

I suppose it was all especially entrancing to Wendy, because those rampagious boys of hers gave her so much to do. Really there were whole weeks when, except perhaps with a stocking in the evening, she was never above ground. The cooking, I can tell you, kept her nose to the pot, and even if there was nothing in it, even though there was no pot, she had to keep watching that it came aboil just the same. You never exactly knew whether there would be a real meal or just a make-believe, it all depended upon Peter's whim: he could eat, really eat, if it was part of a game, but he could not stodge just to feel stodgy, which is what most children like better than anything else; the next best thing being to talk about it. Make-believe was so real to him that during a meal of it you could see him getting rounder. Of course it was trying, but you simply had to follow his lead, and if you could prove to him that you were getting loose for your tree he let you stodge.

Wendy's favourite time for sewing and darning was after they had all gone to bed. Then, as she expressed it, she had a breathing time for herself; and she occupied it in making new things for them, and putting double pieces on the knees, for they were all most frightfully hard on their knees.

When she sat down to a basketful of their stockings, every heel with a hole in it, she would fling up her arms and exclaim, "Oh dear, I am sure I sometimes think spinsters are to be envied!"

Her face beamed when she exclaimed this.

You remember about her pet wolf. Well, it very soon discovered that she had come to the island and found her out, and they just ran into each other's arms. After that it followed her about everywhere.

As time wore on did she think much about the beloved parents she had left behind her? This is a difficult question, because it is quite impossible to say how time does wear on in the Neverland, where it is calculated by moons and suns, and there are ever so many more of them than on the mainland. But I am afraid that Wendy did not really worry about her father and mother, she was absolutely confident that they would always keep the window open for her to fly back by, and this gave her complete ease of mind. What did disturb her at times was that John remembered his parents vaguely only, as people he had once known, while Michael was quite willing to believe that she was really his mother. These things scared her a little, and nobly anxious to do her duty, she tried to fix the old life in their minds by setting them examination papers on it, as like as possible to the ones she used to do at school. The other boys thought this awfully interesting, and insisted on joining, and they made slates for themselves, and sat round the table, writing and thinking hard about the questions she had written on another slate and passed round. They were the most ordinary questions — "What was the colour of Mother's eyes? Which was taller, Father or Mother? Was Mother blonde or brunette? Answer all three questions if possible." "(A) Write an essay of not less than 40 words on How I spent my last Holidays, or The Carakters of Father and Mother compared. Only one of these to be attempted." Or "(1) Describe Mother's laugh; (2) Describe Father's laugh; (3) Describe Mother's Party Dress; (4) Describe the Kennel and its Inmate."

They were just everyday questions like these, and when you could not answer them you were told to make a cross; and it was really dreadful what a number of crosses even John made. Of course the only boy who replied to every question was Slightly, and no one could have been more hopeful of coming out first, but his answers were perfectly ridiculous, and he really came out last: a melancholy thing.

Peter did not compete. For one thing he despised all mothers except Wendy, and for another he was the only boy on the island who could neither write nor spell; not the smallest word. He was above all that sort of thing.

By the way, the questions were all written in the past tense. What was the colour of Mother's eyes, and so on. Wendy, you see, had been forgetting too.

Adventures, of course, as we shall see, were of daily occurrence; but about this time Peter invented, with Wendy's help, a new game that fascinated him enormously, until he suddenly had no more interest in it, which, as you have been told, was what always happened with his games. It consisted in pretending not to have adventures, in doing the sort of thing John and Michael had been doing all their lives, sitting on stools flinging balls in the air, pushing each other, going out for walks and coming back without having killed so much as a grizzly. To see Peter doing nothing on a stool was a great sight; he could not help looking solemn at such times, to sit still seemed to him such a comic thing to do. He boasted that he had gone a walk for the good of his health. For several suns these were the most novel of all adventures to him; and John and Michael had to pretend to be delighted also; otherwise he would have treated them severely.

He often went out alone, and when he came back you were never absolutely certain whether he had had an adventure or not. He might have forgotten it so completely that he said nothing about it; and then when you went out you found the body; and, on the other hand, he might say a great deal about it, and yet you could not find the body. Sometimes he came home with his head bandaged, and then Wendy cooed over him and bathed it in lukewarm water, while he told a dazzling tale. But she was never quite sure, you know. There were, however, many adventures which she knew to be true because she was in them herself, and there were still more that were at least partly true, for the other boys were in them and said they were wholly true. To describe them all would require a book as large as an English-Latin, Latin-English Dictionary, and the most we can do is to give one as a specimen of an average hour on the island. The difficulty is which one to choose. Should we take the brush with the redskins at Slightly Gulch? It was a sanguinary affair, and especially interesting as showing one of Peter's peculiarities, which was that in the middle of a fight he would suddenly change sides. At the Gulch, when victory was still in the balance, sometimes leaning this way and sometimes that, he called out, "I'm redskin to-day; what are you, Tootles?" And Tootles answered, "Redskin; what are you, Nibs?" and Nibs said, "Redskin; what are you, Twin?" and so on; and they were all redskin; and of course this would have ended the fight had not the real redskins, fascinated by Peter's methods, agreed to be lost boys for that once, and so at it they all went again, more fiercely than ever.

The extraordinary upshot of this adventure was — but we have not decided yet that this is the adventure we are to narrate. Perhaps a better one would be the night attack by the redskins on the house under the ground, when several of them stuck in the hollow trees and had to be pulled out like corks. Or we might tell how Peter saved Tiger Lily's life in the Mermaids' Lagoon, and so made her his ally.

Or we could tell of that cake the pirates cooked so that the boys might eat it and perish; and how they placed it in one cunning spot after another; but always Wendy snatched it from the hands of her children, so that in time it lost its succulence, and became as hard as stone, and was used as a missile, and Hook fell over it in the dark.

Or suppose we tell of the birds that were Peter's friends, particularly of the Never bird that built in a tree overhanging the lagoon, and how the nest fell into the water, and still the bird sat on her eggs, and Peter gave orders that she was not to be disturbed. That is a pretty story, and the end shows how grateful a bird can be; but if we tell it we must also tell the whole adventure of the lagoon, which would of course be telling two adventures rather than just one. A shorter adventure, and quite as exciting, was Tinker Bell's attempt, with the help of some street fairies, to have the sleeping Wendy conveyed on a great floating leaf to the mainland. Fortunately the leaf gave way and Wendy woke, thinking it was bath-time, and swam back. Or again, we might choose Peter's defiance of the lions, when he drew a circle round him on the ground with an arrow and dared them to cross it; and though he waited for hours, with the other boys and Wendy looking on breathlessly from trees, not one of them would accept his challenge.

Which of these adventures shall we choose? The best way will be to toss for it.

I have tossed, and the lagoon has won. This almost makes one wish that the gulch or the cake or Tink's leaf had won. Of course I could do it again, and make it best out of three; however, perhaps fairest to stick to the lagoon.

CHAPTER VIII

THE MERMAIDS' LAGOON

f you shut your eyes and are a lucky one, you may see at times a shapeless pool of lovely pale colours suspended in the darkness; then if you squeeze your eyes tighter, the pool begins to take shape, and the colours become so vivid that with another squeeze they must go on fire. But just before they go on fire you see the lagoon. This is the nearest you ever get to it on the mainland, just one heavenly moment; if there could be two moments you might see the surf and hear the mermaids singing.

The children often spent long summer days on this lagoon, swimming or floating most of the time, playing the mermaid games in the water, and so forth. You must not think from this that the mermaids were on friendly terms with them: on the contrary, it was among Wendy's lasting regrets that all the time she was on the island she never had a civil word from one of them. When she stole softly to the edge of the lagoon she might see them by the score, especially on Marooners' Rock, where they loved to bask, combing out their hair in a lazy way that quite irritated her; or she might even swim, on tiptoe as it were, to within a yard of them, but then they saw her and dived, probably splashing her with their tails, not by accident, but intentionally.

They treated all the boys in the same way, except of course Peter, who chatted with them on Marooners' Rock by the hour and sat on their tails when they got cheeky. He gave Wendy one of their combs.

The most haunting time at which to see them is at the turn of the moon, when they utter strange wailing cries; but the lagoon is dangerous for mortals then, and until the evening of which we have now to tell, Wendy had never seen the lagoon by moonlight, less from fear, for of

course Peter would have accompanied her, than because she had strict rules about every one being in bed by seven. She was often at the lagoon, however, on sunny days after rain, when the mermaids come up in extraordinary numbers to play with their bubbles. The bubbles of many colours made in rainbow water they treat as balls, hitting them gaily from one to another with their tails, and trying to keep them in the rainbow till they burst. The goals are at each end of the rainbow, and the keepers only are allowed to use their hands. Sometimes a dozen of these games will be going on in the lagoon at a time, and it is quite a pretty sight.

But the moment the children tried to join in they had to play by themselves, for the mermaids immediately disappeared. Nevertheless we have proof that they secretly watched the interlopers, and were not above taking an idea from them; for John introduced a new way of hitting the bubble, with the head instead of the hand, and the mermaids adopted it. This is the one mark that John has left on the Neverland.

It must also have been rather pretty to see the children resting on a rock for half an hour after their mid-day meal. Wendy insisted on their doing this, and it had to be a real rest even though the meal was make-believe. So they lay there in the sun, and their bodies glistened in it, while she sat beside them and looked important.

It was one such day, and they were all on Marooners' Rock. The rock was not much larger than their great bed, but of course they all knew how not to take up much room, and they were dozing or at least lying with their eyes shut, and pinching occasionally when they thought Wendy was not looking. She was very busy stitching.

While she stitched a change came to the lagoon. Little shivers ran over it, and the sun went away and shadows stole across the water, turning it cold. Wendy could no longer see to thread her needle, and when she looked up, the lagoon that had always hitherto been such a laughing place seemed formidable and unfriendly.

It was not, she knew, that night had come, but something as dark as night had come. No, worse than that. It had not come, but it had sent that shiver through the sea to say that it was coming. What was it?

There crowded upon her all the stories she had been told of Marooners' Rock, so called because evil captains put sailors on it and leave them there to drown. They drown when the tide rises, for then it is submerged.

Of course she should have roused the children at once; not merely because of the unknown that was stalking toward them, but because it was no longer good for them to sleep on a rock grown chilly. But she was a young mother and she did not know this; she thought you simply must stick to your rule about half an hour after the mid-day meal. So, though fear was upon her, and she longed to hear male voices, she would not waken them. Even when she heard the sound of muffled oars, though her heart was in her mouth, she did not waken them. She stood over them 'to let them have their sleep out. Was it not brave of Wendy?

It was well for those boys then that there was one among them who could sniff danger even in his sleep. Peter sprang erect, as wide awake at once as a dog, and with one warning cry he roused the others.

He stood motionless, one hand to his ear. "Pirates!" he cried. The others came closer to him. A strange smile was playing about his face, and Wendy saw it and shuddered. While that smile was on his face no one dared address him; all they could do was to stand ready to obey. The order came sharp and incisive.

"Dive!"

There was a gleam of legs, and instantly the lagoon seemed deserted. Marooners' Rock stood alone in the forbidding waters, as if it were itself marooned.

The boat drew nearer. It was the pirate dinghy, with three figures in her, Smee and Starkey, and the third a captive, no other than Tiger Lily. Her hands and ankles were tied, and she knew what was to be her fate. She was to be left on the rock to perish, an end to one of her race more terrible than death by fire or torture, for is it not written in the book of the tribe that there is no path through water to the happy hunting-ground? Yet her face was impassive; she was the daughter of a chief, she must die as a chief's daughter, it is enough.

They had caught her boarding the pirate ship with a knife in her mouth. No watch was kept on the ship, it being Hook's boast that the wind of his name guarded the ship for a mile around. Now her fate would help to guard it also. One more wail would go the round in that wind by night.

In the gloom that they brought with them the two pirates did not see the rock till they crashed into it.

"Luff, you lubber," cried an Irish voice that was Smee's; "here's the rock. Now, then, what we have to do is to hoist the redskin on to it and leave her there to drown."

It was the work of one brutal moment to land the beautiful girl on the rock; she was too proud to offer a vain resistance.

Quite near the rock, but out of sight, two heads were bobbing up and down, Peter's and Wendy's. Wendy was crying, for it was the first tragedy she had seen. Peter had seen many tragedies, but he had forgotten them all. He was less sorry than Wendy for Tiger Lily: it was two against one that angered him, and he meant to save her. An easy way would have been to wait until the pirates had gone, but he was never one to choose the easy way.

There was almost nothing he could not do, and he now imitated the voice of Hook.

"Ahoy there, you lubbers!" he called. It was a marvellous imitation.

"The captain!" said the pirates, staring at each other in surprise.

"He must be swimming out to us," Starkey said, when they had looked for him in vain.

"We are putting the redskin on the rock," Smee called out.

"Set her free," came the astonishing answer.

"Free!"

"Yes, cut her bonds and let her go."

"But, captain—"

"At once, d'ye hear," cried Peter, "or I'll plunge my hook in you."

"This is queer!" Smee gasped.

"Better do what the captain orders," said Starkey nervously.

"Ay, ay," Smee said, and he cut Tiger Lily's cords. At once like an eel she slid between Starkey's legs into the water.

Of course Wendy was very elated over Peter's cleverness; but she knew that he would be elated also and very likely crow and thus betray himself, so at once her hand went out to cover his mouth. But it was stayed even in the act, for "Boat ahoy!" rang over the lagoon in Hook's voice, but this time it was not Peter who had spoken.

Peter may have been about to crow, but his face puckered in a whistle of surprise instead.

"Boat ahoy!" again came the voice.

Now Wendy understood. The real Hook was also in the water.

He was swimming to the boat, and as his men showed a light to guide him he had soon reached them. In the light of the lantern Wendy saw his hook grip the boat's side; she saw his evil swarthy face as he rose dripping from the water, and, quaking, she would have liked to swim away, but Peter would not budge. He was tingling with life and also top-heavy with conceit. "Am I not a wonder, oh, I am a wonder!" he whispered to her, and though she thought so also, she was really glad for the sake of his reputation that no one heard him except herself.

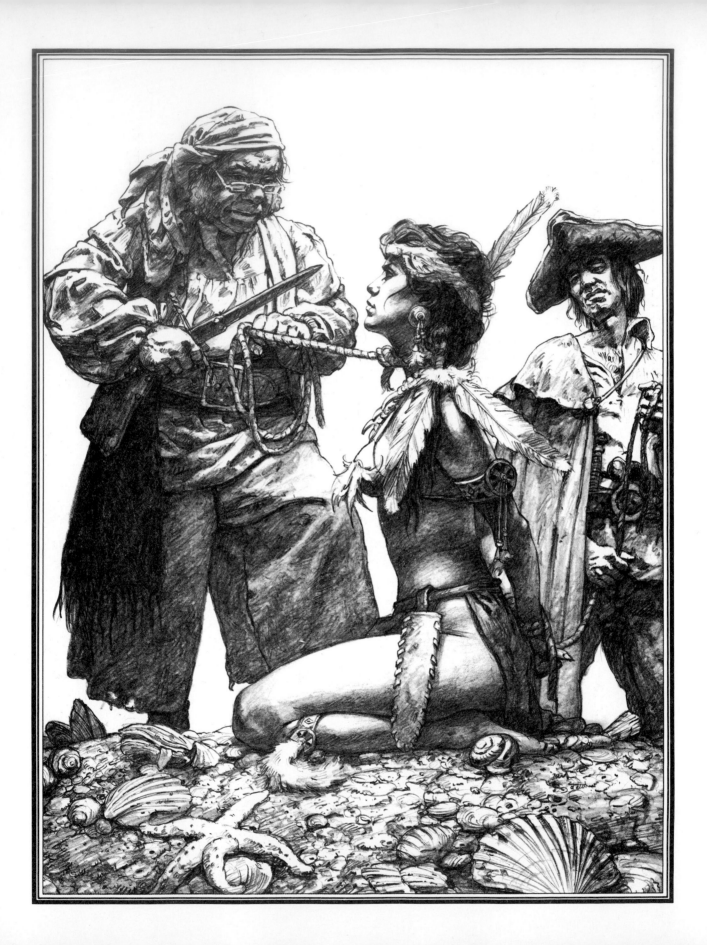

He signed to her to listen.

The two pirates were very curious to know what had brought their captain to them, but he sat with his head on his hook in a position of profound melancholy.

"Captain, is all well?" they asked timidly, but he answered with a hollow moan.

"He sighs," said Smee.

"He sighs again," said Starkey.

"And yet a third time he sighs," said Smee.

"What's up, captain?"

Then at last he spoke passionately.

"The game's up," he cried, "those boys have found a mother."

Affrighted though she was, Wendy swelled with pride.

"O evil day!" cried Starkey.

"What's a mother?" asked the ignorant Smee.

Wendy was so shocked that she exclaimed, "He doesn't know!" and always after this she felt that if you could have a pet pirate Smee would be her one.

Peter pulled her beneath the water, for Hook had started up, crying, "What was that?"

"I heard nothing," said Starkey, raising the lantern over the waters, and as the pirates looked they saw a strange sight. It was the nest I have told you of, floating on the lagoon, and the Never bird was sitting on it.

"See," said Hook in answer to Smee's question, "that is a mother. What a lesson! The nest must have fallen into the water, but would the mother desert her eggs? No."

There was a break in his voice, as if for a moment he recalled innocent days when — but he brushed away this weakness with his hook.

Smee, much impressed, gazed at the bird as the nest was borne past, but the more suspicious Starkey said, "If she is a mother, perhaps she is hanging about here to help Peter."

Hook winced. "Ay," he said, "that is the fear that haunts me."

He was roused from this dejection by Smee's eager voice.

"Captain," said Smee, "could we not kidnap these boys' mother and make her our mother?"

"It is a princely scheme," cried Hook, and at once it took practical shape in his great brain. "We will seize the children and carry them to the boat: the boys we will make walk the plank, and Wendy shall be our mother."

Again Wendy forgot herself.

"Never!" she cried, and bobbed.

"What was that?"

But they could see nothing. They thought it must have been but a leaf in the wind. "Do you agree, my bullies?" asked Hook.

"There is my hand on it," they both said.

"And there is my hook. Swear."

They all swore. By this time they were on the rock, and suddenly Hook remembered Tiger Lily.

"Where is the redskin?" he demanded abruptly.

He had a playful humour at moments, and they thought this was one of the moments.

"That is all right, captain," Smee answered complacently; "we let her go."

"Let her go!" cried Hook.

"'Twas your own orders," the bo'sun faltered.

"You called over the water to us to let her go," said Starkey.

"Brimstone and gall," thundered Hook, "what cozening is here!" His face had gone black with rage, but he saw that they believed their words, and he was startled. "Lads," he said, shaking a little, "I gave no such order."

"It is passing queer," Smee said, and they all fidgeted uncomfortably. Hook raised his voice, but there was a quiver in it.

"Spirit that haunts this dark lagoon to-night," he cried, "dost hear me?"

Of course Peter should have kept quiet, but of course he did not. He immediately answered in Hook's voice:

"Odds, bobs, hammer and tongs, I hear you."

In that supreme moment Hook did not blanch, even at the gills, but Smee and Starkey clung to each other in terror.

"Who are you, stranger, speak?" Hook demanded.

"I am James Hook," replied the voice, "captain of the *Jolly Roger.*"

"You are not; you are not," Hook cried hoarsely.

"Brimstone and gall," the voice retorted, "say that again, and I'll cast anchor in you."

Hook tried a more ingratiating manner. "If you are Hook," he said almost humbly, "come tell me, who am I?"

"A codfish," replied the voice, "only a codfish."

"A codfish!" Hook echoed blankly, and it was then, but not till then, that his proud spirit broke. He saw his men draw back from him.

"Have we been captained all this time by a codfish!" they muttered. "It is lowering to our pride."

They were his dogs snapping at him, but, tragic figure though he had become, he scarcely heeded them. Against such fearful evidence it was not their belief in him that he needed, it was his own. He felt his ego slipping from him. "Don't desert me, bully," he whispered hoarsely to it.

In his dark nature there was a touch of the feminine, as in all the greatest pirates, and it sometimes gave him intuitions. Suddenly he tried the guessing game.

"Hook," he called, "have you another voice?"

Now Peter could never resist a game, and he answered blithely in his own voice, "I have."

"And another name?"

"Ay, ay."

"Vegetable?" asked Hook.

"No."

"Mineral?"

"No."

"Animal?"

"Yes."

"Man?"

"No!" This answer rang out scornfully.

"Boy?"

"Yes."

"Ordinary boy?"

"No!"

"Wonderful boy?"

To Wendy's pain the answer that rang out this time was "Yes."

"Are you in England?"

"No."

"Are you here?"

"Yes."

Hook was completely puzzled. "You ask him some questions," he said to the others, wiping his damp brow.

Smee reflected. "I can't think of a thing ," he said regretfully.

"Can't guess, can't guess!" crowed Peter. "Do you give it up?"

Of course in his pride he was carrying the game too far, and the miscreants saw their chance.

"Yes, yes," they answered eagerly.

"Well, then," he cried, "I am Peter Pan!"

Pan!

In a moment Hook was himself again, and Smee and Starkey were his faithful henchmen.

"Now we have him," Hook shouted. "Into the water, Smee. Starkey, mind the boat. Take him dead or alive!"

He leaped as he spoke, and simultaneously came the gay voice of Peter.

"Are you ready, boys?"

"Ay, ay" from various parts of the lagoon.

"Then lam into the pirates."

The fight was short and sharp. First to draw blood was John, who gallantly climbed into the boat and held Starkey. There was a fierce struggle, in which the cutlass was torn from the pirate's grasp. He wriggled overboard and John leapt after him. The dinghy drifted away.

Here and there a head bobbed up in the water, and there was a flash of steel followed by a cry or a whoop. In the confusion some struck at their own side. The corkscrew of Smee got Tootles in the fourth rib, but he was himself pinked in turn by Curly. Farther from the rock Starkey was pressing Slightly and the twins hard.

Where all this time was Peter? He was seeking bigger game.

The others were all brave boys, and they must not be blamed for backing from the pirate captain. His iron claw made a circle of dead water round him, from which they fled like affrighted fishes.

But there was one who did not fear him: there was one prepared to enter that circle.

Strangely, it was not in the water that they met. Hook rose to the rock to breathe, and at the same moment Peter scaled it on the opposite side. The rock was slippery as a ball, and they had to crawl rather than climb. Neither knew that the other was coming. Each feeling for a grip met the other's arm: in surprise they raised their heads; their faces were almost touching; so they met.

Some of the greatest heroes have confessed that just before they fell to they had a sinking. Had it been so with Peter at that moment I would admit it. After all, this was the only man that the Sea-Cook had feared. But Peter had no sinking, he had one feeling only, gladness; and he gnashed his pretty teeth with joy. Quick as thought he snatched a knife from Hook's belt and was about to drive it home, when he saw that he was higher up the rock than his foe. It would not have been fighting fair.

He gave the pirate a hand to help him up.

It was then that Hook bit him.

Not the pain of this but its unfairness was what dazed Peter. It made him quite helpless. He could only stare, horrified. Every child is affected thus the first time he is treated unfairly. All he thinks he has a right to when he comes to you to be yours is fairness. After you have been unfair to him he will love you again, but he will never afterwards be quite the same boy. No one ever gets over the first unfairness; no one except Peter. He often met it, but he always forgot it. I suppose that was the real difference between him and all the rest.

So when he met it now it was like the first time; and he could just stare, helpless. Twice the iron hand clawed him.

A few minutes afterwards the other boys saw Hook in the water striking wildly for the ship; no elation on his pestilent face now, only white fear, for the crocodile was in dogged pursuit of him. On ordinary occasions the boys would have swum alongside cheering; but now they were uneasy, for they had lost both Peter and Wendy, and were scouring the lagoon for them, calling them by name. They found the dinghy and went home in it, shouting "Peter, Wendy" as they went, but no answer came save mocking laughter from the mermaids. "They must be swimming back or flying," the boys concluded. They were not very anxious, they had such faith in Peter. They chuckled, boylike, because they would be late for bed; and it was all mother Wendy's fault!

When their voices died away there came cold silence over the lagoon, and then a feeble cry.

"Help, help!"

Two small figures were beating against the rock; the girl had fainted and lay on the boy's arm. With a last effort Peter pulled her up the rock and then lay down beside her. Even as he also fainted he saw that the water was rising. He knew that they would soon be drowned, but he could do no more.

As they lay side by side a mermaid caught Wendy by the feet, and began pulling her softly into the water. Peter, feeling her slip from him, woke with a start, and was just in time to draw her back. But he had to tell her the truth.

"We are on the rock, Wendy," he said, "but it is growing smaller. Soon the water will be over it."

She did not understand even now.

"We must go," she said, almost brightly.

"Yes," he answered faintly.

"Shall we swim or fly, Peter?"

He had to tell her.

"Do you think you could swim or fly as far as the island, Wendy, without my help?"

She had to admit that she was too tired.

He moaned.

"What is it?" she asked, anxious about him at once.

"I can't help you, Wendy. Hook wounded me. I can neither fly nor swim."

"Do you mean we shall both be drowned?"

"Look how the water is rising."

They put their hands over their eyes to shut out the sight. They thought they would soon be no more. As they sat thus something brushed against Peter as light as a kiss, and stayed there, as if saying timidly, "Can I be of any use?"

It was the tail of a kite, which Michael had made some days before. It had torn itself out of his hand and floated away.

"Michael's kite," Peter said without interest, but next moment he had seized the tail, and was pulling the kite toward him.

"It lifted Michael off the ground," he cried; "why should it not carry you?"

"Both of us!"

"It can't lift two; Michael and Curly tried."

"Let us draw lots," Wendy said bravely.

"And you a lady; never." Already he had tied the tail round her. She clung to him; she refused to go without him; but with a "Good-bye, Wendy," he pushed her from the rock; and in a few minutes she was borne out of his sight. Peter was alone on the lagoon.

The rock was very small now; soon it would be submerged. Pale rays of light tiptoed across the waters; and by and by there was to be heard a sound at once the most musical and the most melancholy in the world: the mermaids calling to the moon.

Peter was not quite like other boys; but he was afraid at last. A tremor ran through him, like a shudder passing over the sea; but on the sea one shudder follows another till there are hundreds of them, and Peter felt just the one. Next moment he was standing erect on the rock again, with that smile on his face and a drum beating within him. It was saying, "To die will be an awfully big adventure."

CHAPTER IX

THE NEVER BIRD

he last sounds Peter heard before he was quite alone were the mermaids retiring one by one to their bedchambers under the sea. He was too far away to hear their doors shut; but every door in the coral caves where they live rings a tiny bell when it opens or closes (as in all the nicest houses on the mainland), and he heard the bells.

Steadily the waters rose till they were nibbling at his feet; and to pass the time until they made their final gulp, he watched the only thing moving on the lagoon. He thought it was a piece of floating paper, perhaps part of the kite, and wondered idly how long it would take to drift ashore.

Presently he noticed as an odd thing that it was undoubtedly out upon the lagoon with some definite purpose, for it was fighting the tide, and sometimes winning; and when it won, Peter, always sympathetic to the weaker side, could not help clapping; it was such a gallant piece of paper.

It was not really a piece of paper; it was the Never bird, making desperate efforts to reach Peter on her nest. By working her wings, in a way she had learned since the nest fell into the water, she was able to some extent to guide her strange craft, but by the time Peter recognised her she was very exhausted. She had come to save him, to give him her nest, though there were eggs in it. I rather wonder at the bird, for though he had been nice to her, he had also sometimes tormented her. I can suppose only that, like Mrs. Darling and the rest of them, she was melted because he had all his first teeth.

She called out to him what she had come for, and he called out to her what was she doing there; but of course neither of them understood the other's language. In fanciful stories people can talk to the birds freely, and I wish for the moment I could pretend that this was such a story, and say that Peter replied intelligently to the Never bird; but truth is best, and I want to tell only what really happened. Well, not only could they not understand each other, but they forgot their manners.

"I — want — you — to — get — into — the — nest," the bird called, speaking as slowly and distinctly as possible, "and — then — you — can — drift — ashore, but — I — am — too — tired — to — bring — it — any — nearer — so — you — must — try — to — swim — to — it."

"What are you quacking about?" Peter answered. "Why don't you let the nest drift as usual?"

"I — want — you —" the bird said, and repeated it all over.

Then Peter tried slow and distinct.

"What — are — you — quacking — about?" and so on.

The Never bird became irritated; they have very short tempers.

"You dunderheaded little jay," she screamed, "why don't you do as I tell you?"

Peter felt that she was calling him names, and at a venture he retorted hotly:

"So are you!"

Then rather curiously they both snapped out the same remark.

"Shut up!"

"Shut up!"

Nevertheless the bird was determined to save him if she could, and by one last mighty effort she propelled the nest against the rock. Then up she flew; deserting her eggs, so as to make her meaning clear.

Then at last he understood, and clutched the nest and waved his thanks to the bird as she fluttered overhead. It was not to receive his thanks, however, that she hung there in the sky; it was not even to watch him get into the nest; it was to see what he did with her eggs.

There were two large white eggs, and Peter lifted them up and reflected. The bird covered her face with her wings, so as not to see the last of them; but she could not help peeping between the feathers.

I forget whether I have told you that there was a stave on the rock, driven into it by some buccaneers of long ago to mark the site of buried treasure. The children had discovered the glittering hoard, and when in mischievous mood used to fling showers of moidores, diamonds, pearls and pieces of eight to the gulls, who pounced upon them for food, and then flew away, raging at the scurvy trick that had been played upon them. The stave was still there, and on it Starkey had hung his hat, a deep tarpaulin, watertight, with a broad brim. Peter put the eggs into this hat and set it on the lagoon. It floated beautifully.

The Never bird saw at once what he was up to, and screamed her admiration of him; and, alas, Peter crowed his agreement with her. Then he got into the nest, reared the stave in it as a mast, and hung up his shirt for a sail. At the same moment the bird fluttered down upon the hat and once more sat snugly on her eggs. She drifted in one direction, and he was borne off in another, both cheering.

Of course when Peter landed he beached his barque in a place where the bird would easily find it; but the hat was such a great success that she abandoned the nest. It drifted about till it went to pieces, and often Starkey came to the shore of the lagoon, and with many bitter feelings watched the bird sitting on his hat. As we shall not see her again, it may be worth mentioning here that all Never birds now build in that shape of nest, with a broad brim on which the youngsters take an airing.

Great were the rejoicings when Peter reached the home under the ground almost as soon as Wendy, who had been carried hither and thither by the kite. Every boy had adventures to tell; but perhaps the biggest adventure of all was that they were several hours late for bed. This so inflated them that they did various dodgy things to get staying up still longer, such as demanding bandages; but Wendy, though glorying in having them all home again safe and sound, was scandalised by the lateness of the hour, and cried, "To bed, to bed," in a voice that had to be obeyed. Next day, however, she was awfully tender, and gave out bandages to every one, and they played till bed-time at limping about and carrying their arms in slings.

CHAPTER X

THE HAPPY HOME

One important result of the brush on the lagoon was that it made the redskins their friends. Peter had saved Tiger Lily from a dreadful fate, and now there was nothing she and her braves would not do for him. All night they sat above, keeping watch over the home under the ground and awaiting the big attack by the pirates which obviously could not be much longer delayed. Even by day they hung about, smoking the pipe of peace, and looking almost as if they wanted tit-bits to eat.

They called Peter the Great White Father, prostrating themselves before him; and he liked this tremendously, so that it was not really good for him.

"The great white father," he would say to them in a very lordly manner, as they grovelled at his feet, "is glad to see the Piccaninny warriors protecting his wigwam from the pirates."

"Me Tiger Lily," that lovely creature would reply, "Peter Pan save me, me his velly nice friend. Me no let pirates hurt him."

She was far too pretty to cringe in this way, but Peter thought it his due, and he would answer condescendingly, "It is good. Peter Pan has spoken."

Always when he said, "Peter Pan has spoken," it meant that they must now shut up, and they accepted it humbly in that spirit; but they were by no means so respectful to the other boys, whom they looked upon as just ordinary braves. They said "How-do?" to them, and things like that; and what annoyed the boys was that Peter seemed to think this all right.

Secretly Wendy sympathised with them a little, but she was far too loyal a housewife to listen to any complaints against father. "Father knows best," she always said, whatever her private opinion must be. Her private opinion was that the redskins should not call her a squaw.

We have now reached the evening that was to be known among them as the Night of Nights, because of its adventures and their upshot. The day, as if quietly gathering its forces, had been almost uneventful, and now the redskins in their blankets were at their posts above, while, below, the children were having their evening meal; all except Peter, who had gone out to get the time. The way you got the time on the island was to find the crocodile, and then stay near him till the clock struck.

This meal happened to be a make-believe tea, and they sat round the board, guzzling in their greed; and really, what with their chatter and recriminations, the noise, as Wendy said, was positively deafening. To be sure, she did not mind noise, but she simply would not have them grabbing things, and then excusing themselves by saying that Tootles had pushed their elbow. There was a fixed rule that they must never hit back at meals, but should refer the matter of dispute to Wendy by raising the right arm politely and saying, "I complain of so-and-so"; but what usually happened was that they forgot to do this or did it too much.

"Silence," cried Wendy when for the twentieth time she had told them that they were not all to speak at once. "Is your mug empty, Slightly darling?"

"Not quite empty, mummy," Slightly said, after looking into an imaginary mug.

"He hasn't even begun to drink his milk," Nibs interposed.

This was telling, and Slightly seized his chance.

"I complain of Nibs," he cried promptly.

John, however, had held up his hand first.

"Well, John?"

"May I sit in Peter's chair, as he is not here?"

"Sit in father's chair, John!" Wendy was scandalised. "Certainly not."

"He is not really our father," John answered.

"He didn't even know how a father does till I showed him."

This was grumbling. "We complain of John," cried the twins.

Tootles held up his hand. He was so much the humblest of them, indeed he was the only humble one, that Wendy was specially gentle with him.

"I don't suppose," Tootles said diffidently, "that I could be father."

"No, Tootles."

Once Tootles began, which was not very often, he had a silly way of going on.

"As I can't be father," he said heavily, "I don't suppose, Michael, you would let me be baby?"

"No, I won't," Michael rapped out. He was already in his basket.

"As I can't be baby," Tootles said, getting heavier and heavier, "do you think I could be a twin?"

"No, indeed," replied the twins; "it's awfully difficult to be a twin."

"As I can't be anything important," said Tootles, "would any of you like to see me do a trick?"

"No," they all replied.

Then at last he stopped. "I hadn't really any hope," he said.

The hateful telling broke out again.

"Slightly is coughing on the table."

"The twins began with cheese-cakes."

"Curly is taking both butter and honey."

"Nibs is speaking with his mouth full."

"I complain of the twins."

"I complain of Curly."

"I complain of Nibs."

"Oh dear, oh dear," cried Wendy, "I'm sure I sometimes think that spinsters are to be envied."

She told them to clear away, and sat down to her work-basket, a heavy load of stockings and every knee with a hole in it as usual.

"Wendy," remonstrated Michael, "I'm too big for a cradle."

"I must have somebody in a cradle," she said almost tartly, "and you are the littlest. A cradle is such a nice homely thing to have about a house."

While she sewed they played around her; such a group of happy faces and dancing limbs lit up by that romantic fire. It had become a very familiar scene this in the home under the ground, but we are looking on it for the last time.

There was a step above, and Wendy, you may be sure, was the first to recognise it.

"Children, I hear your father's step. He likes you to meet him at the door."

Above, the redskins crouched before Peter.

"Watch well, braves. I have spoken."

And then, as so often before, the gay children dragged him from his tree. As so often before, but never again.

He had brought nuts for the boys as well as the correct time for Wendy.

"Peter, you just spoil them, you know," Wendy simpered.

"Ah, old lady," said Peter, hanging up his gun.

"It was me told him mothers are called old lady," Michael whispered to Curly.

"I complain of Michael," said Curly instantly.

The first twin came to Peter. "Father, we want to dance."

"Dance away, my little man," said Peter, who was in high good humour.

"But we want you to dance."

Peter was really the best dancer among them, but he pretended to be scandalised.

"Me! My old bones would rattle!"

"And mummy too."

"What!" cried Wendy, "the mother of such an armful, dance!"

"But on a Saturday night," Slightly insinuated.

It was not really Saturday night, at least it may have been, for they had long lost count of the days; but always if they wanted to do anything special they said this was Saturday night, and then they did it.

"Of course it is Saturday night, Peter," Wendy said, relenting.

"People of our figure, Wendy!"

"But it is only among our own progeny."

"True, true."

So they were told they could dance, but they must put on their nighties first.

"Ah, old lady," Peter said aside to Wendy, warming himself by the fire and looking down at her as she sat turning a heel, "there is nothing more pleasant of an evening for you and me when the day's toil is over than to rest by the fire with the little ones near by."

"It is sweet, Peter, isn't it?" Wendy said, frightfully gratified. "Peter, I think Curly has your nose."

"Michael takes after you."

She went to him and put her hand on his shoulder.

"Dear Peter," she said, "with such a large family, of course, I have now passed my best, but you don't want to change me, do you?"

"No, Wendy."

Certainly he did not want a change, but he looked at her uncomfortably, blinking, you know, like one not sure whether he was awake or asleep.

"Peter, what is it?"

"I was just thinking," he said, a little scared. "It is only make-believe, isn't it, that I am their father?"

"Oh yes," Wendy said primly.

"You see," he continued apologetically, "it would make me seem so old to be their real father."

"But they are ours, Peter, yours and mine."

"But not really, Wendy?" he asked anxiously.

"Not if you don't wish it," she replied; and she distinctly heard his sigh of relief. "Peter," she asked, trying to speak firmly, "what are your exact feelings to me?"

"Those of a devoted son, Wendy."

"I thought so," she said, and went and sat by herself at the extreme end of the room.

"You are so queer," he said, frankly puzzled, "and Tiger Lily is just the same. There is something she wants to be to me, but she says it is not my mother."

"No, indeed, it is not," Wendy replied with frightful emphasis. Now we know why she was prejudiced against the redskins.

"Then what is it?"

"It isn't for a lady to tell."

"Oh, very well," Peter said, a little nettled. "Perhaps Tinker Bell will tell me."

"Oh yes, Tinker Bell will tell you," Wendy retorted scornfully. "She is an abandoned little creature."

Here Tink, who was in her bedroom, eavesdropping, squeaked out something impudent.

"She says she glories in being abandoned," Peter interpreted.

He had a sudden idea. "Perhaps Tink wants to be my mother?"

"You silly ass!" cried Tinker Bell in a passion.

She had said it so often that Wendy needed no translation.

"I almost agree with her," Wendy snapped. Fancy Wendy snapping! But she had been much tried, and she little knew what was to happen before the night was out. If she had known she would not have snapped.

None of them knew. Perhaps it was best not to know. Their ignorance gave them one more glad hour; and as it was to be their last hour on the island, let us rejoice that there were sixty glad minutes in it. They sang

and danced in their night-gowns. Such a deliciously creepy song it was, in which they pretended to be frightened at their own shadows, little witting that so soon shadows would close in upon them, from whom they would shrink in real fear. So uproariously gay was the dance, and how they buffeted each other on the bed and out of it! It was a pillow fight rather than a dance, and when it was finished, the pillows insisted on one bout more, like partners who know that they may never meet again. The stories they told, before it was time for Wendy's good-night story! Even Slightly tried to tell a story that night, and the beginning was so fearfully dull that it appalled not only the others but himself, and he said happily:

"Yes, it is a dull beginning. I say, let us pretend that it is the end."

And then at last they all got into bed for Wendy's story, the story they loved best, the story Peter hated. Usually when she began to tell this story, he left the room or put his hands over his ears; and possibly if he had done either of those things this time they might all still be on the island. But to-night he remained on his stool; and we shall see what happened.

CHAPTER XI

WENDY'S STORY

"Listen then," said Wendy, settling down to her story, with Michael at her feet and seven boys in the bed. "There was once a gentleman — "

"I had rather he had been a lady," Curly said.

"I wish he had been a white rat," said Nibs.

"Quiet," their mother admonished them. "There was a lady also, and — "

"O mummy," cried the first twin, "you mean that there is a lady also, don't you? She is not dead, is she?"

"Oh no."

"I am awfully glad she isn't dead," said Tootles. "Are you glad, John?"

"Of course I am."

"Are you glad, Nibs?"

"Rather."

"Are you glad, Twins?"

"We are just glad."

"Oh dear," sighed Wendy.

"Little less noise there," Peter called out, determined that she should have fair play, however beastly a story it might be in his opinion.

"The gentleman's name," Wendy continued, "was Mr. Darling, and her name was Mrs. Darling."

"I knew them," John said, to annoy the others.

"I think I knew them," said Michael rather doubtfully.

"They were married, you know," explained Wendy, "and what do you think they had?"

"White rats!" cried Nibs, inspired.

"No."

"It's awfully puzzling," said Tootles, who knew the story by heart.

"Quiet, Tootles. They had three descendants."

"What is descendants?"

"Well, you are one. Twin."

"Do you hear that, John? I am a descendant."

"Descendants are only children," said John.

"Oh dear, oh dear," sighed Wendy. "Now these three children had a faithful nurse called Nana; but Mr. Darling was angry with her and chained her up in the yard, and so all the children flew away."

"It's an awfully good story," said Nibs.

"They flew away," Wendy continued, "to the Neverland, where the lost children are."

"I just thought they did," Curly broke in excitedly. "I don't know how it is, but I just thought they did!"

"O Wendy," cried Tootles, "was one of the lost children called Tootles?"

"Yes, he was."

"I am in a story, Hurrah, I am in a story, Nibs."

"Hush. Now I want you to consider the feelings of the unhappy parents with all their children flown away."

"Oo!" they all moaned, though they were not really considering the feelings of the unhappy parents one jot.

"Think of the empty beds!"

"Oo!"

"It's awfully sad," the first twin said cheerfully.

"I don't see how it can have a happy ending," said the second twin. "Do you, Nibs?"

"I'm frightfully anxious."

"If you knew how great is a mother's love," Wendy told them triumphantly, "you would have no fear." She had now come to the part that Peter hated.

"I do like a mother's love," said Tootles, hitting Nibs with a pillow. "Do you like a mother's love, Nibs?"

"I do just," said Nibs, hitting back.

"You see," Wendy said complacently, "our heroine knew that the mother would always leave the window open for her children to fly back by; so they stayed away for years and had a lovely time."

"Did they ever go back?"

"Let us now," said Wendy, bracing herself up for her finest effort, "take a peep into the future"; and they all gave themselves the twist that makes peeps into the future easier. "Years have rolled by, and who is this elegant lady of uncertain age alighting at London Station?"

"O Wendy, who is she?" cried Nibs, every bit as excited as if he didn't know.

"Can it be — yes — no — it is — the fair Wendy!"

"Oh!"

"And who are the two noble portly figures accompanying her, now grown to man's estate? Can they be John and Michael? They are!"

"Oh!"

"See, dear brothers," says Wendy, pointing upwards, "there is the window still standing open. Ah, now we are rewarded for our sublime faith in a mother's love. So up they flew to their mummy and daddy, and pen cannot describe the happy scene, over which we draw a veil."

That was the story, and they were as pleased with it as the fair narrator herself. Everything just as it should be, you see. Off we skip like the most heartless things in the world, which is what children are, but so attractive; and we have an entirely selfish time, and then when we have need of special attention we nobly return for it, confident that we shall be rewarded instead of smacked.

So great indeed was their faith in a mother's love that they felt they could afford to be callous for a bit longer.

But there was one there who knew better, and when Wendy finished he uttered a hollow groan.

"What is it, Peter?" she cried, running to him, thinking he was ill. She felt him solicitously, lower down than his chest. "Where is it, Peter?"

"It isn't that kind of pain," Peter replied darkly.

"Then what kind is it?"

"Wendy, you are wrong about mothers."

They all gathered round him in affright, so alarming was his agitation; and with a fine candour he told them what he had hitherto concealed.

"Long ago," he said, "I thought like you that my mother would always keep the window open for me, so I stayed away for moons, and moons and moons, and then flew back; but the window was barred, for mother had forgotten all about me, and there was another little boy sleeping in my bed."

I am not sure that this was true, but Peter thought it was true; and it scared them.

"Are you sure mothers are like that?"

"Yes."

So this was the truth about mothers. The toads!

Still it is best to be careful; and no one knows so quickly as a child when he should give in. "Wendy, let us go home," cried John and Michael together.

"Yes," she said, clutching them.

"Not to-night?" asked the lost boys bewildered. They knew in what they called their hearts that one can get on quite well without a mother, and that it is only the mothers who think you can't.

"At once," Wendy replied resolutely, for the horrible thought had come to her: "Perhaps mother is in half mourning by this time."

This dread made her forgetful of what must be Peter's feelings, and she said to him rather sharply, "Peter, will you make the neccessary arrangements?"

"If you wish it," he replied, as coolly as if she had asked him to pass the nuts.

Not so much as a sorry-to-lose-you between them! If she did not mind the parting, he was going to show her, was Peter, that neither did he.

But of course he cared very much; and he was so full of wrath against grown-ups, who, as usual, were spoiling everything, that as soon as he got inside his tree he breathed intentionally quick short breaths at the rate of about five to a second. He did this because there is a saying in the Neverland that, every time you breathe, a grown-up dies; and Peter was killing them off vindictively as fast as possible.

Then having given the necessary instructions to the redskins he returned to the home, where an unworthy scene had been enacted in his absence. Panic-stricken at the thought of losing Wendy the lost boys had advanced upon her threateningly.

"It will be worse than before she came," they cried.

"We shan't let her go."

"Let's keep her prisoner."

"Ay, chain her up."

In her extremity an instinct told her to which of them to turn.

"Tootles," she cried, "I appeal to you."

Was it not strange? she appealed to Tootles, quite the silliest one.

Grandly, however, did Tootles respond. For that one moment he dropped his silliness and spoke with dignity.

"I am just Tootles," he said, "and nobody minds me. But the first who does not behave to Wendy like an English gentleman I will blood him severely."

He drew his hanger; and for that instant his sun was at noon. The others held back uneasily. Then Peter returned, and they saw at once that they would get no support from him. He would keep no girl in the Neverland against her will.

"Wendy," he said, striding up and down, "I have asked the redskins to guide you through the wood, as flying tires you so."

"Thank you, Peter."

"Then," he continued, in the short sharp voice of one accustomed to be obeyed, "Tinker Bell will take you across the sea. Wake her, Nibs."

Nibs had to knock twice before he got an answer, though Tink had really been sitting up in bed listening for some time.

"Who are you? How dare you? Go away," she cried.

"You are to get up, Tink," Nibs called, "and take Wendy on a journey."

Of course Tink had been delighted to hear that Wendy was going; but she was jolly well determined not to be her courier, and she said so in still more offensive language. Then she pretended to be asleep again.

"She says she won't!" Nibs exclaimed, aghast at such insubordination, whereupon Peter went sternly toward the young lady's chamber.

"Tink," he rapped out, "if you don't get up and dress at once I will open the curtains, and then we shall all see you in your *negligée*."

This made her leap to the floor. "Who said I wasn't getting up?" she cried.

In the meantime the boys were gazing very forlornly at Wendy, now equipped with John and Michael for the journey. By this time they were dejected, not merely because they were about to lose her, but also because they felt that she was going off to something nice to which they had not been invited. Novelty was beckoning to them as usual.

Crediting them with a nobler feeling, Wendy melted.

"Dear ones," she said, "if you will all come with me I feel almost sure I can get my father and mother to adopt you."

The invitation was meant specially for Peter, but each of the boys was thinking exclusively of himself, and at once they jumped with joy.

"But won't they think us rather a handful?" Nibs asked in the middle of his jump.

"Oh no," said Wendy, rapidly thinking it out, "it will only mean having a few beds in the drawing-room; they can be hidden behind screens on first Thursdays."

"Peter, can we go?" they all cried imploringly. They took it for granted that if they went he would go also, but really they scarcely cared. Thus children are ever ready, when novelty knocks, to desert their dearest ones.

"All right," Peter replied with a bitter smile, and immediately they rushed to get their things.

"And now, Peter," Wendy said, thinking she had put everything right, "I am going to give you your medicine before you go." She loved to give them medicine, and undoubtedly gave them too much. Of course it was only water, but it was out of a bottle, and she always shook the bottle and counted the drops, which gave it a certain medicinal quality. On this occasion, however, she did not give Peter his draught, for just as she had prepared it, she saw a look on his face that made her heart sink.

"Get your things, Peter," she cried, shaking.

"No," he answered, pretending indifference, "I am not going with you, Wendy."

"Yes, Peter."

"No."

To show that her departure would leave him umoved, he skipped up and down the room, playing gaily on his heartless pipes. She had to run about after him, though it was rather undignified.

"To find your mother," she coaxed.

Now, if Peter had ever quite had a mother, he no longer missed her. He could do very well without one. He had thought them out, and remembered only their bad points.

"No, no," he told Wendy decisively; "perhaps she would say I was old, and I just want always to be a little boy and to have fun."

"But, Peter — "

"No."

And so the others had to be told.

"Peter isn't coming."

Peter not coming! They gazed blankly at him, their sticks over their backs, and on each stick a bundle. Their first thought was that if Peter was not going he had probably changed his mind about letting them go.

But he was far too proud for that. "If you find your mothers," he said darkly, "I hope you will like them."

The awful cynicism of this made an uncomfortable impression, and most of them began to look rather doubtful. After all, their faces said, were they not noodles to want to go?

"Now then," cried Peter, "no fuss, no blubbering; good-bye, Wendy"; and he held out his hand cheerily, quite as if they must really go now, for he had something important to do.

She had to take his hand, as there was no indication that he would prefer a thimble.

"You will remember about changing your flannels, Peter?" she said, lingering over him. She was always so particular about their flannels.

"Yes."

"And you will take your medicine?"

"Yes."

That seemed to be everything, and an awkward pause followed. Peter, however, was not the kind that breaks down before people. "Are you ready, Tinker Bell?" he called out.

"Ay! ay!"

"Then lead the way."

Tink darted up the nearest tree; but no one followed her, for it was at this moment that the pirates made their dreadful attack upon the redskins. Above, where all had been so still, the air was rent with shrieks and the clash of steel. Below, there was dead silence. Mouths opened and remained open. Wendy fell on her knees, but her arms were extended toward Peter. All arms were extended to him, as if suddenly blown in his direction; they were beseeching him mutely not to desert them. As for Peter, he seized his sword, the same he thought he had slain Barbecue with, and the lust of battle was in his eye.

CHAPTER XII

THE CHILDREN ARE CARRIED OFF

he pirate attack had been a complete surpise: a sure proof that the unscrupulous Hook had conducted it improperly, for to surprise redskins fairly is beyond the wit of the white man.

By all the unwritten laws of savage warfare it is always the redskin who attacks, and with the wiliness of his race he does it just before the dawn, at which time he knows the courage of the whites to be at its lowest ebb. The white men have in the meantime made a rude stockade on the summit of yonder undulating ground, at the foot of which a stream runs, for it is destruction to be too far from water. There they await the onslaught, the inexperienced ones clutching their revolvers and treading on twigs, but the old hands sleeping tranquilly until just before the dawn. Through the long black night the savage scouts wriggle, snake-like, among the grass without stirring a blade. The brushwood closes behind them as silently as sand into which a mole has dived. Not a sound is to be heard, save when they give vent to a wonderful imitation of the lonely call of the coyote. The cry is answered by other braves; and some of them do it even better than the coyotes, who are not very good at it. So the chill hours wear on, and the long suspense is horribly trying to the paleface who has to live through it for the first time; but to the trained hand those ghastly calls and still ghastlier silences are but an intimation of how the night is marching.

That this was the usual procedure was so well-known to Hook that in disregarding it he cannot be excused on the plea of ignorance.

The Piccaninnies, on their part, trusted implicitly to his honour, and their whole action of the night stands out in marked contrast to his. They left nothing undone that was consistent with the reputation of their tribe. With that alertness of the senses which is at once the marvel and despair of civilised peoples, they knew that the pirates were on the island from the moment one of them trod on a dry stick; and in an incredibly short space of time the coyote cries began. Every foot of ground between the spot where Hook had landed his forces and the home under the trees was stealthily examined by braves wearing their moccasins with the heels in front. They found only one hillock with a stream at its base, so that Hook had no choice; here he must establish himself and wait for just before the dawn. Everything being thus mapped out with almost diabolical cunning, the main body of the redskins folded their blankets around them, and in the phlegmatic manner that is to them the pearl of manhood squatted above the children's home, awaiting the cold moment when they should deal pale death.

Here dreaming, though wide-awake, of the exquisite tortures to which they were to put him at break of day, those confiding savages were found by the treacherous Hook. From the accounts afterwards supplied by such of the scouts as escaped the carnage, he does not seem even to have paused at the rising ground, though it is certain that in the grey light he must have seen it: no thought of waiting to be attacked appears from first to last to have visited his subtle mind; he would not even hold off till the night was nearly spent; on he pounded with no policy but to fall to. What could the bewildered scouts do, masters as they were of every war-like artifice save this one, but trot helplessly after him, exposing themselves fatally to view, the while they gave pathetic utterance to the coyote cry.

Around the brave Tiger Lily were a dozen of her stoutest warriors, and they suddenly saw the perfidious pirates bearing down upon them. Fell from their eyes then the film through which they had looked at victory. No more would they torture at the stake. For them the happy hunting-grounds now. They knew it; but as their fathers' sons they acquitted themselves. Even then they had time to gather in a phalanx that would have been hard to break had they risen quickly, but this they were forbidden to do by the traditions of their race. It is written that the noble savage must never express surpise in the presence of the white. Thus terrible as the sudden appearance of the pirates must have been to them, they remained stationary for a moment, not a muscle moving; as if the

foe had come by invitation. Then, indeed, the tradition gallantly upheld, they seized their weapons, and the air was torn with the war-cry; but it was now too late.

It is no part of ours to describe what was a massacre rather than a fight. Thus perished many of the flower of the Piccaninny tribe. Not all unavenged did they die, for with Lean Wolf fell Alf Mason, to disturb the Spanish Main no more, and among others who bit the dust were Geo. Scourie, Chas. Turley, and the Alsatian Foggerty. Turley fell to the toma-hawk of the terrible Panther, who ultimately cut a way through the pirates with Tiger Lily and a small remnant of the tribe.

To what extent Hook is to blame for his tactics on this occasion is for the historian to decide. Had he waited on the rising ground till the proper hour he and his men would probably have been butchered; and in judging him it is only fair to take this into account. What he should perhaps have done was to acquaint his opponents that he proposed to follow a new method. On the other hand, this, as destroying the element of surprise, would have made his strategy of no avail, so that the whole question is beset with difficulties. One cannot at least withhold a reluctant admira-tion for the wit that had conceived so bold a scheme, and the fell genius with which it was carried out.

What were his own feelings about himself at the triumphant moment? Fain would his dogs have known, as breathing heavily and wip-ing their cutlasses, they gathered at a discreet distance from his hook, and squinted through their ferret eyes at this extraordinary man. Elation must have been in his heart, but his face did not reflect it: ever a dark and solitary enigma, he stood aloof from his followers in spirit as in sub-stance.

The night's work was not yet over, for it was not the redskins he had come out to destroy; they were but the bees to be smoked, so that he should get at the honey. It was Pan he wanted, Pan and Wendy and their band, but chiefly Pan.

Peter was such a small boy that one tends to wonder at the man's hatred of him. True he had flung Hook's arm to the crocodile, but even this and the increased insecurity of life to which it led, owing to the croc-odile's pertinacity, hardly account for a vindictiveness so relentless and malignant. The truth is that there was a something about Peter which goaded the pirate captain to frenzy. It was not his courage, it was not his engaging appearance, it was not —. There is no beating about the bush, for we know quite well what it was, and have got to tell. It was Peter's cockiness.

This had got on Hook's nerves; it made his iron claw twitch, and at night it disturbed him like an insect. While Peter lived, the tortured man felt that he was a lion in a cage into which a sparrow had come.

The question now was how to get down the trees, or how to get his dogs down? He ran his greedy eyes over them, searching for the thinnest ones. They wriggled uncomfortably, for they knew he would not scruple to ram them down with poles.

In the meantime, what of the boys? We have seen them at the first clang of weapons, turned as it were into stone figures, open-mouthed, all appealing with outstretched arms to Peter; and we return to them as their mouths close, and their arms fall to their sides. The pandemonium above has ceased almost as suddenly as it arose, passed like a fierce gust of wind; but they know that in the passing it has determined their fate.

Which side had won?

The pirates, listening avidly at the mouths of the trees, heard the question put by every boy, and alas, they also heard Peter's answer.

"If the redskins have won," he said, "they will beat the tom-tom; it is always their sign of victory."

Now Smee had found the tom-tom, and was at that moment sitting on it. "You will never hear the tom-tom again," he muttered, but inaudibly of course, for strict silence had been enjoined. To his amazement Hook signed to him to beat the tom-tom, and slowly there came to Smee an understanding of the dreadful wickedness of the order. Never, probably, had this simple man admired Hook so much.

Twice Smee beat upon the instrument, and then stopped to listen gleefully.

"The tom-tom," the miscreants heard Peter cry; "an Indian victory!"

The doomed children answered with a cheer that was music to the black hearts above, and almost immediately they repeated their good-byes to Peter. This puzzled the pirates, but all their other feelings were swallowed by a base delight that the enemy were about to come up the trees. They smirked at each other and rubbed their hands. Rapidly and silently Hook gave his orders: one man to each tree, and the others to arrange themselves in a line two yards apart.

CHAPTER XIII

DO YOU BELIEVE IN FAIRIES?

he more quickly this horror is disposed of the better. The first to emerge from his tree was Curly. He rose out of it into the arms of Cecco, who flung him to Smee, who flung him to Starkey, who flung him to Bill Jukes, who flung him to Noodler, and so he was tossed from one to another till he fell at the feet of the black pirate. All the boys were plucked from their trees in this ruthless manner; and several of them were in the air at a time, like bales of goods flung from hand to hand.

A different treatment was accorded to Wendy, who came last. With ironical politeness Hook raised his hat to her, and, offering her his arm, escorted her to the spot where the others were being gagged. He did it with such an air, he was so frightfully *distingué*, that she was too fascinated to cry out. She was only a little girl.

Perhaps it is tell-tale to divulge that for a moment Hook entranced her, and we tell on her only because her slip led to strange results. Had she haughtily unhanded him (and we should have loved to write it of her), she would have been hurled through the air like the others, and then Hook would probably not have been present at the tying of the children; and had he not been at the tying he would not have discovered Slightly's secret, and without the secret he could not presently have made his foul attempt on Peter's life.

They were tied to prevent their flying away, doubled up with their knees close to their ears; and for this job the black pirate had cut a rope into nine equal pieces. All went well with the trussing until Slightly's turn came, when he was found to be like those irritating parcels that use up all the string in going round and leave no tags with which to tie a knot. The pirates kicked him in their rage, just as you kick the parcel (though in fairness you should kick the string); and strange to say it was Hook who told them to belay their violence. His lip was curled with malicious triumph. While his dogs were merely sweating because every time they tried to pack the unhappy lad tight in one part he bulged out in another, Hook's master mind had gone far beneath Slightly's surface, probing not for effects but for causes; and his exultation showed that he had found them. Slightly, white to the gills, knew that Hook had surprised his secret, which was this, that no boy so blown out could use a tree wherein an average man need stick. Poor Slightly, most wretched of all the children now, for he was in a panic about Peter, bitterly regretted what he had done. Madly addicted to the drinking of water when he was hot, he had swelled in consequence to his present girth, and instead of reducing himself to fit his tree he had, unknown to the others, whittled his tree to make it fit him.

Sufficient of this Hook guessed to persuade him that Peter at last lay at his mercy, but no word of the dark design that now formed in the subterranean caverns of his mind crossed his lips; he merely signed that the captives were to be conveyed to the ship, and that he would be alone.

How to convey them? Hunched up in their ropes they might indeed be rolled down hill like barrels, but most of the way lay through a morass. Again Hook's genius surmounted difficulties. He indicated that the little house must be used as a conveyance. The children were flung into it, four stout pirates raised it on their shoulders, the others fell in behind, and singing the hateful pirate chorus the strange procession set off through the wood. I don't know whether any of the children were crying; if so, the singing drowned the sound; but as the little house disappeared in the forest, a brave though tiny jet of smoke issued from its chimney as if defying Hook.

Hook saw it, and it did Peter a bad service. It dried up any trickle of pity for him that may have remained in the pirate's infuriated breast.

The first thing he did on finding himself alone in the fast falling night was to tiptoe to Slightly's tree, and make sure that it provided him with a passage. Then for long he remained brooding; his hat of ill omen on the sward, so that a gentle breeze which had arisen might play refreshingly through his hair. Dark as were his thoughts his blue eyes were as soft as the periwinkle. Intently he listened for any sound from the nether world, but all was as silent below as above; the house under the ground seemed to be but one more empty tenement in the void. Was that boy asleep, or did he stand waiting at the foot of Slightly's tree, with his dagger in his hand?

There was no way of knowing, save by going down. Hook let his cloak slip softly to the ground, and then biting his lips till a lewd blood stood on them, he stepped into the tree. He was a brave man, but for a moment he had to stop there and wipe his brow, which was dripping like a candle. Then silently he let himself go into the unknown.

He arrived unmolested at the foot of the shaft, and stood still again, biting at his breath, which had almost left him. As his eyes became accustomed to the dim light various objects in the home under the trees took shape; but the only one on which his greedy gaze rested, long sought for and found at last, was the great bed. On the bed lay Peter fast asleep.

Unaware of the tragedy being enacted above, Peter had continued, for a little time after the children left, to play gaily on his pipes: no doubt rather a forlorn attempt to prove to himself that he did not care. Then he decided not to take his medicine, so as to grieve Wendy. Then he lay down on the bed outside the coverlet, to vex her still more; for she had always tucked them inside it, because you never know that you may not grow chilly at the turn of the night. Then he nearly cried; but it struck him how indignant she would be if he laughed instead; so he laughed a haughty laugh and fell asleep in the middle of it.

Sometimes, though not often, he had dreams, and they were more painful than the dreams of other boys. For hours he could not be separated from these dreams, though he wailed piteously in them. They had to do, I think, with the riddle of his existence. At such times it had been Wendy's custom to take him out of bed and sit with him on her lap, soothing him in dear ways of her own invention, and when he grew calmer to put him back to bed before he quite woke up, so that he should not know of the indignity to which she had subjected him. But on this occasion he had fallen at once into a dreamless sleep. One arm dropped over the edge of the bed, one leg was arched, and the unfinished part of his laugh was stranded on his mouth, which was open, showing the little pearls.

Thus defenceless Hook found him. He stood silent at the foot of the tree looking across the chamber at his enemy. Did no feeling of compassion stir his sombre breast? The man was not wholly evil; he loved flowers (I have been told) and sweet music (he was himself no mean performer on the harpsichord); and, let it be frankly admitted, the idyllic nature of the scene shook him profoundly. Mastered by his better self he would have returned reluctantly up the tree, but for one thing.

What stayed him was Peter's impertinent appearance as he slept. The open mouth, the drooping arm, the arched knee: they were such a personification of cockiness as, taken together, will never again one may hope be presented to eyes so sensitive to their offensiveness. They steeled Hook's heart. If his rage had broken him into a hundred pieces every one of them would have disregarded the incident, and leapt at the sleeper.

Though a light from the one lamp shone dimly on the bed Hook stood in darkness himself, and at the first stealthy step forward he discovered an obstacle, the door of Slightly's tree. It did not entirely fill the aperture, and he had been looking over it. Feeling for the catch, he found to his fury that it was low down, beyond his reach. To his disordered brain it seemed then that the irritating quality in Peter's face and figure visibly increased, and he rattled the door and flung himself against it. Was his enemy to escape him after all?

But what was that? The red in his eye had caught sight of Peter's medicine standing on a ledge within easy reach. He fathomed what it was straightway, and immediately he knew that the sleeper was in his power.

Lest he should be taken alive, Hook always carried about his person a dreadful drug, blended by himself of all the death-dealing rings that had come into his possession. These he had boiled down into a yellow liquid quite unknown to science, which was probably the most virulent poison in existence.

Five drops of this he now added to Peter's cup. His hand shook, but it was in exultation rather than in shame. As he did it he avoided glancing at the sleeper, but not lest pity should unnerve him; merely to avoid spilling. Then one long gloating look he cast upon his victim, and turning, wormed his way with difficulty up the tree. As he emerged at the top he looked the very spirit of evil breaking from its hole. Donning his hat at its most rakish angle, he wound his cloak around him, holding one end in front as if to conceal his person from the night, of which it was the blackest part, and muttering strangely to himself stole away through the trees.

Peter slept on. The light guttered and went out, leaving the tenement in darkness; but still he slept. It must have been not less than ten o'clock by the crocodile, when he suddenly sat up in his bed, wakened by he knew not what. It was a soft cautious tapping on the door of his tree.

Soft and cautious, but in that stillness it was sinister. Peter felt for his dagger till his hand gripped it. Then he spoke.

"Who is that?"

For long there was no answer: then again the knock.

"Who are you?"

No answer.

He was thrilled, and he loved being thrilled. In two strides he reached his door. Unlike Slightly's door it filled the aperture, so that he could not see beyond it, nor could the one knocking see him.

"I won't open unless you speak," Peter cried.

Then at last the visitor spoke, in a lovely bell-like voice.

"Let me in, Peter."

It was Tink, and quickly he unbarred to her. She flew in excitedly, her face flushed and her dress stained with mud.

"What is it?"

"Oh, you could never guess!" she cried, and offered him three guesses. "Out with it!" he shouted, and in one ungrammatical sentence, as long as the ribbons conjurers pull from their mouths, she told of the capture of Wendy and the boys.

Peter's heart bobbed up and down as he listened. Wendy bound, and on the pirate ship; she who loved everything to be just so!

"I'll rescue her!" he cried, leaping at his weapons. As he leapt he thought of something he could do to please her. He could take his medicine.

His hand closed on the fatal draught.

"No!" shrieked Tinker Bell, who had heard Hook muttering about his deed as he sped through the forest.

"Why not?"

"It is poisoned."

"Poisoned! Who could have poisoned it?"

"Hook."

"Don't be silly. How could Hook have got down here?"

Alas, Tinker Bell could not explain this, for even she did not know the dark secret of Slightly's tree . Nevertheless Hook's words had left no room for doubt. The cup was poisoned.

"Besides," said Peter, quite believing himself, "I never fell asleep."

He raised the cup. No time for words now; time for deeds, and with one of her lightning movements Tink got between his lips and the draught, and drained it to the dregs.

"Why, Tink, how dare you drink my medicine?"

But she did not answer. Already she was reeling in the air.

"What is the matter with you?" cried Peter, suddenly afraid.

"It was poisoned, Peter," she told him softly; "and now I am going to be dead."

"O Tink, did you drink it to save me?"

"Yes."

"But why, Tink?"

Her wings would scarcely carry her now, but in reply she alighted on his shoulder and gave his nose a loving bite. She whispered in his ear "you silly ass," and then, tottering to her chamber, lay down on the bed.

His head almost filled the fourth wall of her little room as he knelt near her in distress. Every moment her light was growing fainter; and he knew that if it went out she would be no more. She liked his tears so much that she put out her beautiful finger and let them run over it.

Her voice was so low that at first he could not make out what she said. Then he made it out. She was saying that she thought she could get well again if children believed in fairies.

Peter flung out his arms. There were no children there, and it was night time; but he addressed all who might be dreaming of the Neverland, and who were therefore nearer to him than you think: boys and girls in their nighties, and naked papooses in their baskets hung from trees.

"Do you believe?" he cried.

Tink sat up in bed almost briskly to listen to her fate.

She fancied she heard answers in the affirmative, and then again she wasn't sure.

"What do you think?" she asked Peter.

"If you believe," he shouted to them, "clap your hands; don't let Tink die."

Many clapped.

Some didn't

A few little beasts hissed.

The clapping stopped suddenly; as if countless mothers had rushed to their nurseries to see what on earth was happening; but already Tink was saved. First her voice grew strong, then she popped out of bed, then she was flashing through the room more merry and impudent than ever.

she was flashing through the room more merry and impudent than ever. She never thought of thanking those who believed, but she would have liked to get at the ones who had hissed.

"And now to rescue Wendy!"

The moon was riding in a cloudy heaven when Peter rose from his tree, begirt with weapons and wearing little else, to set out upon his perilous quest. It was not such a night as he would have chosen. He had hoped to fly, keeping not far from the ground so that nothing unwonted should escape his eyes; but in that fitful light to have flown low would have meant trailing his shadow through the trees, thus disturbing the birds and acquainting a watchful foe that he was astir.

He regretted now that he had given the birds of the island such strange names that they are very wild and difficult of approach.

There was no other course but to press forward in redskin fashion, at which happily he was an adept. But in what direction, for he could not be sure that the children had been taken to the ship? A slight fall of snow had obliterated all footmarks; and a deathly silence pervaded the island, as if for a space Nature stood still in horror of the recent carnage. He had taught the children something of the forest lore that he had himself learned from Tiger Lily and Tinker Bell, and knew that in their dire hour they were not likely to forget it. Slightly, if he had an opportunity, would blaze the trees, for instance, Curly would drop seeds, and Wendy would leave her handkerchief at some important place. But morning was needed to search for such guidance, and he could not wait. The upper world had called him, but would give no help.

The crocodile passed him, but not another living thing, not a sound, not a movement; and yet he knew well that sudden death might be at the next tree, or stalking him from behind.

He swore this terrible oath: "Hook or me this time."

Now he crawled forward like a snake; and again, erect, he darted across a space on which the moonlight played, one finger on his lip and his dagger at the ready. He was frightfully happy.

CHAPTER XIV

THE PIRATE SHIP

ne green light squinting over Kidd's Creek, which is near the mouth of the pirate river, marked where the brig, the *Jolly Roger,* lay, low in the water; a rakish-looking craft foul to the hull, every beam in her detestable like ground strewn with mangled feathers. She was the cannibal of the seas, and scarce needed that watchful eye, for she floated immune in the horror of her name.

She was wrapped in the blanket of night, through which no sound from her could have reached the shore. There was little sound, and none agreeable save the whir of the ship's sewing machine at which Smee sat, ever industrious and obliging, the essence of the commonplace, pathetic Smee. I know not why he was so infinitely pathetic, unless it were because he was so pathetically unaware of it; but even strong men had to turn hastily from looking at him, and more than once on summer evenings he had touched the fount of Hook's tears and made it flow. Of this, as of almost everything else, Smee was quite unconscious.

A few of the pirates leant over the bulwarks drinking in the miasma of the night; others sprawled by barrels over games of dice and cards; and the exhausted four who had carried the little house lay prone on the deck, where even in their sleep they rolled skilfully to this side or that out of Hook's reach, lest he should claw them mechanically in passing.

Hook trod the deck in thought. O man unfathomable. It was his hour of triumph. Peter had been removed forever from his path, and all the other boys were on the brig, about to walk the plank. It was his grimmest deed since the days when he had brought Barbecue to heel; and knowing as we do how vain a tabernacle is man, could we be surprised had he now paced the deck unsteadily, bellied out by the winds of his success?

But there was no elation in his gait, which kept pace with the action of his sombre mind. Hook was profoundly dejected.

He was often thus when communing with himself on board ship in the quietude of the night. It was because he was so terribly alone. This inscrutable man never felt more alone than when surrounded by his dogs. They were socially so inferior to him.

Hook was not his true name. To reveal who he really was would even at this date set the country in a blaze; but as those who read between the lines must already have guessed, he had been at a famous public school; and its traditions still clung to him like garments, with which indeed they are largely concerned. Thus it was offensive to him even now to board a ship in the same dress in which he grappled her, and he still adhered in his walk to the school's distinguished slouch. But above all he retained the passion for good form.

Good form! However much he may have degenerated, he still knew that this is all that really matters.

From far within him he heard a creaking as of rusty portals, and through them came a stern tap-tap-tap, like hammering in the night when one cannot sleep. "Have you been good form to-day?" was their eternal question.

"Fame, fame, that glittering bauble, it is mine!" he cried.

"Is it quite good form to be distinguished at anything?" the tap-tap from his school replied.

"I am the only man whom Barbecue feared," he urged, "and Flint himself feared Barbecue."

"Barbecue, Flint — what house?" came the cutting retort.

Most disquieting reflection of all, was it not bad form to think about good form?

His vitals were tortured by this problem. It was a claw within him sharper than the iron one; and as it tore him, the perspiration dripped down his tallow countenance and streaked his doublet. Ofttimes he drew his sleeve across his face, but there was no damming that trickle.

Ah, envy not Hook.

There came to him a presentiment of his early dissolution. It was as if Peter's terrible oath had boarded the ship. Hook felt a gloomy desire to make his dying speech, lest presently there should be no time for it.

"Better for Hook," he cried, "if he had had less ambition!" It was in his darkest hours only that he referred to himself in the third person.

"No little children love me!"

Strange that he should think of this, which had never troubled him before; perhaps the sewing machine brought it to his mind. For long he muttered to himself, staring at Smee, who was hemming placidly, under the conviction that all children feared him.

Feared him! Feared Smee! There was not a child on board the brig that night who did not already love him. He had said horrid things to them and hit them with the palm of his hand, because he could not hit with his fist, but they had only clung to him the more. Michael had tried on his spectacles.

To tell poor Smee that they thought him lovable! Hook itched to do it, but it seemed too brutal. Instead, he revolved this mystery in his mind: why do they find Smee lovable? He pursued the problem like the sleuth-hound that he was. If Smee was lovable, what was it that made him so? A terrible answer suddenly presented itself — "Good form?"

Had the bo'sun good form without knowing it, which is the best form of all?

He remembered that you have to prove you don't know you have it before you are eligible for Pop.

With a cry of rage he raised his iron hand over Smee's head; but he did not tear. What arrested him was this reflection:

"To claw a man because he is good form, what would that be?"

"Bad form!"

The unhappy Hook was as impotent as he was damp, and he fell forward like a cut flower.

His dogs thinking him out of the way for a time, discipline instantly relaxed; and they broke into a bacchanalian dance, which brought him to his feet at once, all traces of human weakness gone, as if a bucket of water had passed over him.

"Quiet, you scugs," he cried, "or I'll cast anchor in you"; and at once the din was hushed. "Are all the children chained, so that they cannot fly away?"

"Ay, ay."

"Then hoist them up."

The wretched prisoners were dragged from the hold, all except Wendy, and ranged in line in front of him. For a time he seemed unconscious of their presence. He lolled at his ease, humming, not unmelodiously, snatches of a rude song, and fingering a pack of cards. Ever and anon the light from his cigar gave a touch of colour to his face.

"Now then, bullies," he said briskly, "six of you walk the plank to-night, but I have room for two cabin boys. Which of you is it to be?"

"Don't irritate him unnecessarily," had been Wendy's instructions in the hold; so Tootles stepped forward politely. Tootles hated the idea of signing under such a man, but an instinct told him that it would be prudent to lay the responsibility on an absent person; and though a somewhat silly boy, he knew that mothers alone are always willing to be the buffer. All children know this about mothers, and despise them for it, but make constant use of it.

So Tootles explained prudently, "You see, sir, I don't think my mother would like me to be a pirate. Would your mother like you to be a pirate, Slightly?"

He winked at Slightly, who said mournfully, "I don't think so," as if he wished things had been otherwise. "Would your mother like you to be a pirate, Twin?"

"I don't think so," said the first twin, as clever as the others. "Nibs, would — "

"Stow this gab," roared Hook, and the spokesmen were dragged back. "You, boy," he said, addressing John, "you look as if you had a little pluck in you. Didst never want to be a pirate, my hearty?"

Now John had sometimes experienced this hankering at maths. prep.; and he was struck by Hook's picking him out.

"I once thought of calling myself Red-handed Jack," he said diffidently.

"And a good name too. We'll call you that here, bully, if you join."

"What do you think, Michael?" asked John.

"What would you call me if I join?" Michael demanded.

"Blackbeard Joe."

Michael was naturally impressed. "What do you think, John?" He wanted John to decide, and John wanted him to decide.

"Shall we still be respectful subjects of the King?" John inquired.

Through Hook's teeth came the answer: "You would have to swear, 'Down with the King.' "

Perhaps John had not behaved very well so far, but he shone out now.

"Then I refuse!" he cried, banging the barrel in front of Hook.

"And I refuse," cried Michael.

"Rule Britannia!" squeaked Curly.

The infuriated pirates buffeted them in the mouth; and Hook roared out, "That seals your doom. Bring up their mother. Get the plank ready."

They were only boys, and they went white as they saw Jukes and Cecco preparing the fatal plank. But they tried to look brave when Wendy was brought up.

No words of mine can tell you how Wendy despised those pirates. To the boys there was at least some glamour in the pirate calling; but all that she saw was that the ship had not been tidied for years. There was not a porthole on the grimy glass of which you might not have written with your finger "Dirty pig"; and she had already written it on several. But as the boys gathered round her she had no thought, of course, save for them.

"So, my beauty," said Hook, as if he spoke in syrup, "you are to see your children walk the plank."

Fine gentleman though he was, the intensity of his communings had soiled his ruff, and suddenly he knew that she was gazing at it. With a hasty gesture he tried to hide it, but he was too late.

"Are they to die?" asked Wendy, with a look of such frightful contempt that he nearly fainted.

"They are," he snarled. "Silence all," he called gloatingly, "for a mother's last words to her children."

At this moment Wendy was grand. "These are my last words, dear boys," she said firmly. "I feel that I have a message to you from your real mothers, and it is this: 'We hope our sons will die like English gentlemen.'"

Even the pirates were awed, and Tootles cried out hysterically, "I am going to do what my mother hopes. What are you to do, Nibs?"

"What my mother hopes. What are you to do, Twin?"

"What my mother hopes. John, what are — "

But Hook had found his voice again.

"Tie her up!" he shouted.

It was Smee who tied her to the mast. "See here, honey," he whispered, "I'll save you if you promise to be my mother."

But not even for Smee would she make such a promise. "I would almost rather have no children at all," she said disdainfully.

It is sad to know that not a boy was looking at her as Smee tied her to the mast; the eyes of all were on the plank: that last little walk they were about to take. They were no longer able to hope that they would walk it manfully, for the capacity to think had gone from them; they could stare and shiver only.

Hook smiled on them with his teeth closed, and took a step toward Wendy. His intention was to turn her face so that she should see the boys walking the plank one by one. But he never reached her, he never heard the cry of anguish he hoped to wring from her. He heard something else instead.

It was the terrible tick-tick of the crocodile.

They all heard it — pirates, boys, Wendy — and immediately every head was blown in one direction; not to the water whence the sound proceeded, but toward Hook. All knew that what was about to happen concerned him alone, and that from being actors they were suddenly become spectators.

Very frightful was it to see the change that came over him. It was as if he had been clipped at every joint. He fell in a little heap.

The sound came steadily nearer; and in advance of it came this ghastly thought, "the crocodile is about to board the ship"!

Even the iron claw hung inactive; as if knowing that it was no intrinsic part of what the attacking force wanted. Left so fearfully alone, any other man would have lain with his eyes shut where he fell: but the gigantic brain of Hook was still working, and under its guidance he crawled on his knees along the deck as far from the sound as he could go. The pirates respectfully cleared a passage for him, and it was only when he brought up against the bulwarks that he spoke.

"Hide me!" he cried hoarsely.

They gathered round him, all eyes averted from the thing that was coming aboard. They had no thought of fighting it. It was Fate.

Only when Hook was hidden from them did curiosity loosen the limbs of the boys so that they could rush to the ship's side to see the crocodile climbing it. Then they got the strangest surprise of this Night of Nights; for it was no crocodile that was coming to their aid. It was Peter.

He signed to them not to give vent to any cry of admiration that might arouse suspicion. Then he went on ticking.

CHAPTER XV

"HOOK OR ME THIS TIME"

Odd things happen to all of us on our way through life without our noticing for a time that they have happened. Thus, to take an instance, we suddenly discover that we have been deaf in one ear for we don't know how long, but, say, half an hour. Now such an experience had come that night to Peter. When last we saw him he was stealing across the island with one finger to his lips and his dagger at the ready. He had seen the crocodile pass by without noticing anything peculiar about it, but by and by he remembered that it had not been ticking. At first he thought this eerie, but soon he concluded rightly that the clock had run down.

Without giving a thought to what might be the feelings of a fellow-creature thus abruptly deprived of its closest companion, Peter began to consider how he could turn the catastrophe to his own use; and he decided to tick, so that wild beasts should believe he was the crocodile and let him pass unmolested. He ticked superbly, but with one unforeseen result. The crocodile was among those who heard the sound, and it followed him, though whether with the purpose of regaining what it had lost, or merely, as a friend under the belief that it was again ticking itself, will never be certainly known, for, like all slaves to a fixed idea, it was a stupid beast.

Peter reached the shore without mishap, and went straight on, his legs encountering the water as if quite unaware that they had entered a new element. Thus many animals pass from land to water, but no other human of whom I know. As he swam he had but one thought: "Hook or me this time." He had ticked so long that he now went on ticking without knowing that he was doing it. Had he known he would have stopped, for to board the brig by the help of the tick, though an ingenious idea, had not occurred to him.

On the contrary, he thought he had scaled her side as noiseless as a mouse; and he was amazed to see the pirates cowering from him, with Hook in their midst as abject as if he had heard the crocodile.

The crocodile! No sooner did Peter remember it than he heard the ticking. At first he thought the sound did come from the crocodile, and he looked behind him swiftly. Then he realized that he was doing it himself, and in a flash he understood the situation. "How clever of me!" he thought at once, and signed to the boys not to burst into applause.

It was at this moment that Ed Teynte the quartermaster emerged from the forecastle and came along the deck. Now, reader, time what happened by your watch. Peter struck true and deep. John clapped his hands on the ill-fated pirate's mouth to stifle the dying groan. He fell forward. Four boys caught him to prevent the thud. Peter gave the signal, and the carrion was cast overboard. There was a splash, and then silence. How long has it taken?

"One!" (Slightly had begun to count.)

None too soon, Peter, every inch of him on tip-toe, vanished into the cabin; for more than one pirate was screwing up his courage to look round. They could hear each other's distressed breathing now, which showed them that the more terrible sound had passed.

"It's gone, captain," Smee said, wiping his spectacles. "All's still again."

Slowly Hook let his head emerge from his ruff, and listened so intently that he could have caught the echo of the tick. There was not a sound, and he drew himself up firmly to his full height.

"Then here's to Johnny Plank!" he cried brazenly, hating the boys more than ever because they had seen him unbend. He broke into the villainous ditty:

> "Yo ho, yo ho, the frisky plank,
> You walks along it so,
> Till it goes down and you goes down
> To Davy Jones below!"

To terrorise the prisoners the more, though with a certain loss of dignity, he danced along an imaginary plank, grimacing at them as he sang; and when he finished he cried, "Do you want a touch of the cat before you walk the plank?"

At that they fell on their knees. "No, no!" they cried so piteously that every pirate smiled.

"Fetch the cat, Jukes," said Hook, "it's in the cabin."

The cabin! Peter was in the cabin! The children gazed at each other.

"Ay, ay," said Jukes blithely, and he strode into the cabin. They followed him with their eyes; they scarce knew that Hook had resumed his song, his dogs joining in with him:

"Yo ho, yo ho, the scratching cat,
Its tails are nine, you know,
And when they're writ upon your back—"

What was the last line will never be known, for of a sudden the song was stayed by a dreadful screech from the cabin. It wailed through the ship, and died away. Then was heard a crowing sound which was well understood by the boys, but to the pirates was almost more eerie than the screech.

"What was that?" cried Hook.

"Two," said Slightly solemnly.

The Italian Cecco hesitated for a moment and then swung into the cabin. He tottered out, haggard.

"What's the matter with Bill Jukes, you dog?" hissed Hook, towering over him.

"The matter wi' him is he's dead, stabbed," replied Cecco in a hollow voice.

"Bill Jukes dead!" cried the startled pirates.

"The cabin's as black as a pit," Cecco said, almost gibbering, "but there is something terrible in there: the thing you heard crowing."

The exultation of the boys, the lowering looks of the pirates, both were seen by Hook.

"Cecco," he said in his most steely voice, "go back and fetch me out that doodle-doo."

Cecco, bravest of the brave, cowered before his captain, crying, "No, no"; but Hook was purring to his claw.

"Did you say you would go, Cecco?" he said musingly.

Cecco went, first flinging up his arms despairingly. There was no more singing, all listened now; and again came a death-screech and again a crow.

No one spoke except Slightly. "Three," he said.

Hook rallied his dogs with a gesture. "S' death and odds fish," he thundered, "who is to bring me that doodle-doo?"

"Wait till Cecco comes out," growled Starkey, and the others took up the cry.

"I think I heard you volunteer, Starkey," said Hook, purring again.

"No, by thunder!" Starkey cried.

"My hook thinks you did," said Hook, crossing to him. "I wonder if it would not be advisable, Starkey, to humour the hook?"

"I'll swing before I go in there," replied Starkey doggedly, and again he had the support of the crew.

"Is it mutiny?" asked Hook more pleasantly than ever. "Starkey's ringleader!"

"Captain, mercy!" Starkey whimpered, all of a tremble now.

"Shake hands, Starkey," said Hook, proffering his claw.

Starkey looked round for help, but all deserted him. As he backed Hook advanced, and now the red spark was in his eye. With a despairing scream the pirate leapt upon Long Tom and precipitated himself into the sea.

"Four," said Slightly.

"And now," Hook asked courteously, "did any other gentleman say mutiny?" Seizing a lantern and raising his claw with a menacing gesture, "I'll bring out that doodle-doo myself," he said, and sped into the cabin.

"Five." How Slightly longed to say it. He wetted his lips to be ready, but Hook came staggering out, without his lantern.

"Something blew out the light," he said a little unsteadily.

"Something!" echoed Mullins.

"What of Cecco?" demanded Noodler.

"He's as dead as Jukes," said Hook shortly.

His reluctance to return to the cabin impressed them all unfavourably, and the mutinous sounds again broke forth. All pirates are superstitious, and Cookson cried, "They do say the surest sign a ship's accurst is when there's one on board more than can be accounted for."

"I've heard," muttered Mullins, "he always boards the pirate craft at last. Had he a tail, captain?"

"They say," said another, looking viciously at Hook, "that when he comes it's in the likeness of the wickedest man aboard."

"Had he a hook, captain?" asked Cookson insolently; and one after another took up the cry, "The ship's doomed!" At this the children could not resist raising a cheer. Hook had well-nigh forgotten his prisoners, but as he swung round on them now his face lit up again.

"Lads," he cried to his crew, "here's a notion. Open the cabin door and drive them in. Let them fight the doodle-doo for their lives. If they kill him, we're so much the better; if he kills them, we're none the worse."

For the last time his dogs admired Hook, and devotedly they did his bidding. The boys, pretending to struggle, were pushed into the cabin and the door was closed on them.

"Now, listen!" cried Hook, and all listened. But not one dared to face the door. Yes, one, Wendy, who all this time had been bound to the mast. It was for neither a scream nor a crow that she was watching, it was for the reappearance of Peter.

She had not long to wait. In the cabin he had found the thing for which he had gone in search: the key that would free the children of their manacles, and now they all stole forth, armed with such weapons as they could find. First signing to them to hide, Peter cut Wendy's bonds, and then nothing could have been easier than for them all to fly off together; but one thing barred the way, an oath, "Hook or me this time." So when he had freed Wendy, he whispered to her to conceal herself with the others, and himself took her place by the mast, her cloak around him so that he should pass for her. Then he took a great breath and crowed.

To the pirates it was a voice crying that all the boys lay slain in the cabin; and they were panic-stricken. Hook tried to hearten them, but like the dogs he had made them they showed him their fangs, and he knew that if he took his eyes off them now they would leap at him.

"Lads," he said, ready to cajole or strike as need be, but never quailing for an instant, "I've thought it out. There's a Jonah aboard."

"Ay," they snarled, "a man wi' a hook."

"No, lads, no, it's the girl. Never was luck on a pirate ship wi' a woman on board. We'll right the ship when she's gone."

Some of them remembered that this had been a saying of Flint's. "It's worth trying," they said doubtfully.

"Fling the girl overboard," cried Hook; and they made a rush at the figure in the cloak.

"There's none can save you now, missy," Mullins hissed jeeringly.

"There's one," replied the figure.

"Who's that?"

"Peter Pan the avenger!" came the terrible answer; and as he spoke

Peter flung off his cloak. Then they all knew who 'twas that had been undoing them in the cabin, and twice Hook essayed to speak and twice he failed. In that frightful moment I think his fierce heart broke.

At last he cried, "Cleave him to the brisket!" but without conviction.

"Down, boys, and at them!" Peter's voice rang out; and in another moment the clash of arms was resounding through the ship. Had the pirates kept together it is certain that they would have won; but the onset came when they were all unstrung, and they ran hither and thither, striking wildly, each thinking himself the last survivor of the crew. Man to man they were the stronger; but they fought on the defensive only, which enabled the boys to hunt in pairs and choose their quarry. Some of the miscreants leapt into the sea, others hid in dark recesses, where they were found by Slightly, who did not fight, but ran about with a lantern which he flashed in their faces, so that they were half blinded and fell an easy prey to the reeking swords of the other boys. There was little sound to be heard but the clang of weapons, an occasional screech or splash, and Slightly monotonously counting — five — six — seven — eight — nine — ten — eleven.

I think all were gone when a group of savage boys surrounded Hook, who seemed to have a charmed life, as he kept them at bay in that circle of fire. They had done for his dogs, but this man alone seemed to be a match for them all. Again and again they closed upon him, and again and again he hewed a clear space. He had lifted up one boy with his hook, and was using him as a buckler, when another, who had just passed his sword through Mullins, sprang into the fray.

"Put up your swords, boys," cried the newcomer, "this man is mine."

Thus suddenly Hook found himself face to face with Peter. The others drew back and formed a ring round them.

For long the two enemies looked at one another, Hook shuddering slightly, and Peter with the strange smile upon his face.

"So, Pan," said Hook at last, "this is all your doing."

"Ay, James Hook," came the stern answer, "it is all my doing."

"Proud and insolent youth," said Hook, "prepare to meet thy doom."

"Dark and sinister man," Peter answered, "have at thee."

Without more words they fell to, and for a space there was no advantage to either blade. Peter was a superb swordsman, and parried with dazzling rapidity; ever and anon he followed up a feint with a lunge that got past his foe's defence, but his shorter reach stood him in ill stead, and he could not drive the steel home. Hook, scarcely his inferior in bril-

liancy, but not quite so nimble in wrist play, forced him back by the weight of his onset, hoping suddenly to end all with a favourite thrust, taught him long ago by Barbecue at Rio; but to his astonishment he found this thrust turned aside again and again. Then he sought to close and give the quietus with his iron hook, which all this time had been pawing the air; but Peter doubled under it and, lunging fiercely, pierced him in the ribs. At sight of his own blood, whose peculiar colour, you remember, was offensive to him, the sword fell from Hook's hand, and he was at Peter's mercy.

"Now!" cried all the boys, but with a magnificent gesture Peter invited his opponent to pick up his sword. Hook did so instantly, but with a tragic feeling that Peter was showing good form.

Hitherto he had thought it was some fiend fighting him, but darker suspicions assailed him now.

"Pan, who and what art thou?" he cried huskily.

"I'm youth, I'm joy," Peter answered at a venture, "I'm a little bird that has broken out of the egg."

This, of course, was nonsense; but it was proof to the unhappy Hook that Peter did not know in the least who or what he was, which is the very pinnacle of good form.

"To't again," he cried despairingly.

He fought now like a human flail, and every sweep of that terrible sword would have severed in twain any man or boy who obstructed it; but Peter fluttered round him as if the very wind it made blew him out of the danger zone. And again and again he darted in and pricked.

Hook was fighting now without hope. That passionate breast no longer asked for life; but for one boon it craved: to see Peter bad form before it was cold forever.

Abandoning the fight he rushed into the powder magazine and fired it.

"In two minutes," he cried, "the ship will be blown to pieces."

Now, now, he thought, true form will show.

But Peter issued from the powder magazine with the shell in his hands, and calmly flung it overboard.

What sort of form was Hook himself showing? Misguided man though he was, we may be glad, without sympathising with him, that in the end he was true to the traditions of his race. The other boys were flying around him now, flouting, scornful; and as he staggered about the deck striking up at them impotently, his mind was no longer with them; it was slouching in the playing fields of long ago, or being sent up for good, or watching the wall-game from a famous wall. And his shoes were right, and his waistcoat was right, and his tie was right, and his socks were right.

James Hook, thou not wholly unheroic figure, farewell.

For we have come to his last moment.

Seeing Peter slowly advancing upon him through the air with dagger poised, he sprang upon the bulwarks to cast himself into the sea.

He did not know that the crocodile was waiting for him; for we purposely stopped the clock that this knowledge might be spared him: a little mark of respect from us at the end.

He had one last triumph, which I think we need not grudge him. As he stood on the bulwark looking over his shoulder at Peter gliding through the air, he invited him with a gesture to use his foot. It made Peter kick instead of stab.

At last Hook had got the boon for which he craved.

"Bad form," he cried jeeringly, and went content to the crocodile.

Thus perished James Hook.

"Seventeen," Slightly sang out; but he was not quite correct in his figures. Fifteen paid the penalty for their crimes that night; but two reached the shore: Starkey to be captured by the redskins, who made him nurse for all their papooses, a melancholy come-down for a pirate; and Smee, who henceforth wandered about the world in his spectacles, making a precarious living by saying he was the only man that Jas. Hook had feared.

Wendy, of course, had stood by taking no part in the fight, though watching Peter with glistening eyes; but now that all was over she became prominent again. She praised them equally, and shuddered delightfully when Michael showed her the place where he had killed one; and then she took them into Hook's cabin and pointed to his watch which was hanging on a nail. It said "half-past one"!

The lateness of the hour was almost the biggest thing of all. She got them to bed in the pirates' bunks pretty quickly, you may be sure; all but Peter, who strutted up and down on deck, until at last he fell asleep by the side of Long Tom. He had one of his dreams that night, and cried in his sleep for a long time, and Wendy held him tight.

CHAPTER XVI

THE RETURN HOME

y three bells next morning they were all stirring their stumps. For there was a big sea running, and Tootles, the bo'sun, was among them, with a rope's end in his hand and chewing tobacco. They all donned pirate clothes cut off at the knee, shaved smartly, and tumbled up, with the true nautical roll and hitching their trousers.

It need not be said who was the captain. Nibs and John were first and second mate. There was a woman aboard. The rest were tars before the mast, and lived in the fo'c'sle. Peter had already lashed himself to the wheel; but he piped all hands and delivered a short address to them; said he hoped they would do their duty like gallant hearties, but that he knew they were the scum of Rio and the Gold Coast, and if they snapped at him he would tear them. His bluff strident words struck the note sailors understand, and they cheered him lustily. Then a few sharp orders were given, and they turned the ship round, and nosed her for the mainland.

Captain Pan calculated, after consulting the ship's chart, that if this weather lasted, they should strike the Azores about the 21st of June, after which it would save time to fly.

Some of them wanted it to be an honest ship and others were in favour of keeping it a pirate; but the captain treated them as dogs, and they dared not express their wishes to him even in a round robin. Instant obedience was the only safe thing. Slightly got a dozen for looking perplexed when told to take soundings. The general feeling was that Peter was honest just now to lull Wendy's suspicions, but that there might be a change when the new suit was ready, which, against her will, she was making for him out of some of Hook's wickedest garments. It was afterwards whispered among them that on the first night he wore this suit he sat long in the cabin with Hook's cigar-holder in his mouth and one hand clenched, all but the forefinger, which he bent and held threateningly aloft like a hook.

Instead of watching the ship, however, we must now return to that desolate home from which three of our characters had taken heartless flight so long ago. It seems a shame to have neglected No. 14 all this time; and yet we may be sure that Mrs. Darling does not blame us. If we had returned sooner to look with sorrowful sympathy at her, she would probably have cried, "Don't be silly, what do I matter? Do go back and keep an eye on the children." So long as mothers are like this their children will take advantage of them; and they may lay to that.

Even now we venture into that familiar nursery only because its lawful occupants are on their way home; we are merely hurrying on in advance of them to see that their beds are properly aired and that Mr. and Mrs. Darling do not go out for the evening. We are no more than servants. Why on earth should their beds be properly aired, seeing that they left them in such a thankless hurry? Would it not serve them jolly well right if they came back and found that their parents were spending the week-end in the country? It would be the moral lesson they have been in need of ever since we met them; but if we contrived things in this way Mrs. Darling would never forgive us.

One thing I should like to do immensely, and that is to tell her, in the way authors have, that the children are coming back, that indeed they will be here on Thursday week. This would spoil so completely the surprise to which Wendy and John and Michael are looking forward. They have been planning it out on the ship: mother's rapture, father's shout of joy, Nana's leap through the air to embrace them first, when what they ought to be preparing for is a good hiding. How delicious to spoil it all by breaking the news in advance; so that when they enter enter grandly Mrs. Darling may not even offer Wendy her mouth, and Mr. Darling may exclaim pettishly, "Dash it all, here are those boys again." However, we should get no thanks even for this. We are beginning to know Mrs. Darling by this time, and may be sure that she would upbraid us for depriving the children of their little pleasure.

"But, my dear madam, it is ten days till Thursday week; so that by telling you what's what, we can save you ten days of unhappiness."

"Yes, but at what a cost! By depriving the children of ten minutes of delight."

"Oh, if you look at it in that way!"

"What other way is there in which to look at it?"

You see, the woman had no proper spirit. I had meant to say extraordinarily nice things about her; but I despise her, and not one of them will I say now. She does not really need to be told to have things ready, for they are ready. All the beds are aired, and she never leaves the house, and observe, the window is open. For all the use we are to her, we might go back to the ship. However, as we are here we may as well stay and look on. That is all we are, lookers-on. Nobody really wants us. So let us watch and say jaggy things, in the hope that some of them will hurt.

The only change to be seen in the night-nursery is that between nine and six the kennel is no longer there. When the children flew away, Mr. Darling felt in his bones that all the blame was his for having chained Nana up, and that from first to last she had been wiser than he. Of course, as we have seen, he was quite a simple man; indeed he might have passed for a boy again if he had been able to take his baldness off; but he had also a noble sense of justice and a lion courage to do what seemed right to him; and having thought the matter out with anxious care after the flight of the children, he went down on all fours and crawled into the kennel. To all Mrs. Darling's dear invitations to him to come out he replied sadly but firmly:

"No, my own one, this is the place for me."

In the bitterness of his remorse he swore that he would never leave the kennel until his children came back. Of course this was a pity; but whatever Mr. Darling did he had to do in excess, otherwise he soon gave up doing it. And there never was a more humble man than the once proud George Darling, as he sat in the kennel of an evening talking with his wife of their children and all their pretty ways.

Very touching was his deference to Nana. He would not let her come into the kennel, but on all other matters he followed her wishes implicitly.

Every morning the kennel was carried with Mr. Darling in it to a cab, which conveyed him to his office, and he returned home in the same way at six. Something of the strength of character of the man will be seen if we remember how sensitive he was to the opinion of neighbours: this man whose every movement now attracted surprised attention. Inwardly he must have suffered torture; but he preserved a calm exterior even when the young criticised his little home, and he always lifted his hat courteously to any lady who looked inside.

It may have been quixotic, but it was magnificent. Soon the inward meaning of it leaked out, and the great heart of the public was touched. Crowds followed the cab, cheering it lustily; charming girls scaled it to get his autograph; interviews appeared in the better class of papers, and society invited him to dinner and added, "Do come in the kennel."

On that eventful Thursday week Mrs. Darling was in the night-nursery awaiting George's return home: a very sad-eyed woman. Now that we look at her closely and remember the gaiety of her in the old days, all gone now just because she has lost her babes, I find I won't be able to say nasty things about her after all. If she was too fond of her rubbishy children she couldn't help it. Look at her in her chair, where she has fallen asleep. The corner of her mouth, where one looks first, is almost withered up. Her hand moves restlessly on her breast as if she had a pain there. Some like Peter best and some like Wendy best, but I like her best. Suppose, to make her happy, we whisper to her in her sleep that the brats are coming back. They are really within two miles of the window now, and flying strong, but all we need whisper is that they are on the way. Let's.

It is a pity we did it, for she has started up, calling their names; and there is no one in the room but Nana.

"O Nana, I dreamt my dear ones had come back."

Nana had filmy eyes, but all she could do was to put her paw gently on her mistress's lap, and they were sitting together thus when the kennel was brought back. As Mr. Darling puts his head out at it to kiss his wife, we see that his face is more worn than of yore, but has a softer expression.

He gave his hat to Liza, who took it scornfully; for she had no imagination, and was quite incapable of understanding the motives of such a man. Outside, the crowd who had accompanied the cab home were still cheering, and he was naturally not unmoved.

"Listen to them," he said; "it is very gratifying."

"Lot of little boys," sneered Liza.

"There were several adults to-day," he assured her with a faint flush; but when she tossed her head he had not a word of reproof for her. Social success had not spoilt him; it had made him sweeter. For some time he sat with his head out of the kennel, talking with Mrs. Darling of this success, and pressing her hand reassuringly when she said she hoped his head would not be turned by it.

"But if I had been a weak man," he said. "Good heavens, if I had been a weak man!"

"And, George," she said timidly, "you are as full of remorse as ever, aren't you?"

"Full of remorse as ever, dearest! See my punishment: living in a kennel."

"But it is punishment, isn't it, George? You are sure you are not enjoying it?"

"My love!"

You may be sure she begged his pardon; and then, feeling drowsy, he curled round in the kennel.

"Won't you play me to sleep," he asked, "on the nursery piano?" and as she was crossing to the day-nursery he added thoughtlessly, "and shut that window. I feel a draught."

"O George, never ask me to do that. The window must always be left open for them, always, always."

Now it was his turn to beg her pardon; and she went into the day-nursery and played, and soon he was asleep; and while he slept, Wendy and John and Michael flew into the room.

Oh no. We have written it so, because that was the charming arrangement planned by them before we left the ship; but something must have happened since then, for it is not they who have flown in, it is Peter and Tinker Bell.

Peter's first words tell all.

"Quick, Tink," he whispered, "close the window; bar it! That's right. Now you and I must get away by the door; and when Wendy comes she will think her mother has barred her out, and she will have to go back with me."

Now I understand what had hitherto puzzled me, why when Peter had exterminated the pirates he did not return to the island and leave Tink to escort the children to the mainland. This trick had been in his head all the time.

Instead of feeling that he was behaving badly he danced with glee; then he peeped into the day-nursery to see who was playing. He whispered to Tink, "It's Wendy's mother! She is a pretty lady, but not so pretty as my mother. Her mouth is full of thimbles, but not so full as my mother's was."

Of course he knew nothing whatever about his mother; but he sometimes bragged about her.

He did not know the tune, which was "Home, Sweet Home," but he knew it was saying, "Come back, Wendy, Wendy, Wendy"; and he cried exultantly. "You will never see Wendy again, lady, for the window is barred!"

He peeped in again to see why the music had stopped, and now he saw that Mrs. Darling had laid her head on the box, and that two tears were sitting on her eyes.

"She wants me to unbar the window," thought Peter, "but I won't, not I!"

He peeped again, and the tears were still there, or another two had taken their place.

"She's awfully fond of Wendy," he said to himself. He was angry with her now for not seeing why she could not have Wendy.

The reason was so simple: "I'm fond of her too. We can't both have her, lady."

But the lady would not make the best of it, and he was unhappy. He ceased to look at her, but even then she would not let go of him. He skipped about and made funny faces, but when he stopped it was just as if she were inside him, knocking.

"Oh, all right," he said at last, and gulped. Then he unbarred the window. "Come on, Tink," he cried, with a frightful sneer at the laws of nature: "we don't want any silly mothers"; and he flew away.

Thus Wendy and John and Michael found the window open for them after all, which of course was more than they deserved. They alighted on the floor, quite unashamed of themselves, and the youngest one had already forgotten his home.

"John," he said looking around him doubtfully, "I think I have been here before."

"Of course you have, you silly. There is your old bed."

"So it is," Michael said, but not with much conviction.

"I say," cried John, "the kennel!" and he dashed across to look into it.

"Perhaps Nana is inside it," Wendy said.

But John whistled. "Hullo," he said, "there's a man inside it."

"It's father!" exclaimed Wendy.

"Let me see father." Michael begged eagerly, and he took a good look. "He is not so big as the pirate I killed," he said with such frank disappointment that I am glad Mr. Darling was asleep; it would have been sad if those had been the first words he heard his little Michael say.

Wendy and John had been taken aback somewhat at finding their

father in the kennel.

"Surely," said John, like one who had lost faith in his memory, "he used not to sleep in the kennel?"

"John," Wendy said falteringly, "perhaps we don't remember the old life as well as we thought we did."

A chill fell upon them; and serve them right.

"It is very careless of mother," said the young scoundrel John, "not to be here when we come back."

It was then that Mrs. Darling began playing again.

"It's mother!" cried Wendy, peeping.

"So it is!" said John.

"Then are you not really our mother, Wendy?" asked Michael, who was surely sleepy.

"Oh dear!" exclaimed Wendy, with her first real twinge of remorse, "it was quite time we came back."

"Let us creep in," John suggested, "and put our hands over her eyes."

But Wendy, who saw that they must break the joyous news more gently, had a better plan.

"Let us all slip into our beds, and be there when she comes in, just as if we had never been away."

And so when Mrs. Darling went back to the night-nursery to see if her husband was asleep, all the beds were occupied. The children waited for her cry of joy, but it did not come. She saw them, but she did not believe they were there. You see, she saw them in their beds so often in her dreams that she thought this was just the dream hanging around her still.

She sat down in the chair by the fire, where in the old days she had nursed them.

They could not understand this, and a cold fear fell upon all the three of them.

"Mother!" Wendy cried.

"That's Wendy," she said, but still she was sure it was a dream.

"Mother!"

"That's John," she said.

"Mother!" cried Michael. He knew her now.

"That's Michael," she said, and she stretched out her arms for the three little selfish children they would never envelop again. Yes, they did, they went round Wendy and John and Michael, who had slipped out of bed and run to her.

"George, George!" she cried when she could speak; and Mr. Darling woke to share her bliss, and Nana came rushing in. There could not have been a lovelier sight; but there was none to see it except a little boy who was staring in at the window. He had ecstasies innumerable that other children can never know; but he was looking through the window at the one joy from which he must be forever barred.

CHAPTER XVII

WHEN WENDY GREW UP

I hope you want to know what became of the other boys. They were waiting below to give Wendy time to explain about them, and when they had counted five hundred they went up. They went up by the stair, because they thought this would make a better impression. They stood in a row in front of Mrs. Darling, with their hats off, and wishing they were not wearing their pirate clothes. They said nothing, but their eyes asked her to have them. They ought to have looked at Mr. Darling also, but they forgot about him.

Of course Mrs. Darling said at once that she would have them; but Mr. Darling was curiously depressed, and they saw that he considered six a rather large number.

"I must say," he said to Wendy, "that you don't do things by halves," a grudging remark which the twins thought was pointed at them.

The first twin was the proud one, and he asked, flushing, "Do you think we should be too much of a handful, sir? Because if so we can go away."

"Father!" Wendy cried, shocked; but still the cloud was on him. He knew he was behaving unworthily, but he could not help it.

"We could lie doubled up," said Nibs.

"I always cut their hair myself," said Wendy.

"George!" Mrs. Darling exclaimed, pained to see her dear one showing himself in such an unfavourable light.

Then he burst into tears, and the truth came out. He was as glad to have them as she was, he said, but he thought they should have asked his consent as well as hers, instead of treating him as a cypher in his own house.

"I don't think he is a cypher," Tootles cried instantly. "Do you think he is a cypher, Curly?"

"No I don't. Do you think he is a cypher, Slightly?"

"Rather not. Twin, what do you think?"

It turned out that not one of them thought him a cypher; and he was absurdly gratified, and said he would find space for them all in the drawing-room if they fitted in.

"We'll fit in, sir," they assured him.

"Then follow the leader," he cried gaily. "Mind you, I am not sure that we have a drawing-room, but we pretend we have, and it's all the same. Hoop la!"

He went off dancing through the house, and they all cried "Hoop la!" and danced after him, searching for the drawing-room; and I forget whether they found it, but at any rate they found corners, and they all fitted in.

As for Peter, he saw Wendy once again before he flew away. He did not exactly come to the window, but he brushed against it in passing, so that she could open it if she liked and call to him. That was what she did.

"Hullo, Wendy, good-bye," he said.

"Oh dear, are you going away?"

"Yes."

"You don't feel, Peter," she said falteringly, "that you would like to say anything to my parents about a very sweet subject?"

"No."

"About me, Peter?"

"No."

Mrs. Darling came to the window, for at present she was keeping a sharp eye on Wendy. She told Peter that she had adopted all the other boys, and would like to adopt him also.

"Would you send me to school?" he inquired craftily.

"Yes."

"And then to an office?"

"I suppose so."

"Soon I should be a man?"

"Very soon."

"I don't want to go to school and learn solemn things," he told her passionately. "I don't want to be a man. O Wendy's mother, if I was to wake up and feel there was a beard!"

"Peter," said Wendy the comforter, "I should love you in a beard;" and Mrs. Darling stretched out her arms to him, but he repulsed her.

"Keep back, lady, no one is going to catch me and make me a man."

"But where are you going to live?"

"With Tink in the house we built for Wendy. The fairies are to put it high up among the tree tops where they sleep at nights."

"How lovely," cried Wendy so longingly that Mrs. Darling tightened her grip.

"I thought all the fairies were dead," Mrs. Darling said.

"There are always a lot of young ones," explained Wendy, who was now quite an authority, "because you see when a new baby laughs for the first time a new fairy is born, and as there are always new babies there are always new fairies. They live in nests on the tops of trees; and the mauve ones are boys and the white ones are girls, and the blue ones are just little sillies who are not sure what they are."

"I shall have such fun," said Peter, with one eye on Wendy.

"It will be rather lonely in the evening," she said, "sitting by the fire."

"I shall have Tink."

"Tink can't go a twentieth part of the way round," she reminded him a little tartly.

"Sneaky tell-tale!" Tink called out from somewhere round the corner.

"It doesn't matter," Peter said.

"O Peter, you know it matters."

"Well, then, come with me to the little house."

"May I, mummy?"

"Certainly not. I have got you home again, and I mean to keep you."

"But he does so need a mother."

"So do you, my love."

"Oh, all right," Peter said, as if he had asked her from politeness merely; but Mrs. Darling saw his mouth twitch, and she made this handsome offer: to let Wendy go to him for a week every year and do his spring cleaning. Wendy would have preferred a more permanent arrangement, and it seemed to her that spring would be long in coming, but this promise sent Peter away quite gay again. He had no sense of time, and was so full of adventures that all I have told you about him is only a halfpenny worth of them. I suppose it was because Wendy knew this that her last words to him were these rather plaintive ones:

"You won't forget me, Peter, will you, before spring-cleaning time comes?"

Of course Peter promised, and then he flew away. He took Mrs. Darling's kiss with him. The kiss that had been for no one else Peter took quite easily. Funny. But she seemed satisfied.

Of course all the boys went to school; and most of them got into Class III, but Slightly was put first into Class IV and then into Class V. Class I is the top class. Before they had attended school a week they saw what goats they had been not to remain on the island; but it was too late now, and soon they settled down to being as ordinary as you or me or Jenkins minor. It is sad to have to say that the power to fly gradually left them. At first Nana tied their feet to the bed-posts so that they should not fly away in the night; and one of their diversions by day was to pretend to fall off buses; but by and by they ceased to tug at their bonds in bed, and found that they hurt themselves when they let go of the bus. In time they could not even fly after their hats. Want of practice, they called it; but what it really meant was that they no longer believed.

Michael believed longer than the other boys, though they jeered at him; so he was with Wendy when Peter came for her at the end of the first year. She flew away with Peter in the frock she had woven from leaves and berries in the Neverland, and her one fear was that he might notice how short it had become, but he never noticed, he had so much to say about himself.

She had looked forward to thrilling talks with him about old times, but new adventures had crowded the old ones from his mind.

"Who is Captain Hook?" he asked with interest when she spoke of the arch enemy.

"Don't you remember," she asked, amazed, "how you killed him and saved all our lives?"

"I forget them after I kill them," he replied carelessly.

When she expressed a doubtful hope that Tinker Bell would be glad to see her he said, "Who is Tinker Bell?"

"O Peter!" she said, shocked; but even when she explained he could not remember.

"There are such a lot of them," he said. "I expect she is no more."

I expect he was right, for fairies don't live long, but they are so little that a short time seems a good while to them.

Wendy was pained too to find that the past year was but as yesterday to Peter; it had seemed such a long year of waiting to her. But he was exactly as fascinating as ever, and they had a lovely spring cleaning in the little house on the tree tops.

Next year he did not come for her. She waited in a new frock because the old one simply would not meet, but he never came.

"Perhaps he is ill," Michael said.

"You know he is never ill."

Michael came close to her and whispered, with a shiver, "Perhaps there is no such person, Wendy!" and then Wendy would have cried if Michael had not been crying.

Peter came next spring cleaning; and the strange thing was that he never knew he had missed a year.

That was the last time the girl Wendy ever saw him. For a little longer she tried for his sake not to have growing pains; and she felt she was untrue to him when she got a prize for general knowledge. But the years came and went without bringing the careless boy; and when they met again Wendy was a married woman, and Peter was no more to her than a little dust in the box in which she had kept her toys. Wendy was grown up. You need not be sorry for her. She was one of the kind that likes to grow up. In the end she grew up of her own free will a day quicker than other girls.

All the boys were grown up and done for by this time; so it is scarcely worth while saying anything more about them. You may see the twins and Nibs and Curly any day going to an office, each carrying a little bag and an umbrella. Michael is an engine-driver. Slightly married a lady of title, and so he became a lord. You see that judge in a wig coming out at the iron door? That used to be Tootles. The bearded man who doesn't know any story to tell his children was once John.

Wendy was married in white with a pink sash. It is strange to think that Peter did not alight in the church and forbid the banns.

Years rolled on again, and Wendy had a daughter. This ought not to be written in ink but in a golden splash.

She was called Jane, and always had an odd inquiring look, as if from the moment she arrived on the mainland she wanted to ask questions. When she was old enough to ask them they were mostly about Peter Pan. She loved to hear of Peter, and Wendy told her all she could remember in the very nursery from which the famous flight had taken place. It was Jane's nursery now, for her father had bought it at the three percents from Wendy's father, who was no longer fond of stairs. Mrs. Darling was now dead and forgotten.

There were only two beds in the nursery now, Jane's and her nurse's;

and there was no kennel, for Nana also had passed away. She died of old age, and at the end she had been rather difficult to get on with, being very firmly convinced that no one knew how to look after children except herself.

Once a week Jane's nurse had her evening off, and then it was Wendy's part to put Jane to bed. That was the time for stories. It was Jane's invention to raise the sheet over her mother's head and her own, thus making a tent, and in the awful darkness to whisper: —

"What do we see now?"

"I don't think I see anything to-night," says Wendy, with a feeling that if Nana were here she would object to further conversation.

"Yes, you do," says Jane, "you see when you were a little girl."

"That is a long time ago, sweetheart," says Wendy. "Ah me, how time flies!"

"Does it fly," asks the artful child, "the way you flew when you were a little girl?"

"The way I flew! Do you know, Jane, I sometimes wonder whether I ever did really fly."

"Yes, you did."

"The dear old days when I could fly!"

"Why can't you fly now, mother?"

"Because I am grown up, dearest. When people grow up they forget the way."

"Why do they forget the way?"

"Because they are no longer gay and innocent and heartless. It is only the gay and innocent and heartless who can fly."

"What is gay and innocent and heartless? I do wish I was gay and innocent and heartless."

Or perhaps Wendy admits she does see something. "I do believe," she says, "that it is this nursery!"

"I do believe it is!" says Jane. "Go on."

They are now embarked on the great adventure of the night when Peter flew in looking for his shadow.

"The foolish fellow," says Wendy, "tried to stick it on with soap, and when he could not he cried, and that woke me, and I sewed it on for him."

"You have missed a bit," interrupts Jane, who now knows the story better than her mother. "When you saw him sitting on the floor crying what did you say?"

"I sat up in bed and I said, 'Boy, why are you crying?' "

"Yes, that was it," says Jane, with a big breath.

"And then he flew us all away to the Neverland and the fairies and the pirates and the redskins and the mermaids' lagoon, and the home under the ground, and the little house."

"Yes! which did you like best of all?"

"I think I liked the home under the ground best of all."

"Yes, so do I. What was the last thing Peter ever said to you?"

"The last thing he ever said to me was, 'Just always be waiting for me, and then some night you will hear me crowing.' "

"Yes!"

"But, alas, he forgot all about me." Wendy said it with a smile. She was as grown up as that.

"What did his crow sound like?" Jane asked one evening.

"It was like this," Wendy said, trying to imitate Peter's crow.

"No, it wasn't," Jane said gravely, "it was like this"; and she did it ever so much better than her mother.

Wendy was a little startled. "My darling, how can you know?"

"I often hear it when I am sleeping," Jane said.

"Ah yes, many girls hear it when they are sleeping, but I was the only one who heard it awake."

"Lucky you!" said Jane.

And then one night came the tragedy. It was the spring of the year, and the story had been told for the night, and Jane was now asleep in her bed. Wendy was sitting on the floor, very close to the fire so as to see to darn, for there was no other light in the nursery; and while she sat darning she heard a crow. Then the window blew open as of old, and Peter dropped on the floor.

He was exactly the same as ever, and Wendy saw at once that he still had all his first teeth.

He was a little boy, and she was grown up. She huddled by the fire not daring to move, helpless and guilty, a big woman.

"Hullo, Wendy," he said, not noticing any difference, for he was thinking chiefly of himself; and in the dim light her white dress might have been the nightgown in which he had seen her first.

"Hullo, Peter," she replied faintly, squeezing herself as small as possible. Something inside her was crying "Woman, woman, let go of me."

"Hullo, where is John?" he asked, suddenly missing the third bed.

"John is not here now," she gasped.

"Is Michael asleep?" he asked, with a careless glance at Jane.

"Yes," she answered; and now she felt that she was untrue to Jane as well as to Peter.

"That is not Michael," she said quickly, lest a judgment should fall on her.

Peter looked. "Hullo, is it a new one?"

"Yes."

"Boy or girl?"

"Girl."

Now surely he would understand; but not a bit of it.

"Peter," she said, faltering, "are you expecting me to fly away with you?"

"Of course; that is why I have come." He added a little sternly, "Have you forgotten that this is spring-cleaning time?"

She knew it was useless to say that he had let many spring-cleaning times pass.

"I can't come," she said apologetically, "I have forgotten how to fly."

"I'll soon teach you again."

"O, Peter, don't waste the fairy dust on me."

She had risen, and now at last a fear assailed him. "What is it?" he cried, shrinking.

"I will turn up the light," she said, "and then you can see for yourself."

For almost the only time in his life that I know of, Peter was afraid. "Don't turn up the light," he cried.

She let her hands play in the hair of the tragic boy. She was not a little girl heart-broken about him; she was a grown woman smiling at it all, but they were wet smiles.

Then she turned up the light, and Peter saw. He gave a cry of pain; and when the tall beautiful creature stooped to lift him in her arms he drew back sharply.

"What is it?" he cried again.

She had to tell him.

"I am old, Peter. I am ever so much more than twenty. I grew up long ago."

"You promised not to!"

"I couldn't help it. I am a married woman, Peter."

"No, you're not."

"Yes, and the little girl in the bed is my baby."

"No, she's not."

But he supposed she was; and he took a step towards the sleeping child with his fist upraised. Of course he did not strike her. He sat down on the floor and sobbed, and Wendy did not know how to comfort him, though she could have done it so easily once. She was only a woman now, and she ran out of the room to try to think.

Peter continued to cry, and soon his sobs woke Jane. She sat up in bed, and was interested at once.

"Boy," she said, "why are you crying?"

Peter rose and bowed to her, and she bowed to him from the bed.

"Hullo," he said.

"Hullo," said Jane.

"My name is Peter Pan," he told her.

"Yes, I know."

"I came back for my mother," he explained, "to take her to the Neverland."

"Yes, I know," Jane said, "I been waiting for you."

When Wendy returned diffidently she found Peter sitting on the bed-post crowing gloriously, while Jane in her nighty was flying round the room in solemn ecstasy.

"She is my mother," Peter explained; and Jane descended and stood by his side, with the look on her face that he liked to see on ladies when they gazed at him.

"He does so need a mother," Jane said.

"Yes, I know," Wendy admitted, rather forlornly; "no one knows it so well as I."

"Good-bye," said Peter to Wendy; and he rose in the air, and the shameless Jane rose with him; it was already her easiest way of moving about.

Wendy rushed to the window.

"No, no!" she cried.

"It is just for spring-cleaning time," Jane said; "he wants me always to do his spring cleaning."

"If only I could go with you!" Wendy sighed.

"You see you can't fly," said Jane.

Of course in the end Wendy let them fly away together. Our last glimpse of her shows her at the window, watching them receding into the sky until they were as small as stars.

As you look at Wendy you may see her hair becoming white, and her

figure little again, for all this happened long ago. Jane is now a common grown-up, with a daughter called Margaret; and every spring-cleaning time, except when he forgets, Peter comes for Margaret and takes her to the Neverland, where she tells him stories about himself, to which he listens eagerly. When Margaret grows up she will have a daughter, who is to be Peter's mother in turn; and so it will go on, so long as children are gay and innocent and heartless.

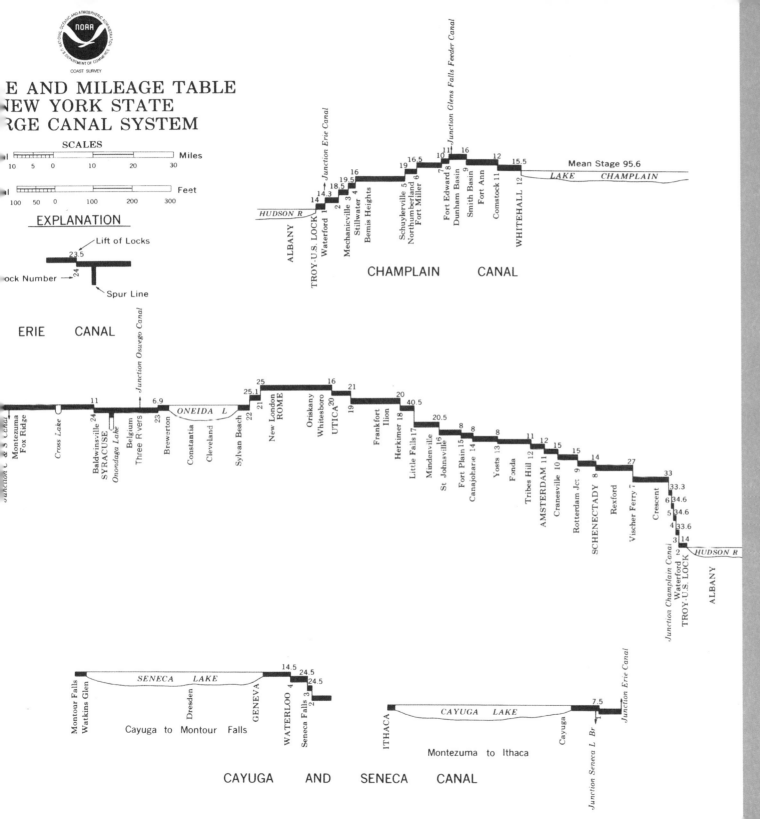

CRUISING AMERICA'S WATERWAYS™

THE ERIE CANAL

CRUISING AMERICA'S WATERWAYS™
THE ERIE CANAL

Debbie Daino Stack and Captain Ronald S. Marquisee

with a foreword by ANDREW CUOMO

MEDIA ARTISTS INC. / *Manlius, NY*

Copyright © 2001 Media Artists Inc.
4673 Brickyard Falls Road
Manlius, New York 13104
www. cruisingamerica. com
All rights reserved

Design and composition by B. Williams & Associates
Printed and bound in Spain by Bookprint, S.L., Barcelona
All photos by Ronald S. Marquisee unless otherwise noted
The "See It on PBS" logo is a trademark of the
Public Broadcasting Service and is used with permission

Library of Congress Control Number: 2001116604
ISBN 0-9708886-0-0

5   4   3   2   1

CONTENTS

Sunrise on the Erie Canal, as a boat prepares to lock through.

DEDICATION

I dedicate this book to my mother, Diane Daino. She always loved the water and was pleased when canal boat rides were a part of our travels together. She had the innate ability to appreciate the beauty in the world around her, including the enchantment found in a well-constructed sentence. It is to her that I owe my love for the written word. —*Debbie*

I dedicate this book to my father, Lionel Marquisee, who first introduced me to photography, boating, and the Erie Canal. When he arrived in Syracuse in the 1920s, the old Erie Canal was being "filled in" to make way for Erie Boulevard. He was more impressed by what was being dumped into that channel than what it signified for the future. A few years ago, at age ninety-five, he made his last day-cruise on the canal, helping me move my boat from Cayuga Lake winter storage to Oneida Lake for the summer. It seems that people age much faster than the canal. He thoroughly enjoyed that trip, and the canal probably enjoyed seeing an old friend for the last time. Thanks, Dad. —*Ron*

FOREWORD

At the dawn of the twenty-first century, the information superhighway is transforming our nation's economy and our daily lives. Nearly 200 years ago, however, another superhighway—the Erie Canal—also fundamentally changed our nation's destiny, opening the western United States to a new generation of Americans.

Governor DeWitt Clinton of New York can justifiably lay claim to both the vision and the achievement of New York's extraordinary system of canals when, as far back as 1816, he first suggested a shipping lane that would link the Port of New York to the eastern shore of Lake Erie in Buffalo and beyond. Not everyone, however, shared the governor's vision. President Thomas Jefferson, himself a brilliant visionary, characterized the notion of a hand-dug canal from Albany to Buffalo as "just short of madness." But that madness built dozens of cities, towns, and villages across New York State and transformed New York into the nation's primary artery of east-west commerce.

For much of the past century New York's canals—the Erie, the Oswego, the Champlain, and the Cayuga-Seneca—lay dormant, bypassed by rail lines, interstate highways, and air transportation. More recently, even in the face of a booming national economy, upstate New York communities that once prospered alongside the canals have struggled from the loss of manufacturing jobs, lagging job growth, and a declining population.

The canals, however, have endured, and today these linkages to our past are pointing the way to a vibrant future, as Americans from across the country and visitors from around the globe discover the unparalleled natural beauty, history, and culture of New York's Canal Corridor.

The rebirth of the Erie Canal and its sister waterways did not happen by accident. Here and throughout the country, communities are discovering the "magic of water" as a magnet for tourism, economic growth, and environmental restoration. As the nation's Secretary of Housing and Urban Development, I have been privileged to initiate an unprecedented federal effort to partner with local governments and businesses along New York's canals in an effort to increase tourism and private sector investment, protect the irreplaceable natural and historic resources of the canals, and—perhaps most importantly—improve the quality of life throughout the region so as to retain and attract residents to upstate New York.

At the heart of our Canal Corridor Initiative has been an effort to build a "regional synergy" along the canals—a shared sense of identity and purpose among larger cities and smaller municipalities that share a common heritage centered around the canals. The investment of nearly $400 million of federal funds has leveraged an additional $400 million from other public and private sources, with assistance to high-tech manufacturers in Newark, construction of

This plaque is part of a monument located in the median of Erie Boulevard in Syracuse.

restaurants and marinas in Ithaca, and support for innovative educational resources like the Capital District Maritime Center in Glenville—all reflecting the diversity of the canals themselves.

Cornell University has estimated that these investments can create more than 27,000 new jobs throughout the region; and the new sense of shared identity and opportunities among canal communities was cemented this year with President Clinton's signature of a new law designating the Erie Canal as a National Heritage Corridor.

So just what is it that makes New York's canals so special? This extraordinary book and the PBS television series *Cruising America's Waterways* highlight in beautiful photography and prose some of the magnificent opportunities that await boaters, hikers, cyclists, motorists, and families along every leg of the Canal Corridor.

Many of my personal favorites are featured here, including the "double" flight of locks at Lockport. But don't miss the 3,000-acre Montezuma National Wildlife Preserve between the Erie and Cayuga-Seneca Canals; the world's only remaining weighlock building in Syracuse; the spectacular Oswego waterfront; the National Women's Rights Museum in Seneca Falls; historic Fort Stanwix in Rome; the highest lock on the canal at Little Falls; beautifully restored Quackenbush Square in Albany; the Feeder Canal bike path in Warren County; or Catskill Point in Greene County.

The Erie Canal of towpaths and flat barges is today a misty memory confined to museums and folklore. But the canal itself speaks to us in an ancient language that reminds us of our past, addresses the challenges of today, and presents new opportunities for tomorrow. The New York State Canal System is a vibrant waterway pulsing with rich history, new life, and unexplored opportunities. In the end, it's a perfect reflection of the people and ideals of the Empire State, proving once again that, like DeWitt Clinton, New Yorkers don't just dream—we work to make dreams come true.

Andrew Cuomo, January 2001

ACKNOWLEDGMENTS

*T*he following have contributed to the development of this book: Joseph Touchstone, Richard and Celia Averson, Jerry Scholder, Joyce Garber, The Voumards (Industrial Color Labs), John Platt, Robert Brooks, John King, Kristen Hanifin, Tom Prindle, the Wiles family, Elizabeth Mann, Nancy Roberts, Marc and Jackie Sacco, Jonathan and Cece Edwards, Patrick and Bonnie Connelly, Vicki Quigley, Paul Mathis, Peter Daino, Ken and Diane Stack, David Aitken, Ken Nichols, Bernie Uebelhoer, Ellen Mitchell, Paul Tater, Gene Johnson, Allen Williams, Howard Lavine, Mary Krause, Pearle, and the Marquisees: Elise, Joseph, Mark, Rose, Georgie, and Evan.

An eastbound sailboat prepares to lock through. Its mast has been lowered to facilitate passage under bridges as an inboard engine powers it along the Erie Canal.

(Left) An aqueduct on the Enlarged Erie carried boats over the Seneca River. Photo Courtesy: Erie Canal Museum, Syracuse, N.Y.

(Above) Today, the remains of the aqueduct can be seen while traveling the "canalized" Seneca River, which is a part of the Erie near its junction with the Cayuga-Seneca Canal.

INTRODUCTION

THE ERIE CANAL is one of four current interconnected canals that facilitate travel by water from New York's interior to ports all over the world. This New York State Canal System also includes the Oswego, Champlain, and the Cayuga-Seneca Canals. This book is a look at this system, still referred to by many as the Erie Canal, as it operates today, set in an historic perspective. It's our hope that present and future generations will be able to pick up this volume and see what the legendary Erie Canal offered at the start of this new millennium. All of the photography, with the exception of historic images, was done in the year 2000. Change is the

A lighthouse and green daymark 65 looking north on the Hudson River.

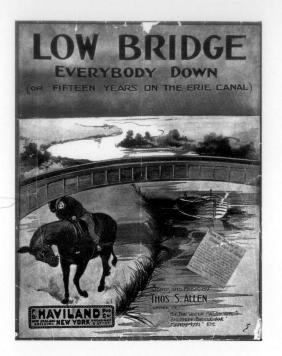

Courtesy: Vincent Motto Music Library, Fayetteville Free Library.

LOW BRIDGE!—EVERYBODY DOWN
(or Fifteen Years On The Erie Canal)

I've got an old mule and her name is Sal,
Fifteen years on the Erie Canal.
She's a good old worker and a good old pal,
Fifteen years on the Erie Canal.
We've hauled some barges in our day,
Filled with lumber, coal and hay,
And ev'ry inch of the way I know,
From Albany to Buffalo.

[Chorus]
Low bridge, everybody down,
Low bridge, we must be getting near a town
You can always tell your neighbor,
You can always tell your pal,
If he's ever navigated on the Erie Canal.

We'd better look 'round for a job old gal,
Fifteen years on the Erie Canal.
You bet your life I wouldn't part with Sal,
Fifteen years on the Erie Canal.
Giddap there gal we've passed that lock,
We'll make Rome 'fore six o'clock,
So one more trip and then we'll go,
Right straight back to Buffalo.

[Chorus]

Low bridge, everybody down,
Low bridge, I've got the finest mule in town,
Once a man named Mike McGinty tried to put it over Sal,
Now he's way down at the bottom of the Erie Canal.

Oh, where would I be if I lost my pal?
Fifteen years on the Erie Canal.
Oh, I'd like to see a mule as good as Sal,
Fifteen years on the Erie Canal.
A friend of mine once got her sore,
Now, he's got a broken jaw.

'Cause she let fly with her iron toe
And kicked him into Buffalo.

[Chorus]

Low bridge, everybody down,
Low bridge, I've got the finest mule in town,
If you're looking 'round for trouble, better stay away from
    Sal,
She's the only fighting donkey on the Erie Canal.
I don't have to call when I want my Sal,
Fifteen years on the Erie Canal,
She trots from her stall like a good old gal,
Fifteen years on the Erie Canal,
I eat my meals with Sal each day
I eat beef and she eats hay,
She ain't so slow if you want to know,
She put the "Buff" in Buffalo.

[Chorus]

Low bridge, everybody down,
Low bridge, I've got the finest mule in town;
Eats a bale of hay for dinner, and on top of that, my Sal
Tries to drink up all the water in the Erie Canal.
You'll soon hear them sing all about my gal,
Fifteen years on the Erie Canal,
It's a darned fool ditty 'bout my darned fool Sal,
Fifteen years on the Erie Canal.
Oh, every band will play it soon,
Darned fool words and darned fool tune;
You'll hear it sung everywhere you go,
From Mexico to Buffalo.

[Chorus]

Low bridge, everybody down,
Low bridge, I've got the finest mule in town,
She's a perfect, perfect lady, and she blushes like a gal,
If she hears you sing about her and the Erie Canal.

nature of things, so as you read this book understand that the specific attractions we visit today may be gone tomorrow. And new attractions will continue to appear as the canal system evolves over time.

The canals are as functional today as they were in the early 1800s, when first conceived. Once the key to commerce and the geographic development of a nation, today's canals are a unique recreational and tourism resource. This book looks at samples of the richness to be found in the historic Canal Corridor villages and cities, and the stretches of unspoiled countryside that reflect the American experience. If we hadn't inherited this canal system from earlier generations, it wouldn't be built today—due to financial, political, and environmental concerns.

We have chosen to include the Hudson River in our look at the New York State Canal System for two reasons. First, the upper Hudson is part of the Champlain Canal. And second, the main purpose of the Erie Canal was to link the Port of New York on the Atlantic Ocean with the Great Lakes, via the Hudson River, which it has done for almost 200 years. New York City thus became the chief port of entry into these United States, shaping the growth of the nation and making New York the "Empire State."

When the idea for this book was first suggested to a friend, he was concerned that the book would be a dull collection of images of locks and river, all of which would look about the same. This was akin to saying that a book about *Route 66* would show nothing but paved highway. In fact, the Erie Canal and *Route 66* share many things. Both were visionary, changed the way we travel, inspired songs, developed groups of aficionados and preservationists, helped us understand our country,

and illustrate a basic human need: to explore beyond our place and time, sifting ideas from first-hand experiences with which to build our own lives. And both are icons of our affection for freedom, be it the open road, the open seas, or an open book. The real difference is that the Erie Canal has retained its essence, still inviting us to cruise and explore . . . while *Route 66* fades from the landscape.

This book is an overview of the New York State Canal System, written by two people who love what it has to offer, and who want to share this treasure with you. If you're a boater, you'll need charts; if you come by car, you'll want maps; hikers and bikers will use trail guides; and those who elect a cruise experience on a commercial carrier . . . well, just pack your bags. No matter how you choose to enjoy these canals, you will.

CRUISING AMERICA'S WATERWAYS™

THE ERIE CANAL

The Erie Canal made it possible for steamers on the Great Lakes to continue shipments via canal boats to markets between Buffalo and New York City, and on to the rest of the world through the Port of New York—and vice versa. Courtesy: Erie Canal Museum, Syracuse, N.Y.

A VERY SHORT HISTORY OF NEW YORK'S CANALS

THERE EXIST MANY GOOD HISTORIES of New York's canals, so our *very short* history touches only upon the events that everyone should be aware of when they consider this legendary waterway. The Erie Canal, the centerpiece of the New York State Canal System, has been around for such a long time that it precedes still photography, movies, and television. Its history begins in a very different era, a time when the word, the painting, and the drawing recorded—or perhaps we should say interpreted—historic events. Information, and everything else, moved at a much slower pace. Time has a way of clouding the past, but most agree on the key events that led to the engineering and cultural marvel of its day—the Erie Canal.

Most great inventions begin with a *need,* followed by an *idea* that can resolve that need if its implementation is feasible. With a populous eastern seaboard, America *needed* a path to its interior if it was to grow and take advantage of the riches to the west—farmland and unimagined natural resources including lumber, coal, and minerals. The problem was that the Appalachian Mountains were a seemingly insurmountable barrier. There was, however, one route that could take advantage of relatively friendly natural topography; it ran from the Hudson River near Albany, New York, through the center of the state all the way to Lake Erie, thus linking the Atlantic Ocean with the Great Lakes. The distance exceeded 350 miles, and as a journey by land at that time, it was an impossible route over which to sustain commerce.

A number of politicos favored the construction of a canal, but the federal government lacked the will and resources to undertake such a project. And whatever westward route was chosen would favor the growth of some states and thereby disadvantage others, furthering the political struggle. So it came down to the resolve of one state, New York, to finance and undertake the construction of a westward canal. It was Governor DeWitt Clinton who, by championing his idea for the canal in the state legislature, was able to get authorization for the $7 million needed to build the Erie. This was a particularly brave undertaking for New York for many reasons: it was an expensive project, there were no professional engineering and construction companies in existence to build such a canal, and there was no precedent by which to estimate the potential for the project's success. With an incredibly optimistic look into the future, the canal project began its physical growth with the turning of a shovel of dirt in Rome on July 4, 1817. More than the start of a canal, this moment was a symbol of American entrepreneurship and vision—the same vision that would establish America as a leader in both scientific and cultural evolution for generations.

animals met the challenges of clearing trees, removing stumps, blasting channels through solid rock, forming canal sections through swamps, and removing immeasurable quantities of dirt and stone. To expedite the process, many private contractors, often farmers, were hired to dig small sections of the canal. It was completed in October 1825—with celebrations all along its route. The *Seneca Chief* departed Buffalo with DeWitt Clinton and other dignitaries on board, carrying kegs of water from Lake Erie, along the canal, to be poured into New York Harbor for the Wedding of the Waters ceremonies. The trip took ten days and captured the attention of a jubilant people as no other public works event had.

Other major canals—laterals—extended the reach of the Erie.

Surveying teams worked their way through the wilderness, laying out improved routes for transportation. Courtesy: Erie Canal Museum, Syracuse, N.Y.

An historic marker at Erie Canal Village near Rome identifies the spot where construction of the Erie Canal began.

The route for the Erie Canal was laid out by three self-made engineers: Benjamin Wright, James Geddes, and Charles G. Broadhead. Together they would oversee the entire project. This was the *first* Erie Canal, today referred to as the Old Erie. It was a ditch 40 feet wide at the top, 4 feet deep, and 28 feet wide at the bottom. On one side there was a 5-foot-wide berm, and on the other side a 12-foot-wide towpath to accommodate the mules and horses—guided by people called hoggees (Scottish word for worker)—that pulled the boats along the canal's 363-mile route from Albany to Buffalo. It would take eight years to complete the "ditch," with its 18 aqueducts (to carry the canal over rivers and streams), and 83 locks (90 feet long and 15 feet wide) that were needed to raise boats 565 feet from the Hudson River to Lake Erie.

Construction inventiveness was the order of the day, as men and

Animals were the source of power for boats on both the Erie and the Enlarged Erie. Courtesy: Erie Canal Museum, Syracuse, N.Y.

The double flight of locks at Lockport, an engineering and construction triumph, carried boats over the Niagara Escarpment. Courtesy: Erie Canal Museum, Syracuse, N.Y.

(Above) The salt industry in Syracuse flourished with the canal's low-cost transportation to distant markets. The sun was used to evaporate water from the brine pumped from the salt wells near Onondaga Lake, producing salt for shipment. Courtesy: Erie Canal Museum, Syracuse, N.Y.

(Right) Clinton Square in downtown Syracuse looks very much the same today, except that the "road of water" has been filled in and paved over to serve automotive traffic. Courtesy: Erie Canal Museum, Syracuse, N.Y.

The Champlain Canal ran from Albany to Lake Champlain, the Oswego Canal linked the mid-section of the Erie to Lake Ontario, and the Cayuga-Seneca Canal provided a connection to the Finger Lakes. Canals were being built along routes that would tie communities all over the state to the Erie, The Grand Canal. This was a link that meant life or death for many towns.

The Erie Canal was the undisputed engineering marvel of its day, the implementation of technology on a grand scale to promote the commerce of a developing nation. And it worked. The cost of moving freight from Albany to Buffalo dropped from $100 a ton to $4 a ton within the first decade of the canal's operation. The canal facilitated the flow of finished goods, raw materials, people, and ideas. It

was a success in every way. Tolls provided the state with helpful revenues upon which to develop, and the towns along the canal grew and flourished. And success follows success. The immediate positive impact of the Erie spurred the construction of more than 2,000 miles of other American canals, some of which survive to this day, but most of which have been abandoned. It wasn't long before plans were being made for the *second* Erie Canal, the Enlarged Erie.

The enlargement of the Erie Canal, while seen to be inevitable, took 27 years and cost about $32 million. The project was, for the most part, completed in 1862. The ditch was now 70 feet wide at the water's surface, 7 feet deep, and 42 feet wide at the bottom. The enlarged towpath was 14 feet wide, and the berm was 10 feet wide.

Locks were extended to 110 feet. The good news was that more traffic, carrying more tonnage, could now use the Erie and its lateral canals. The bad news was that railroads were growing rapidly along many of the canal routes and provided year-round service, whereas the canals were frozen and useless during the winter. It appeared, however, that nothing could match the impact of the *first* Erie.

In the competitive race with the railroads, canal tolls were abolished in 1882. But the railroads far outpaced the canals in tonnage growth, despite their higher rates. While water transportation had the potential of being dramatically less expensive for shipping many important commodities, such as coal and oil, the Enlarged Erie was now too small to meet the demands of the "modern" world. So, in 1905, it was time to build the *third* Erie Canal, which would become the dramatically enlarged and redesigned New York State Barge Canal System.

The new Barge Canal was completed in 1918 at a cost exceeding $150 million. The most modern inland waterway system in the world then, it continues to provide service to this day with few changes—except in name. As barge traffic diminished from the peak year of

The Barge Canal had to promote itself in a struggle with rail and trucking competition. Courtesy: Erie Canal Museum, Syracuse, N.Y.

1951, and as recreational vessels became the primary users, the Barge Canal was renamed the New York State Canal System.

The Barge Canal project began under Governor Theodore Roosevelt's administration. It was to meet the demands of a new age, so it was not to be a simple enlargement of the existing canals but rather the best canal system that current engineering practices would allow—designed to accommodate large, motor-powered barges that could compete in a changing transportation environment. The 30-ton boats that populated the original Erie would be displaced by efficient motor-powered 3,000-ton barges. We had conquered our western frontier and were now rushing through the Industrial Revolution. The new Barge Canal would "canalize" the existing rivers and lakes along its route and link them with "cut" sections to create a wider (averaging 200 feet), deeper (12 to 14 feet) channel, with

The large "modern" locks, such as this one on the Cayuga-Seneca Canal, helped keep the cost of shipping via canal lower than competitive choices.

only 35 locks on the Erie section. Fewer locks meant shorter transport times in an industry where faster is always better. The massive new lock gates would be electrified on the 328-foot-long by 45-foot-wide concrete lock chambers. Forty-three terminals were constructed. Canals that were not a part of the new system would fade from the landscape, and the survivors were the familiar Erie, Oswego, Champlain, and Cayuga-Seneca Canals, now described as "sections" of the system.

While there are places where the earlier canals and the Barge Canal share the same turf, much of the route was altered. Canal communities, where the canal literally ran through the middle of town, were now separated from the waterway that brought them into being and bolstered their economies. On the other hand, towns along the new route stood to benefit from their position on the Barge Canal. Just as interstate highways bypass business districts while providing access to towns along their route, so it is with this superhighway of a canal. The early canal towns are still here with their wonderful architecture, histories, people, and early canal artifacts. But travel today is on the modern (approaching 100 years old) New York State Canal System, also known as the Barge Canal. Most of the equipment is original and designed by engineers who expected the Barge Canal to live forever. There have been changes over the years: for example, the coming of nearby electric utilities led to the decommissioning of the self-contained power generating facilities that provided locks with energy for lighting, gate, and valve operation. And today's focus on recreational boating has been aided by the addition of rope lines along the inside of lock chamber walls. But all of the changes combined have only slightly altered the "feel" of the canal experience. And that's what is so unique about cruising this legendary waterway.

Much of the region's oldest and most interesting architecture can be seen from the water where the route of the Barge Canal is the same as that of the Old Erie, such as here in Lockport.

A recreational locking permit is checked by a lock operator on the Cayuga-Seneca Canal.

2

THE MECHANICS OF
TODAY'S CANAL SYSTEM

WHEN THINKING of the canal system, the first image that comes to mind is that of a lock. It's almost as if the canals are a group of locks connected by water, not vast stretches of water connected by locks. Coupled with dams and other structures, locks provide those relatively current-less, navigable channels of water, or pools, that *are* the canals—offering a safe and usually dependable route for boaters. The engineering challenge is to manage what nature supplies to provide pools of water with a fixed depth, so that craft with a particular "draft" can pass safely. And the water level (surface elevation) has to be held constant, so that craft with a particular height can pass safely under bridges. At the most basic level, the surface elevation can be altered by evaporation, rain, and melting snows; and the depth of the channel can be altered by silting from bank erosion, decaying plant life, and deposits left behind by crossing streams. The canal system is designed with the engineering features needed to maintain its operation under normal weather conditions.

Managing this system is a complex process. With so many variables of nature acting on such a vast waterway, it is not always possible to keep the levels constant and the entire system navigable. And while highway travel usually offers alternate routes if, for example, a bridge is out, the failure of a single canal lock may render the entire system useless for a particular voyage. As you travel the canals, it is interesting to explore the mechanical features that make them work.

While automobiles can change elevation easily by driving up or down hills that are a part of the terrain, boats must travel at one level, accommodating changes in elevation by passing through locks that raise or lower them to a different level. Some routes, such as those followed by the Oswego and Cayuga-Seneca Canals are, respectively, down or uphill all the way. Other routes, such as those of the Erie and Champlain Canals, have their ups and downs to get over topographic ridges, on their way to a final destination and elevation.

Locks and dams are used to "canalize" the Oswego River, making it the Oswego Canal. If we look at the Oswego's profile from its junction with the Erie, at a point known as Three Rivers, to Lake Ontario, there's a drop of about 118 feet. The water continues its trip to sea level through Lake Ontario and the St. Lawrence River, which has also been made navigable through a system of locks and dams, known as the St. Lawrence Seaway.

In its natural state, the Oswego River wasn't navigable due to shallows, rapids, water-level changes, and unpredictable currents. To tame the river, dams were built at critical points along its 23-mile course, forming "pools" of sufficient depth void of strong currents, allowing boat traffic.

Junction Erie Canal

10.2
17.8
27
18
20
14.5
11.1

OSWEGO

Phoenix 1
Fulton 3
Minetto 5
6
7
8

Mean Stage 244.8

LAKE ONTARIO

OSWEGO CANAL

Dams form navigable pools of water, and locks allow boats to move from one pool to the next.

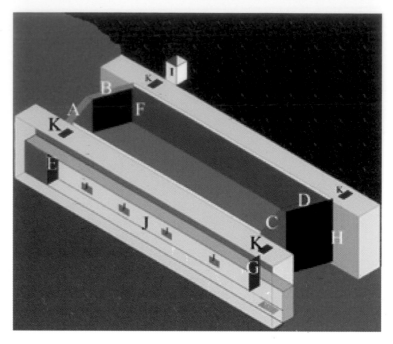

The upper pool is to the left, and the lower pool is to the right. As illustrated, the lock is discharging water into the lower pool.

LOCKS

Since boats can't safely travel over dams, to get from one elevation to the next locks are built beside the dams to gently raise or lower craft to the next level. While there are small variations in design and operation on the canals, for the most part the locks are similar. A lock chamber accommodates a boat that is a maximum of 300 feet long and 43.5 feet wide, or a number of smaller boats that will fit within that space. Many locks have attractive floral displays, picnic facilities, and a wall suitable for docking while you explore the area, or, with permission, spend the night.

A lock's major components are the four hinged gates (A, B, C, D); the four valves that regulate the flow of water into and out of the chamber (E, F, G, H); the controls used by the lock operator (I)

to supply electricity to the eight motors that operate the gates and valves; and the reinforced-cement chamber itself, complete with tunnels (J) to carry water into and out of the chamber. Gravity, not pumps, moves the water into and out of the locks, reducing power consumption, noise, and hardware requirements. Let's look at a "lock cycle" for Lock O-3 on the Oswego Canal for a boat headed downstream (north) to Lake Ontario. In this case the boat will be lowered.

All gates on the lock are closed. Valves G and H are closed and then valves E and F are opened to allow water to fill the chamber through tunnels J. The main tunnel is seven by nine feet in cross section. The valves are guillotines that are pulled up or lowered by electrically powered winches (K) connected by cables. The water enters the chamber through smaller tunnels along the sides of the walls and well below the water line, even when the water level is at its low point (14 feet) in the chamber. Once the chamber is full, valves E and F are closed, and the gates A and B are opened fully by electrically driven geared arms that are attached to each gate, allowing the vessels to enter the chamber. Boats position themselves along the walls of the chamber, holding their positions with lines that hang down along the wall, or by looping lines around the heavy-duty mushroom-like "bollards" at the top of the wall.

Gates A and B are then fully closed. There's always a slight "V" when the gates are closed, that faces the higher pool, to utilize the pressure from this water to help force the gates more tightly together. Next, valves E and F are closed. Then valves G and H are opened, allowing the water in the chamber to discharge into the lower pool. When the water level in the chamber matches the level in the lower pool, gates C and D are opened, and the vessels drop their lines and exit the chamber.

The process is similar when raising a boat, in this case southbound. A vessel enters the chamber and the crew holds onto the lines attached to the walls. Gates C and D are closed and valves G and H are closed. Valves E and F are opened, allowing water into the chamber. When the water level in the chamber matches that of the upper pool, gates A and B are opened, and boats leave the chamber. The difference in elevation between the upper and lower pools is the lock's "lift," which ranges from 6 feet to 40.5 feet on the canal system. Less lift generally means a shorter time locking through.

DAMS

The dams that form the pools of water on the canal are visible at "river section" locks, and vary in design. Some are traditional-looking "fixed" dams, such as the one in Fulton, that work in conjunction with commercial power generation stations. Water may flow over the tops of these dams or be diverted into turbines through large pipes or tunnels, ultimately being discharged into the lower pool. The maximum depth of the retained pool is fixed by the dam's height.

(Left) The rack arm extends from the machinery pit to the gate that it electrically opens and closes powered by a 7- to 10-horsepower motor.

(Below) Taintor gates regulate the flow of water over the dam in Waterloo.

A Canal Corporation employee prepares to adjust a Mohawk-style dam near Amsterdam.

The Court Street Dam in Rochester keeps the Genesee River navigable.

Other dams, such as the one at Mechanicville on the Champlain Canal, employ *crest gates* along the top of the fixed dam section. These can be electrically raised and lowered to adjust the depth of the retained pool. At this site, water is diverted into a hydroelectric plant and then discharged below the dam.

Some dams, such as the one at Waterloo, employ *taintor gates*. These are pie-shaped gates that fit into a notch in the fixed dam, pivoting from the apex to create a larger or smaller spillway. Counterweights may be used to balance the gate, minimizing the motor power needed for adjustment. These gates facilitate lowering the pool created by the fixed dam, providing more water for power generation or a lowered upper pool to reduce the chances of flooding during periods of high runoff.

There are two particularly unusual types of dams used in the canal system. The Court Street Dam in Rochester controls the water level in the Genesee River, which is navigable from its junction with the Erie Canal right into the city. This is a floating dam, and the pool

depth can be regulated by allowing water to flow into the dam, raising it; or water can be let out of the dam, lowering it.

Perhaps the most distinctive dams are the Mohawk-style dams used to control water levels in the eastern portion of the Erie Canal. During the boating season, the dam sections are lowered into cement footings at the bottom of the river, forming the wall that creates the needed pool. Each section incorporates two steel plates. The lower plate creates the nominal pool level. An additional two-foot plate allows adjustment of the pool level to ensure adequate water while reducing potential flooding conditions. These dams were relatively inexpensive to build and have proven their dependability for more than 80 years. Perhaps the most important feature is that the plates can be pulled completely out of the water during periods when the canal is closed for the season, allowing the Mohawk River to run its natural course. This way, nature alone is responsible for flooding that may occur due to the rapid melting of snow and heavy rains in the spring.

GUARD GATES

Guard gates are strategically located along the route of the canal system. Their primary purpose is to protect the waterway from draining in the event of a catastrophic failure of a canal system component. The massive gates would be dropped down, preventing the flow of water past their location. For example, the water from Oneida Lake flows westward through Lock E-23, whose gates maintain the proper level in the upper pool. If a mechanical failure opened both sets of lock gates at the same time, the huge amount of water in Oneida Lake would surge through the canal system on its way to Lake Ontario, creating life-threatening problems for people on or near the channel. So in this application, the guard gates function as an emergency safety device. They also provide additional security, thus helping to prevent potential problems. For example, the guard gate at the top of the Waterford locks is kept down as a precautionary barrier when boats aren't locking through. In a very different role, the gates may be used as an aid in draining a canal section to perform maintenance work.

RESERVOIRS

Reservoirs, such as Delta Reservoir, which was formed by the construction of Delta Dam, provide water to maintain the canal system's depth, especially in unusually dry summer weather. Water is allowed to flow into the system as needed from the reservoir's elevated position many miles from the waterway itself. This and other reservoirs also provide the state with important recreational resources.

Guard gates are frequently found at locks, such as this one at Lock E-23 near Brewerton.

SPILLWAYS, WASTE WEIRS, AND SLUICE GATES

Maintaining a waterway is a balancing act between man and the forces of nature. Water flows into the canal system from rain, melting snow, streams, rivers, and reservoirs. To maintain a relatively fixed level, spillways, waste weirs, and sluice gates are used to drain off the excess water. Spillways and waste weirs are concrete canalside walls that are notched to a level that allows water to flow over

(Left) Delta Dam and an early northern lateral canal.
Courtesy: Erie Canal Museum, Syracuse, N.Y.

(Below) Today the aqueduct remains, and the water from
Delta Lake feeds the current Erie Canal.

them and into a stream when it exceeds the desired water level in the canal system. Another device to control the water level in the canals employs sluice gates. Large culverts drain water from within the channel, through a vertical adjustable gate (much like a lock valve but controlled by a worm gear) into another waterway.

POWERHOUSES

A few locks still have operating powerhouses that can be used in an emergency to power the lock or to provide electric heat during the colder months. These were the primary sources of power at the locks before electricity was widely distributed by utility companies. They take advantage of the differing pool levels, utilizing water-powered turbines and generators.

AQUEDUCTS AND DIVE CULVERTS

Aqueducts were an important part of earlier canal systems. They were troughs of wood that were supported by masonry to carry the canals and boats over rivers and streams. This unusual aqueduct on the current canal system carries the Erie Canal over Culvert Road (a highway, not a body of water), near Medina. There are still many places, however, where the beautiful remains of aqueducts can be seen along the route. In some crossings, the 1825 Erie diverted smaller streams under the canal through U-shaped *dive culverts*. This same technique is still used today.

This 1918 vintage power-generating plant at a lock on the Champlain Canal is still operating.

(Above) Culvert Road passes under the current Erie Canal near Medina. This is the only functioning aqueduct on the New York State Canal System.

(Right) Dive culverts allow small streams to cross under the canals without interruption.

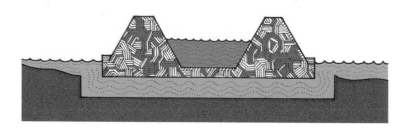

EARTH EMBANKMENTS

While most of the canal system passes natural river shoreline, or through "cut" sections, there are areas where earth embankments were formed to serve as one or both sides of a stretch of canal. Here the boater may ride high above the nearby landscape, looking down on fields and houses. These walls of earth have to be regularly inspected to ensure they will not rupture, flooding nearby property. Animals burrowing into the elevated earthen canal walls have been known to cause leaks that are pathways for expanded erosion and subsequent embankment failure.

BRIDGES

There are three basic types of bridges on the canal system: fixed, lift, and swing. Most of the bridges are fixed, and their height above the water line varies by location and the water level in the system itself. There's one lift bridge on the Oswego Canal at Phoenix that pivots upward from one end with the help of a large counterweight. The other 15 lift bridges are on the western section of the Erie Canal, providing a clearance of 15.5 feet, as they rise parallel to the water's surface (Fairport excepted, where the bridge is on a permanent incline). There's also one swing bridge at Lock O-2, in Fulton, on the Oswego Canal.

BUOYS AND SIGNAGE

Buoys mark the canal system's main channel, where the depth is maintained as stated in NOAA charts. Red "nun" buoys mark one side, and green "can" buoys mark the other. Fixed day markers are used as well, and each has a charted identification number. The buoys are put out in the spring and removed for the winter. Other buoys, of differing colors, are used to mark hazardous locations, such as the tops of dams. Lighthouses are also navigational aids, but you'll find just three of them on the canal system, all automated, and all near Oneida Lake.

The canals and canal-side trails feature a variety of informational signs and historic markers. The information you would expect to find at a lock includes the lock's identification (for example, O-1,

Markers along the canals highlight points of historic interest, such as the 40.5 foot lift at Lock E-17 near Little Falls.

(Top left) This unique lift bridge is located in Phoenix and operated in conjunction with the lock.

(Top right) This swing bridge in Fulton rotates to span the lock chamber.

(Bottom) This is a typical lift bridge on the western Erie in its raised position.

This lighthouse is located in Brewerton, and serves as a navigational aid for the shallow and sometimes treacherous Oneida Lake.

the first lock on the Oswego Canal); the lock's lift; the distance east-bound or westbound to the next lock; the speed limit; and the Lock Limit, an approach zone where passing is not allowed and reduced speed is mandatory. Other signs along the route identify marinas, highways, hidden dangers, no-wake zones, and nearby attractions.

MAINTENANCE

The physical "good looks" and dependable functionality of this canal system that is more than 80 years old are testament to the quality of routine maintenance that has been performed throughout its

(Above) A fleet of vessels is dedicated to maintaining the canal system. These craft are working on the Erie.

(Right) Lock operators maintain their equipment when they're not locking boats, as seen here near Macedon.

Major repairs to the canal system continue through the winter, such as this refurbishing of a lock on the Champlain Canal.

existence, and to the inherent design work by the engineers back in the early 1900s. Today, most parts needed to repair the system have to be custom-fabricated. Attempts at substituting new technology for the components and systems originally specified have generally resulted in reduced performance or shortened component life. Lock operators spend much of their non-locking time cleaning, lubricating, painting, adjusting, and performing minor and preventative repairs on equipment. Major repairs are scheduled throughout the year, rotated throughout the system, and employ appropriate specialists. In fact, much of the heavy work, such as refurbishing gates and cement work, is done when the canal system isn't in operation, right through the winter. Because downtime on the canals inconveniences users, outside contractors may be hired to resolve unanticipated critical failures.

Each canal's channel requires constant maintenance. Dredges remove sediment to maintain the charted depth, floating debris is fished from the water by specially equipped cranes and floated away on barges, vegetation is cut back along the shore, and stones are replaced to reduce bank erosion. There's a constant battle between man and nature to maintain this navigable route that has served us so well for so long a time.

BEYOND MECHANICS

The mechanics of the canal system are only as good as the people who operate all of this hardware to get boaters safely to their destinations—while reducing flood damage and providing water for irrigation and power generation. The New York State Canal Corporation, a division of the New York State Thruway Authority, with administrative offices in Albany, is presently the custodian of this legacy resource, overseeing day-to-day operations and planning the system's future in partnership with many municipalities and organizations along its route. A mechanical marvel, the Erie Canal continues to be an element in New York State's cultural growth.

Looking eastward from Lock E-17 on the Erie.

Biking and hiking trails along many canal sections broaden the recreational opportunities available.

A BOATERS' GUIDE TO
USING THE CANALS

*I*T'S GREAT TO READ about the canals, but it's more fun to use them. This chapter will provide you with what you need to know to take advantage of this unique resource. Yes, there's a great trail system that follows sections of the old and current canals, providing an easy, scenic, and historically interesting path for bikers and hikers. And yes, there are roads that let you drive to locks and ports all along the way. But the New York State Canal System was built as a water route for commercial shipping that has evolved into a premiere recreational boating destination. There are detailed cruising guides that tell you what services and attractions are available along the way, and there are trail guides with helpful maps and advice. The information that is included here provides a broad overview for anyone who wants to better understand the scope of knowledge required to safely travel by water, whether you use your own boat, a self-captained hire boat, or a staffed cruise line.

Most people use a boat to go fishing, swimming, skiing, tubing, or to just enjoy being on the water and they return to their departure point at the end of the day. But the canals invite you to actually go places; to *cruise,* to take a trip along a route that has provided adventure for generations. The canal system is lined with destinations (as described later in this book), and it also serves as a connection to other waterways including the Great Lakes, the St. Lawrence River,

The aft flag on this trawler shows that its home port is in Canada.

and the Atlantic Ocean. And these waterways are connected to other waterways, so you can reach ports all over the world starting anywhere along the system. The canal system is fully operational from late April to mid-November (check with the New York State Canal Corporation for exact dates via their web site or telephone information line: 1-800-4CANAL4).

The beautiful limestone locks and aqueducts of the Enlarged Erie, and other canal remains scattered throughout the state, may give the impression that the canal system has become fragmented and overgrown. But these are remnants of an earlier age, purposely abandoned when they were displaced by the Barge Canal at the beginning of this century. The Barge Canal, now called the New York State Canal System, is fully intact and regularly serving the needs of recreational boaters. It consists of four connected canals: the **Erie**, 338 miles long, which runs from Waterford (and Albany by way of the Hudson River) to Tonawanda (and Buffalo by way of the Niagara River); the **Champlain**, 60 miles long, which runs from Albany to Whitehall at the southern tip of Lake Champlain; the **Oswego**, 24 miles long, that runs from the Three Rivers junction on the Erie to Lake Ontario at the port of Oswego; and the **Cayuga-**

Seneca, 102 miles long including lake sections, that links the Erie, near Montezuma, with Cayuga and Seneca Lakes (which are also considered a part of the system). The canals, including lake sections, are freshwater bodies, not subject to tidal activity. An overview of the canal system is provided in the NOAA chart book (see inside back cover).

CHARTS

Planning a trip by water typically begins with a review of charts. Charts are the boating equivalent of maps used for land travel. The major difference is that they show water depths, overhead clearances, and other potential hazards for boaters. Charts are essential in planning a safe trip by water and are presently available in both paper and electronic forms for most areas. Since electronic devices can fail (a blown fuse, for example), it is recommended that paper charts always be available.

The "official" charts are published by the National Oceanic and Atmospheric Administration (NOAA), which is a part of the U.S. Department of Commerce. Charts can be ordered directly from the government or purchased through catalog and marine retail outlets. Presently, *Recreational Chart 14786, New York State Barge Canal System,* covers the canals, with the exception of the Erie between Lyons and Tonawanda. While buoyed, this "cut" section is so straightforward that it's not included. This chart book, first published in 1948, is presently in its 12th edition, which was released in May 1998.

Connecting U.S. waters are covered in other charts also published by NOAA. Other countries, including Canada, have charts available covering their waterways. Every boater should be familiar with charts, their symbols, and the wealth of information they provide.

The NOAA Chart Book also includes a profile chart, documenting changes in elevation, and a handy mileage table for estimating distances between major locations along the canals (inside front cover).

EQUIPMENT

As you plan to travel on the canals, you'll need to carry Coast Guard-required equipment appropriate for the size of your mechanically propelled or sail-powered recreational craft, such as approved fire extinguishers, life preservers, whistles, and lights. In addition, there is equipment especially helpful when using the canals, above and beyond the general requirements. If you're uncertain about your required equipment, you can invite the Coast Guard Auxiliary to perform a Marine Courtesy Exam. An Auxiliary member will inspect your boat without charge and, if it's in compliance, post a decal. If it's not in compliance, you'll be told what needs to be done to meet legal *and* Auxiliary recommended standards. This is not an enforcement program. Detailed regulations are available in a variety of publications made available by governmental agencies without charge.

Your craft also will have to be currently registered and properly display an identification number (or name and home port if it's a documented vessel) and a registration sticker. If you're going to go

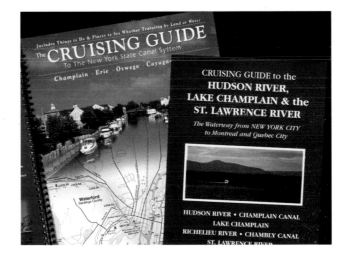

Cruising guides provide detailed, timely information for boaters using the canals.

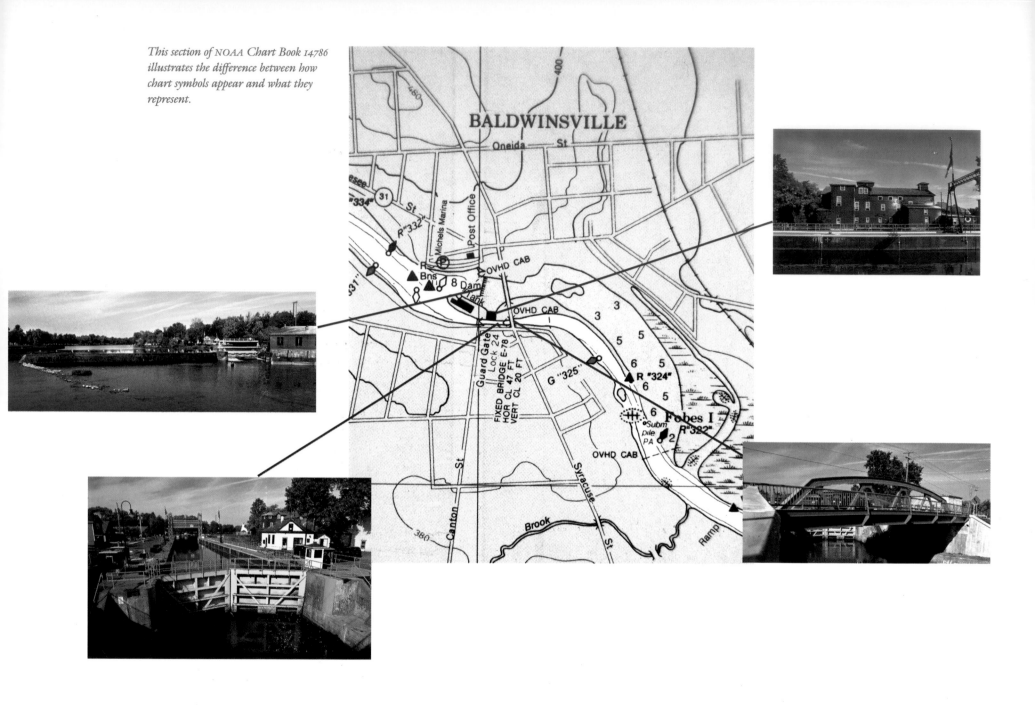

This section of NOAA Chart Book 14786 illustrates the difference between how chart symbols appear and what they represent.

Lock operators, such as this one in Little Falls, sell passes and track boats through the canal system.

through locks or under lift bridges, you'll need to purchase either a two-day pass or a seasonal permit from the New York State Canal Corporation. The cost is modest and in proportion to the length of the vessel. Craft without motors, such as canoes and kayaks, may use the canal system without charge. If your trip doesn't take you through a lock, or require that a bridge be raised, you don't need a pass. Passes may be purchased at locks on a walk-in basis.

Beyond the "legal" equipment, you'll want to have additional items on board to facilitate locking. A VHF **marine radio**, tuned to channel 13, allows you to talk with lock operators and other similarly equipped boats; and those radios equipped to receive the WX channels will have access to helpful weather information. Adequate **fenders** will protect your hull, other boats, and the lock chamber walls from damage. The number and size of the fenders required will vary with the vessel, but it's best to be overprotected. Adequate **lines** are required to hold the boat steady in the lock chamber and secure when docked. A **boat hook** makes it easier to grab lines or fend off a wall. A pair of waterproof **gloves** makes handling the lines a more

pleasant task. And a good pair of waterproof **binoculars** can be helpful in identifying buoys and landmarks. In lake sections, a **compass** is helpful in maintaining a course, especially during periods of restricted visibility.

FLOAT PLAN

An extended trip utilizing the canals should be planned on a day-by-day basis. Once you are underway, changes are common, but a plan should be developed at the outset. Since the speed limit on the canal

Buoys are taken out of the canals during the winter, and then returned to their designated positions early in the spring. Red 134, seen here, marks the western channel in Oneida Lake.

FLOAT PLAN   Complete this plan before going boating and leave it with a reliable person who can be depended upon to notify the Coast Guard, or other rescue organization, should you not return as scheduled. Do not file this plan with the Coast Guard.

TODAY'S DATE_____

1. *NAME OF PERSON REPORTING*_____TELEPHONE NUMBER_____

2. *DESCRIPTION OF BOAT,* TYPE_____ COLOR_____ TRIM_____
REGISTRATION NO._____ LENGTH_____ NAME_____
MAKE_____ OTHER INFO._____

3. *PERSONS ABOARD*_____

NAME	AGE	ADDRESS & TELE. NO.
_____	_____	_____
_____	_____	_____
_____	_____	_____
_____	_____	_____

4. *ENGINE TYPE*_____H.P._____ NO. OF ENGINES_____ FUEL CAPACITY_____

5. *SURVIVAL EQUIPMENT: (CHECK AS APPROPRIATE)*
PFDs_____ FLARES_____ MIRROR_____ SMOKE SIGNALS_____ FLASHLIGHT_____ FOOD_____
PADDLES_____ WATER_____ OTHERS_____
ANCHOR_____ RAFT OR DINGHY_____ EPIRB_____

6. RADIO YES / NO TYPE_____FREQS._____

7. *TRIP EXPECTATIONS:* LEAVE AT_____(DATE / TIME)
FROM_____ GOING TO_____
EXPECT TO RETURN BY_____(DATE / TIME)
AND IN NO EVENT LATER THAN_____

8. ANY OTHER PERTINENT INFO._____

9. AUTOMOBILE LICENSE_____TYPE_____ TRAILER LICENSE_____
COLOR AND MAKE OF AUTO_____ WHERE PARKED_____

10. IF NOT RETURNED BY_____(TIME/DATE) CALL THE COAST GUARD,
OR_____(LOCAL AUTHORITY) TELE. NO._____

Canal	Bridge Clearance	Channel Depth*	Mileage
Erie Canal			
Waterford to Three Rivers	20 Feet	14 Feet	160 Miles
Three Rivers to Tonawanda	15.5 Feet	12 Feet	178 Miles
Oswego Canal	20 Feet	14 Feet	24 Miles
Champlain Canal	15.5 Feet	12 Feet	60 Miles
Cayuga-Seneca Canal	15.5 Feet	12 Feet	102 Miles**

*subject to variations   **lake sections, 90 miles; canal sections, 12 miles

channel depth (draft) and **overhead bridge clearance**, which are described in the above chart.

The canal system was designed for shallow draft, low-profile barges, not high-mast sailing vessels and oceangoing ships. This limitation is built into the system, but like so many things, there are "work-around" tricks that let some larger boats traverse the canals. Sailing vessels can step (lower) their masts to clear bridges. Larger power vessels frequently lower antennas or their entire radar arch, raising them after reaching the Great Lakes or Hudson River, depending on the direction of travel. There are stories of captains who take on maximum water and fuel, and even flood their bilge areas to sneak under bridges. Draft is less flexible. While a reduction in fuel and water carried on board can be used to reduce draft, no one wants to risk running aground.

The official speed limit on the canals is 10 miles an hour. All

system, excluding lake sections, is ten miles an hour, the daily distance traveled is relatively short. A float plan is a document that describes your intended trip, and includes other information that will be of value in a search-and-rescue operation. The plan should be left with a responsible person who will check your progress along the way. If, for example, you are heading from Syracuse, by way of the Oswego Canal and Lake Ontario, to Kingston, Ontario, departing at 6:00 A.M. with an anticipated arrival time of 6:00 P.M. the same day, you would then contact the person holding the float plan to confirm your arrival. If that person did not hear from you in a timely fashion, they would notify authorities that you were missing, providing information from the float plan to aid in a search, and if necessary, a rescue operation. If faced with a problem that creates a delay, a call via cellular phone can update your arrival time and avoid unnecessary concern.

RESTRICTIONS

There are several factors that might prohibit a particular vessel from using the canals. The first concerns are

This bridge on the Cayuga-Seneca Canal illustrates why vessel height is restricted to 15.5 feet. Having a freight train pass two feet over your head is more than exciting.

boats, including personal watercraft, are legally responsible for damage caused by their wakes, so locations near moored boats or in narrow channels may require even slower "no wake" speeds. And if this doesn't slow things down enough, it typically takes about 20 minutes to pass through a lock or under a lift bridge. Unlike a highway used to get somewhere, the canals are destinations unto themselves. The slow pace is a part of their character.

Weather, the boater's traditional nemesis, is less of a problem on the canals than on most open bodies of water. Only the lake sections are subject to significant wave action. Wind, however, can challenge vessels that have broad surfaces subject to a "sail" effect, especially during the more delicate maneuvering required for locking and docking operations. A bow flag can be helpful in determining wind direction and force. The NOAA weather broadcasts on the VHF radio's WX channels provide guidance for both long- and short-term travel planning and recreational small-craft advisories warning boaters of difficult conditions.

MARINAS

Private and publicly owned marinas are found along the canals, and range from full-service operations on down. A description of the services offered at a specific marina is found in the cruising guides that are presently available. Unfortunately, these guides may not be completely accurate by the time they get into your hands. Change is the order of the day along the system. Most marinas are prideful operations that befriend boaters and offer a wide range of on-site or nearby amenities. Selecting the "right" marina, regardless of your needs, can enhance your travel experience. Marinas have two key clienteles: those who reside in their marina as seasonal dockage and transients, those who visit the marina only for services or to spend the night.

Fuel

Marinas may offer gasoline, diesel fuel, or both. The cost of fuel is typically higher in marinas than in gas stations. Fueling should be done with safety as a primary concern. When fueling an outboard with a separate tank, the tank should be placed on the dock, onlook-

(Left) Winter Harbor Marina's gas dock allows pay-at-the-pump credit card service.

(Above) At Winter Harbor, a traveling lift moves boats from the water to heated (50°F) indoor winter storage.

ers should be kept at a distance, and the dispensing nozzle should be in contact with the tank's metal rim (to prevent sparks) as it's filled. Take care not to overfill the tank.

When fueling an inboard, all passengers should be off the boat, ports and hatches should be closed, and all electric devices should be turned off. Care should be taken not to overfill the tank, creating a *spill*. By law, any spill that produces a sheen on the water should be reported immediately to the Coast Guard. After fueling, the bilge area should be inspected for fuel leaks and ventilated before starting engines. Since running out of fuel on the water poses many special dangers, it's recommended that you not allow your craft to get below one-third of its maximum fuel capacity.

Repairs

There's a reason why we describe something that's perfectly maintained as being in "shipshape" condition. The prudent captain knows that the safety of the craft and its passengers is dependent on all systems being fully functional. The marine environment is especially hard on electrical and mechanical systems, so constant vigilance is mandatory. When a malfunction is observed, or even suspected, it should be checked and remedied immediately. The best marinas will have factory-trained *marine* mechanics that are certified on items that need repair. Since mechanical or electrical failures that occur while underway may delay a float for days waiting for parts, it is best to have all systems checked prior to the start of an extended cruise. If you break down on the water, you may reach many marinas by VHF radio (check what channel they monitor) or cellular phone to get advice or a tow. Also, other boaters may be willing to lend a hand and can be contacted by radio. If it appears that your boat will have to be pulled from the water, make sure that the marina's "traveling lift" capacity can accommodate your boat.

Pump-Out

It is against the law to discharge black-water sewage from a boat's holding tanks anywhere along the canal system. Tanks should be emptied at marina pump-out facilities, which are becoming increasingly common thanks to governmental regulation and financial aid for their installation. Some systems are do-it-yourself operations, and others offer assistance. In most cases there's a charge for using the facility. With the exception of Lake Champlain, gray-water (from sinks and showers) can be discharged directly overboard.

Transient Dockage

Marinas may have slips for transient dockage that can be reserved prior to arrival, which is recommended during the peak summer travel period. Before docking it's important to know the water depth in the slip you've been assigned. The cost is generally based on a daily per foot basis, so if a marina charges one dollar a foot, a 23-foot boat would pay $23 per night. Depending on the marina's facilities, this charge may include a potable water hookup, electricity (typically limited to 125 volts, 15 or 30 amps), cable television connections, showers, restrooms, and trash disposal. Pay telephones, laundry rooms, marine stores (offering everything from groceries to propellers), and restaurants may be a part of the total operation. Security and location relative to nearby services and attractions should be considered before reserving a slip. Many marinas on the canal are within a short walk to the center of town, thus making accessible everything from banking and supermarkets to movie theaters, motels, and restaurants.

LOCKING THROUGH

In an earlier chapter you learned how locks work and why they're a part of the canal system. Now we're going to see how you, as a boater, pass through a lock. During the summer season, locks are typically operated from seven in the morning to ten at night (a current schedule is available from the Canal Corporation). While you're still some distance from the lock, you want to check that you have your crew standing by equipped with boat hooks, and, yes, they should know how to tie off to a cleat and know a few basic knots,

Buoys Restaurant *in Brewerton provides dockage and nautical décor for its patrons.*

(Above) Captain Tom Prindle enters a lock from the lower pool on the Champlain Canal.

(Facing page) The lines with blue-and-white floats are conveniently located for boaters at Lock E-23 in Caughdenoy.

such as the *bowline* and *clove hitch*. It's helpful to work with new crew members prior to departure, explaining their role during the locking process and alerting them to potential dangers. A small boat may get by with just a captain but as the size of the vessel increases, one or more crew may be needed. Even though it may not be required by law, having each crew member wear a personal floatation device (life preserver), and a pair of gloves is a good idea. Fenders should be deployed and adjusted to provide maximum protection for your hull. The lock operator is under no obligation to help you lock through, other than to properly operate the lock's equipment.

There are two general locking situations: either you're going up, or you're going down, and each requires a slightly different approach. If you're going up, the boat will be protected from cross winds while entering the chamber, and lines, ladders, pipes, and cables will be easily grabbed by the crew at shoulder level. If you're going down, cross winds will have an effect on the craft, and lines may be more difficult to grab since they'll be just above the water level, often well below the crew's position (thanks for the boat hook!). In the following example, we'll be going up.

As we near the lock we reduce our speed, and observe a "Lock Limit" sign on the shoreline. This is a no wake zone, and vessels must not pass each other. If the gates are open and the control light is green, we may enter the chamber "under control" and make our way to the wall where the crew will grab a line to hold the vessel secure. If the gates are closed, and the control signal is red, it's best to contact the lock operator on VHF channel 13, using proper protocol, to identify yourself and request lockage. The operator will tell you approximately how long it will be until your vessel can enter. If the time is short, you may maintain your position at a safe distance from the gates. If the time is long (rarely more than 20 minutes), you may tie up to the lower wall and wait. The water being discharged to empty the chamber will create an increase in current in the lower pool, so it is best to keep some distance from the gates. And since traffic may be exiting, you don't want to obstruct their passage.

As you enter the chamber, seasonal permits need to be visible, and daily passes need to be ready for inspection by the operator. If there are several vessels locking through together, you want to position yourself so that others will also have room within the chamber. There's no need to hurry. Once you're secure, you may want to shut down your engines to reduce fumes and noise. Ideally, bow and stern lines will be held by each boat to maintain its position parallel to the wall (never tie lines between the boat and the chamber since this can result in tipping the craft when the lock fills or discharges). When everyone is ready, the gates will close and the chamber will slowly fill with water, creating a little turbulence.

When the chamber is full, the gates will slowly open and you'll get a green light indicating that you may exit "under control" and in order. Maintain reduced speed until you pass the "Lock Limit" sign on the upper pool. If you know that you'll be passing through the next lock, inform the operator and they'll attempt to have it ready for you when you arrive. It is that simple.

(Above) Locks receive competitive awards based on the quality of their maintenance and landscaping.

(Right) Gail is probably holding the fore line while Rob, wearing gloves, tends to the aft line.

Most locks have wall sections where you can tie up to visit adjacent parks and attractions, or with permission, spend the night. The good part is that there's no charge for overnight dockage; the bad part is that there's probably no water, electric, or restroom facility available. Often there are nearby picnic tables and grilles, and the lock grounds display the pride of the tenders with neatly manicured lawns and striking floral displays. Helpful literature is also available without charge, covering the canal system and opportunities along the route.

LIFT BRIDGES

The western section of the Erie Canal has 15 lift bridges. The bridge at Fairport is run on a set schedule, while the other bridges operate on demand, like the locks. To get a bridge raised, you can call the operator on VHF Channel 13 as you approach and make your request. Since a single roving operator may run several bridges, there may be a wait for the operator to drive to your location. If this same person operates other bridges along your route, your needs may be anticipated,

speeding your journey. A green light signals that it's safe to pass under the bridge. Since automotive traffic is being held back for you to pass, you shouldn't delay once the bridge is raised. Like locks, walls may be available for tying-up. Most bridges are located in the heart of small villages and are therefore within easy walking distance of the business district and canal-side parks. One lift bridge on the Oswego Canal is adjacent to Lock O-2 and controlled by the lock operator.

RULES OF THE ROAD/LAWS

Many people who operate boats don't realize that there are federal and state rules and laws that govern the operation of sailboats and motor-powered vessels on the navigable inland waterways of the United States. The chief purpose of these rules is to prevent boating accidents, and they are policed by a range of law enforcement personnel. Although you may not be required to hold a boating license, you're responsible for knowing and obeying the laws and rules that apply. Many states offer boating education programs, and some states require attendance for certification of younger operators. Print and computer based publications are available to help you learn, but the better choice may be one or more of the courses offered by the U.S. Coast Guard Auxiliary, the Power Squadron, state parks departments, or such private institutions as the Boating Education Center, in Syracuse. And not only should you know the rules, you should master the *skills* required to safely operate your boat. All of this takes time, but it is the only way known to reduce the injuries and fatalities associated with what can be a very safe recreational activity. The following basic illustrations should help you better understand what you need to know to operate on the canals, and what you can acquire through further study. Just as important as knowledge is attitude.

When this lift bridge on the western Erie is raised, the stairway allows pedestrians to cross the canal while automotive traffic is held back.

All powered vessels on the canals, regardless of size, are governed by the same rules.

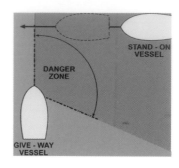

These New York State Troopers are heading out of Trade-A-Yacht Marina to enforce boating laws.

- In a passing situation, where you wish to overtake the vessel in front of you, yours is the *give-way* vessel, and the vessel you are passing is the *stand-on* vessel. First you signal your desire to pass, which can be done by radio (VHF) contact or by using the appropriate whistle signals. For example, to pass on the vessel's port side you would sound two short blasts. The *stand-on* vessel should respond with two short blasts, and, if necessary, reduce its speed to minimize wake problems while being overtaken. Your speed should not exceed the legal limit, and you should pass at sufficient distance to avoid any danger of collision or wake-induced damage.
- In a head-on meeting, both vessels must alter their course to starboard so that each will pass on the port side of the other. Neither vessel has the right-of-way.
- Craft under 16 feet in length are required to carry one wearable, Coast Guard-approved, personal flotation device (PFD, life preserver), in good condition, for each person on board. Craft over 16 feet must also carry a throwable PFD.
- Perhaps most interesting is the Responsibility Rule, which requires that you do whatever is necessary to avoid a collision, even if that means breaking other rules that normally apply to the situation.

ILLUSTRATIVE RULES/LAWS

- Boating While Intoxicated (BWI) and Boating While Ability Impaired (BWAI) convictions can result in significant criminal penalties. More important, these acts put all boaters at risk. The captain has a special responsibility not to consume alcohol or drugs that will affect his ability to properly operate his vessel. Consumption by guests can also threaten their safety and that of others.
- Obey the posted speed limits on the canals, and remember that you're legally responsible for any damage caused by your wake.
- A sailing vessel, under sail, usually has the right of way, or in nautical terms is the *stand-on* vessel. When driven by an engine, the vessel is considered motor powered under the rules.
- In a crossing situation, a motor-powered vessel directly ahead to 22.5 degrees abaft your starboard beam has the right of way and is the *stand-on* vessel, while you are the *give-way* vessel.

LAW ENFORCEMENT

New York State Troopers are assigned to the Canal Corporation to enforce laws and encourage safe boating on the canals. They patrol in uniform on high-speed boats or personal watercraft and issue about 600 citations each year. They receive special training for this voluntary summer duty, and otherwise patrol highways during the winter months. They remind us that you must have a valid registration, operator certification (if applicable), required equipment in operating condition (used as mandated), and a crew that is not impaired by drugs or alcohol. The action they take varies with the situation, but you can be assured that an impaired captain will not be allowed to operate a vessel, even to get back to shore.

Local sheriffs, police, and the U.S. Coast Guard Auxiliary may also patrol waterways and conduct special programs to ensure boater safety and compliance. Nationally, there are far too many boating fatalities each year, most of which are associated with the use of alcohol and imprudent operation of personal watercraft. In short, know and obey New York State's boating requirements when on the canals.

SPECIAL CONCERNS

Bridge Jumping

Young people who have yet to fully appreciate that they're not invincible often climb the superstructure of bridges and jump into the canal waters below. Others swing on ropes and drop into the water or dive from concrete abutments. Such practices are dangerous, against the law, and yet as old as the canals themselves. Since most of the canal system is a relatively narrow channel, especially where bridges cross, the prudent captain needs to keep a keen lookout for people swimming or jumping into the water.

Dams

Keep away from dams. The upper pool poses the risk of your boat running over the dam with disastrous consequences, and the base of a dam may have turbulent currents that can disable or capsize your craft. White and orange buoys typically identify the tops of dams and other hazards as well. From the upper pool, especially at night, the dam may be impossible to see. Charts will identify dams, which may be on either side of a lock. Current will cause unpowered boats to drift naturally toward a dam. In this situation, deployment of an anchor may save lives.

Water lilies and many varieties of wild flowers and trees line the canal banks providing a botanical delight.

These youngsters are jumping from a guard gate near Rome.

Drifting Debris

The canals are lined with beautiful trees that form the habitat for many of the birds you'll see along your route. Of course, trees close to the shore die or are damaged by storms, and end up falling into the channel and drifting, posing a hazard to your hull. The problem is most pronounced early in the spring, when runoff and high water levels pick up the debris of winter and float it into the canal system. Traveling at the proper speed and maintaining a careful watch reduce the potential for damage.

Night Travel

Travel after dark becomes risky on the canal system without the use of specialized equipment, such as night-vision binoculars, radar, and remote-controlled spotlight or floodlight accessories. All required lighting should be checked and on (red port light, green starboard light, masthead, and stern lights, etc.). Lock hours restrict night canal travel. Because it's more work and more dangerous to operate in the dark, trips should be planned to avoid night travel.

Maintenance Vessels

A fleet of manned vessels works to maintain the canal system by dredging and removing shore-side and drifting debris (which builds up behind the Mohawk-style dams). In general, keep away from work vessels and avoid creating a wake in a work zone. Signs may be posted with special instructions indicating, for example, the safe side for passing. Remember that dredges may have pipelines extending from the vessel to the shore (to discard the spoils) that must be avoided. You can contact the working crew by VHF radio if you're uncertain about the best course of action.

Water Quality

Water quality varies widely throughout the canal system by location and circumstance. The most polluted sections are an industrial legacy that is being remedied by environmentally conscious partnerships between industry and government. Check current recommen-

As the sun begins to set, it's a good idea to tie up for the night at one of the many available walls and marinas.

This algae bloom on Oneida Lake is a natural seasonal occurrence.

dations regarding the consumption of fish caught in the system. While Oneida, Cayuga, and Seneca Lakes may offer a safe catch, fish from the Upper Hudson or Onondaga Lake may be tainted. Drinking water should come from reliable shore-side sources. Swimming in the canals is common.

Customs

Through its connected waterways, the canal system facilitates travel in and out of the country. When entering the United States by water, you're required to check in with U.S. Customs. When entering Canadian ports, you'll need to check in with Canadian Customs. The process is simple and can generally be carried out by telephone. Passports and other international documentation should be on board if you're planning to cross international boundaries. There are regulations regarding pets that should be fully understood prior to departure. Dogs are common companions on boats and generally travel well. They need a supply of fresh drinking water and regular walks on the shore, which is easy to do by stopping at walls along the way.

Emergencies

Be prepared. Carry basic first-aid equipment and consider a Red Cross course in CPR. Carry more fire extinguishers than are required, along with all other mandated safety equipment. Have more than one person on board able to captain the vessel. And train your crew on the use of your VHF radio, so that they can do an effective MAYDAY call, should this become necessary (instruction cards, for posting by your radio, are available that describe how to request help in an emergency). If another boat requests your assistance, and you can provide aid with-

Lock E-23 is the busiest lock on the canal system.

Tri-Bridge Marina at sunset. The same spot on the canals looks different every time you pass due to changes in flora, weather, season, and time of day.

Learn the nautical language through further reading, or by attending classes. Either way, you'll enhance both the enjoyment and safety of boating.

Bollard	GPS	Wake	Bowline
Port	Magnetic North	Broach	Fender
Starboard	Bulkhead	LOA	Captain
Aft	Windlass	Head	Freeboard
Stern	Buoy	NOAA	Hatch
Beam	Cleat	Draft	Mast

out endangering your vessel and passengers, the law *requires* that you help. You'll be protected from liability by Good Samaritan laws. Calm and common sense can prevent and resolve problems before they become emergencies. Since the canals pass through a populous corridor, needed services such as medical help are rarely far away.

THE LANGUAGE OF BOATING

Every discipline has its special language, and so it is with boating. The "right" word facilitates communication, which can be important during critical situations. The longer you're a boater, the larger your marine vocabulary. It doesn't really matter whether you steer to the left or to port, so long as everyone understands the *meaning* of the language. Mastery of the skills and terminology associated with boating is the basis for a safe and pleasurable experience.

BOAT RENTALS/CRUISES

Marina Boat Rentals

Some of the marinas along the canals rent boats and personal watercraft. Most rentals of this type are for day use by fishermen, and the boats are very basic. If you decide to rent, be certain that all required equipment is included (such as charts), that insurance coverage is adequate, and that you know how to operate the boat before you leave the marina. If you're renting in an area that isn't familiar, a hand-held VHF radio is recommended. Both public launches and marina ramps allow access for trailered boats, canoes, and personal watercraft.

Hire Boats

Several companies along the canal system specialize in self-captained hire boat rentals. These are typically taken out for a week, from a Saturday afternoon to the following Saturday morning. The most common vessel in service was designed especially for canal travel and utilizes a small diesel engine, tiller, and bow thruster. The boats vary in size and design, but most are about 30 feet long, with sturdy metal

A variety of boats are available for rental along the canals.

This is a portion of the fleet of hire boats maintained by Mid-Lakes Navigation Company.

hulls and feature camplike pine interiors complete with heads (bathrooms), galleys (kitchens), multiple staterooms (bedrooms), and plenty of room to lounge about. The boats are cleaned and refueled for a week's operation prior to your arrival. Everything from bicycles to bed linens and dishes are provided. All you need to supply is food and personal essentials. The hire boat company's representative will take you out and teach you the basics of the boat's operation, answer questions, and make suggestions related to lockage and overnight dockage. The real planning of the trip is up to you. The inherently slow pace of canal travel makes for a laid-back adventure. Select a charter company that's located on the section of the canal system you want to explore.

Cruises

If you want to travel on the canal system, but don't want to operate a boat, there are many cruise opportunities. The largest cruise ships presently traveling the canals are run by the American Canadian Caribbean Line (ACCL). Its ships are specially designed to assume a low profile, allowing them to pass under bridges. These vessels feature individual air-conditioned staterooms with heads and full-meal service in the onboard dining room. The ships travel by day and tie up at night, so passengers don't miss any of the sights along the way. A typical ten-day cruise might take guests from Warren, Rhode Island, through New York Harbor, up the Hudson River, joining the Erie Canal at Waterford, heading west to the Oswego Canal, then north to Lake Ontario and the St. Lawrence River, and on to Montreal, Canada.

Shorter cruises are presently available from Mid-Lakes Navigation Company. Unlike the ACCL cruises, passengers disembark each evening and are bused to a nearby hotel to spend the night. In the morning they return to the boat for breakfast and the continuation of their narrated journey. A typical trip may take three days from Syracuse to Albany, with a bus providing return transportation (about a three-hour trip), while new passengers board in Albany for

(Left) Libby Wiles prepares a hire boat for its next crew.

(Below) This hire boat comes complete with an inventory of basic household items, so the crew has only to supply food and personal items, such as medications.

The ACCL ship Grande Mariner *regularly cruises the canals, offering onboard accommodations and prepared meals.*

the next destination, traveling north on the Champlain Canal or heading west back to Syracuse, or beyond.

The shortest cruises are most readily available, and offer narrated sightseeing, usually including at least one lockage, with or without food available onboard. Dinner cruises, some of which offer live entertainment, are also an easy way to get a taste of canalling.

(Left) The chef and a crew member on the Niagara Prince, *an ACCL ship that fills the chamber as it locks through.*

(Below) The Emita II *on the Cayuga-Seneca Canal, captained by Dan Wiles.*

To get this ship under low bridges (as seen in the background), the pilothouse, antennas, and upper deck items are lowered.

The Colonial Belle *provides narrated sightseeing cruises in the Fairport-Pittsford area.*

THE ADVENTURE

Traveling by boat on the New York State Canal System provides an opportunity that is rare in our culture of synthetic experiences and prefabricated entertainment. You can't predict what will happen on a journey by canal; there are so many variables—like the weather, the appearance of birds, canal-side concerts, unexpected "home-cooking" restaurants, lock remains, local canal festivals, farmers' markets, or new friends discovered in a marina. Travel is slow, a sense of history is pervasive, scenery changes with the season and time of day, and like all boating, the options are limitless. You may plan to spend the night in one place, but being delayed by a walking tour of a town, decide to spend the night in another. The canals are threads that bind people together, whether they live in communities along the route or are cruising by boat. And the Erie is truly America's "mother canal," nurturing generations of people with diverse interests and a common love of this symbolic and functional waterway.

A hire boat passes through the lock at Lyons, heading east.

Wildlife is everywhere on the canals.

TRAVELING THE ERIE CANAL

RAVEL ON New York's canal system is a unique experience. The ever-changing scenery, the blend of rural countryside and urban bustle, and the mechanical workings of locks, dams, and guard gates combine to impress and charm modern-day canallers. But canal travel also holds the mystique of time travel. There's a real sense of going back in time, to an earlier era when travel between two cities 60 miles apart was a day's journey rather than a 60-minute automobile jaunt.

The rewards of successfully adjusting to the slower pace of canal travel are many. There's time to see the blue heron standing at water's edge, appreciate the talents of long-ago masons in the ruins of old aqueducts, and share thoughts with fellow travelers. And there's the camaraderie of waving to passing boats and talking with other boaters, from all over the world, when docking for the evening.

Along the way there are entertaining places to visit and interesting people to meet, often in communities whose names are familiar only because they've been posted on road signs. In canal towns, big and small, there are new restaurants to try, shops to explore on literal "Main" Streets, and things to learn about the state and even yourself, while traveling on the most famous canal of them all—the Erie.

Today's Erie Canal is more than an historic waterway turned recre-

ational opportunity—it is a living legend. When the Erie opened in 1825, its builders were saluted for constructing "the longest canal, in the least time, with the least experience, for the least money, and to the greatest public benefit." It was viewed then as an engineering marvel, and it still is.

The original Erie extended from Albany to Buffalo. Today, it actually begins in Waterford, northeast of Albany, and ends in the Tonawandas. To reach Buffalo, boaters may follow the Niagara River and the Black Rock Canal. Our "book" journey on the Erie will begin in Waterford and continue west to the Tonawandas and Buffalo.

Waterford is a small village, but it sits at an important junction of two canals—the Erie and the Champlain. Waterford has been designated as one of the contemporary canal harbors. A new waterfront visitor's center, at the base of the famed Waterford flight, provides boating and tourism information. Here at Lock E-2 (there is no E-1) the remains of old locks, serving as a spillway today, are an attraction unto themselves.

The original Erie was a totally man-made ditch, but now the Erie consists of canalized natural waterways linked by dug canal sections. By following the path of natural waterways like the Mohawk River, today's route, a result of Barge Canal construction nearly 100 years

The Waterford Flight is a series of five locks that lifts boats more than 150 feet, the highest lift over the shortest distance of any canal in the world.

ago, bypasses many of the original canal towns of the 1800s including Schenectady, just west of Waterford.

Although the Erie doesn't run right through this city of 65,000, there are marinas and floating docks where boaters can tie up and use ground transportation. The influence of the city's Dutch founders is apparent in more than 60 homes, built between 1700 and 1850, located in the historic Stockade District. Schenectady's Union

College, with its beautiful gardens, is considered the first architecturally designed campus in the nation. There are dining and shopping opportunities as well as several museums with exhibits on the area's industry and Dutch heritage.

Continuing west through the Mohawk Valley lies Amsterdam. It became a busy industrial town with the arrival of the Erie Canal and, later, the railroads. Much of the industry has disappeared but the canal still makes its presence known. There's a new wall under construction for boaters near downtown Amsterdam that will offer easy access to shopping. Lock E-11 is just west of the city. Adjacent to the lock is Guy Park State Historic Site, the former home of Guy Johnson, British Superintendent of Indian Affairs at the time of the American Revolution. Site exhibits explore his life and the importance that key transportation routes, including the canal, played in the growth of the Mohawk Valley. Just a few miles west of here is Lock E-12 at Tribe's Hill. It is a short walk from the lock to the National Historic Landmark Schoharie Aqueduct at Schoharie Crossing State Park in Fort Hunter (see Chapter 9).

The canal flows through quiet countryside towards Canajoharie. Within view of the waterway is a large, white factory complex—the Beech-Nut baby food plant. The company was the first to offer baby food in glass jars instead of lead-soldered metal cans, now known to be a health hazard.

Nearby is the Canajoharie Library and Art Gallery. The small gallery, one of the finest in the country, features works by such artists as Homer, Stuart, and Winslow. Bartlett Arkell, the first president of the Beech-Nut Packing Company, gave the village the library and art gallery in the 1920s, donating works from his personal collection. Boaters can tie up at Lock E-14 or at the Canajoharie Terminal Wall to reach the library and the village.

Despite the proximity of nearby towns, this stretch of the canal (Mohawk River) has a serene, rural feeling interrupted at times by the hum of automobile traffic or the roar of a speeding Amtrak train.

(Top) The Canajoharie Library and Art Gallery has a permanent collection of more than 350 paintings and sculpture that reflect the development of American art from colonial times through the mid-twentieth century.

(Bottom) Ryan Parrish and his dog, Minnie, at the entrance of the Canajoharie Library and Art Gallery. Ryan and his family, from Colorado, were traveling on the New York State Thruway and decided to stop and visit.

Impressed by the area's shipping routes and industrial climate, Thomas Edison established his Edison Machine Works, which became the General Electric Company, in Schenectady. Over 4,500 people are employed here by GE Power Systems, one of the world's leading suppliers of power generation technology, energy services, and management systems.

This English Georgian-style mansion was built in 1764 for Nicholas Herkimer and his family. The story of Herkimer and other German immigrants to the Mohawk Valley is the focus of the site's interpretation.

Before arriving at Lock E-17 in Little Falls, the Herkimer Home State Historic Site comes into view. The restored home of American Revolution War General Nicholas Herkimer, hero of the Battle of Oriskany, has a dock available to boaters. It is a short walk to the site, which also includes a visitor's center, a 60-foot monument to Herkimer, and a kitchen garden maintained by costumed interpreters.

Lock E-17, near Little Falls, is the highest lift lock on the canal system and one of the highest in the world. The village of Little Falls is just about a mile from here. Boaters can tie up near the lock or take advantage of places like Rotary Club Park, closer to the village.

Little Falls is fairly large, with fast-food eateries as well as restaurants offering gourmet dining options. Historic Canal Place, along the river, is a restored industrial area featuring antique shops, art galleries, and a visual and performing arts center. An underground walkway links this area to the heart of the village.

The waterway winds through countryside and small communities before reaching Ilion, seven miles east of Lock E-19. The Ilion Marina, with a full range of boater services including a café, is so popular that reservations are recommended. The marina is within walking distance of motels, restaurants, grocery stores, and the Remington Arms Museum. The museum features an outstanding collection of guns and advertising art. Although internationally recognized for the sporting arms it produces today, Remington has also manufactured cash registers, sewing machines, typewriters, and agricultural products. During the 1870s Remington made railroad and highway bridges.

The canal passes north of Utica, a city whose growth was a direct

Lock-watching is especially popular at E-17 with its vertical lift of more than 40 feet.

The New York State Thruway, the longest toll road in the nation, closely parallels the canal's route in many areas.

About six miles west of Lock E-15 is the small community of St. Johnsville. It is clearly boater-friendly, with a municipal marina and a nearby ice cream stand. One of the pleasures of canal travel are pleasant, unexpected surprises, like the miniature lighthouse that greets boaters near the marina's entrance.

The cliffs near Lock E-17 are often lined with rock climbers.

*This restaurant, special-
izing in French and
American cuisine, is
housed in an historic
building near the canal
in Little Falls.*

Priceless oil paintings by artists, including Wyeth and Goodwin, were used in advertisements for Remington products.

Utica's Union Station is a State and National Historic Register site that's still in use.

result of the opening of the Erie. Today, access to the city from the canal is limited. Boaters can tie up at the Utica Canal Terminal Wall at the Utica Harbor Lock or at the Marcy Marina. This city of nearly 70,000 boasts a wide range of attractions including an excellent children's museum, zoo, and the Munson Williams Proctor Art Institute that serves as a museum of art, a school of art, and a performing arts center.

About 11 miles west of Lock E-20 is Rome, home to Erie Canal Village (see Chapter 9) and Fort Stanwix, operated by the National Park Service. It's a short walk from the renovated Rome Terminal Wall into the heart of the city where the fort is located. Originally constructed by the British during the French and Indian War, the fort was rebuilt by American colonial forces to protect the Mohawk Valley.

In a nearby cemetery is the grave of Francis Bellamy, author of our Pledge of Allegiance. Bellamy, a minister and writer, wrote the patriotic pledge for schoolchildren to recite as part of a nationwide celebration in 1892 of the 400th anniversary of Columbus' discovery of America. President Harrison was so inspired by Bellamy's words that he declared Columbus Day a national holiday.

(Above) Tours of Utica's Matt Brewery, founded in 1888, include the seven-story brewhouse where the company's Saranac beers are brewed.

(Left) Fort Stanwix was reconstructed to appear as it did in 1777 when it successfully withstood a three-week siege by British forces.

The public beach is "the" place in Sylvan Beach on a summer day.

Continuing west we come to the summer resort community of Sylvan Beach, on the shores of Oneida Lake. There are many marinas, campgrounds, hotels, and rental cottages in the area. The recently renovated Sylvan Beach Pier is a good place to tie up.

Oneida Lake offers good fishing and is known nationally for walleye pike. The lake, however, can present a challenge for boaters. At 22 miles long and up to 5 miles wide, it is the largest lake entirely within New York State. It is also very shallow, with a maximum depth of 55 feet and an average depth of about 20 feet. When whipped by winds wave heights can quickly reach six feet. A buoyed channel running the length of the lake should be used by boaters unfamiliar with the waters. Charts are a must.

Along the lake's shores are full-service marinas and state parks offering fishing, swimming, and picnicking opportunities. At the

On summer weekends Sylvan Beach hosts a variety of special events. Helicopter rides were part of Canal Days 2000, held in August.

west end of the lake is the community of Brewerton. There are many places to tie up, including Brewerton's Terminal Wall, and plenty of waterfront restaurants to enjoy.

Once across Oneida Lake, the waters return to their more customary tranquility as the canal utilizes the Oneida River. At Lock E-23 there is a park with picnic tables, grilles, and short-term docking. About eight miles west, the Oneida River intersects with the Seneca River and the Oswego River at Three Rivers. The Oswego Canal utilizes the Oswego River to head north to Oswego while the Erie Canal continues westward on the Seneca River.

The Seneca River has a branch that takes boaters past man-made Klein Island to Onondaga Lake. This lake is undergoing major redevelopment, especially at its southern tip, where the city of Syracuse, with a population of nearly 160,000, is located. Previously home to a Barge Canal Terminal, the goal is to transform this area into the biggest and most exciting harbor on the canal system (see Chapter

The Blessing of the Fleet is a time-honored maritime tradition.

Safe dockage at one of the many marinas on Oneida Lake.

(Left) Brewerton's Fire Department maintains a dive team to assist with water rescues.

(Below) In many canal communities such as Brewerton, time seems to hover in the past.

(Above) Cottages and camps line the
banks of the Oneida River.

(Right) Many of the canal system parks,
including this one at Lock E-23, serve
both boaters and land-based travelers.

10). Anchoring the project is the nearby Carousel Center, central New York's largest shopping mall.

The harbor project will provide boaters with easy access to the city and its many attractions, including the Erie Canal Museum (see Chapter 9); the Museum of Science and Technology, home to the only domed IMAX theater in New York State; the Museum of Automobile History (the only automobile museum in the country without a car in it!); and the Everson Museum of Art, internationally recognized for its ceramic collections, all located in the heart of the downtown district. Of course there's plenty of "city life" in the "Salt City."

Syracuse is home to several canal-era businesses including Syracuse China. The city is considered the birthplace of the American candle industry and still has three companies manufacturing candles. The "Salt City" was also the nation's leading producer of salt during the Civil War era. Much of that salt was shipped north to Great Lakes ports via the Oswego Canal, which met the Erie in Syracuse. A small "salt" museum is in Onondaga Lake Park, on the east shore

The Onondaga Lake Inlet is home to Syracuse University's crew team.

The Syracuse Saving Bank was where many tolls from the nineteenth century canals were deposited. The building, now home to Fleet Bank, is located in Clinton Square, named for DeWitt Clinton, considered the Father of the Erie Canal.

The main quadrangle at Syracuse University, founded in 1870.

of Onondaga Lake. The park also features a marina, recreational trails, tram rides, picnicking, and rentals of paddleboats, canoes, roller-blades, and bikes.

Returning to the Erie from Onondaga Lake, boaters continue westward via the Seneca River. There are several marinas en route to Lock E-24 in the community of Baldwinsville, about seven miles away. The village has been developing its waterfront with a new amphitheater, park facilities, and tie-ups for boaters. Baldwinsville has a long canal history; in fact, its privately owned Baldwin Canal, no longer in existence, preceded the Erie.

Beyond Baldwinsville the canal enters Cross Lake. The lake is about four miles long and one mile wide with cottages lining its shores. After Cross Lake, it's back to river cruising with the canal

(Above) The Columbus Bakery, which bakes only Italian bread, has been a Syracuse landmark for more than 100 years.

(Left) The Salt Museum is housed in a recreated salt boiling block.

(Left) Syracuse China is the nation's leading producer of quality restaurant china.

(Below) DeWitt Clinton pattern china was first produced for Los Angeles's Ambassador Hotel in 1936, with orders from the hotel continuing until 1962. The pattern is one of Syracuse China's best sellers and is available here at the Factory Outlet Store.

(Above) Summer means boat trips on the canal for these two Syracuse residents whose combined ages exceed that of the Old Erie.

(Left) Part of the re-development of the canal is the creation of a trail system that provides bikers and hikers with a land-based view.

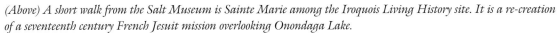

(Above) A short walk from the Salt Museum is Sainte Marie among the Iroquois Living History site. It is a re-creation of a seventeenth century French Jesuit mission overlooking Onondaga Lake.

Dining at the Lock 24 Restaurant includes a view of the workings of Lock E-24.

(Far left) One of the joys of canalling is finding unique places, like this gift shop in Lyons with its display of pharmaceuticals from an earlier era.

(Near left) E-27 lock operator Leon Frazer, a former farmer, has worked on the canal system for more than 13 years.

(Below) Newark's major employer today is IEC Electronics Corporation, which provides broad-based electronics manufacturing services to computer, telecommunications, and industrial equipment companies.

bypassing such former canal towns as Weedsport and Port Byron. Just before reaching Lock E-25 there's signage marking the intersection of the Erie with the Cayuga-Seneca Canal (see Chapter 7).

After Lock E-26 the village of Clyde comes into view. There is dockage near the Clyde Boat Launch. Settled by Scottish immigrants, the village's main street is actually named Glasgow.

Canal-themed murals across from Lock E-27 and many tie-up options welcome boaters to the community of Lyons. During the mid-1800s, Lyons was an international exporter of peppermint, a role

saluted each summer during Peppermint Days. There are museums, restaurants, and shops conveniently located near the waterway.

About two miles west of Lyons is Lock E-28A, where the state maintains a dry dock facility. Next up is Lock E-28B in Newark. Originally, only one lock was planned between Lyons and Newark, but engineers decided two locks were needed. Since lock numbers had already been assigned throughout the system, the locks share the number 28.

Just beyond Lock E-28B is the Newark Canal Park with ample moorings, electricity, picnic tables, and grilles. Overnight dockage is in the heart of the village.

Palmyra is a small community west of Newark with a large dose of pride in its past. Once a busy canal town, it is the birthplace of the Mormon Church. Boaters can tie up at the Palmyra Terminal Wall or west of the village at the Palmyra-Macedon Park near Lock E-29, which features the picture-perfect remains of an aqueduct that once transported the Erie over Ganargua Creek.

In town there is the Alling Coverlet Museum with its collection

The restored interior of the 1828 Grandin Building, where the first 5,000 copies of the Book of Mormon were printed.

There are several Mormon historic sites in Palmyra, including this visitor's center, offering information about the annual Hill Cumorah Pageant, the largest outdoor religious extravaganza in the nation.

(Left) The exterior of the William Phelps General Store Museum. The store on the main floor and the Phelps home on the upper floors are furnished with original Phelps family artifacts and furniture.

(Below) Merchandise from 1880 through 1940, including eggs, still lines store shelves.

of more than 200 nineteenth century coverlets and quilts and the Book of Mormon Historic Publication Site. The architecturally charming Main Street is lined with shops, restaurants, and churches.

Lock E-30 in Macedon is adjacent to a state canal park with picnic areas, boating facilities, and an observation deck. A trail takes visitors to the remains of historic Lock 60, built in the mid-1800s as part of the Erie's enlargement.

After Lock E-30 there are only four more locks heading west on the Erie, but there are 15 lift bridges. The first lift bridge is in Fairport, a community that has wholeheartedly embraced the canal. Here tour boat excursions, restaurants, shops, and services line the canal's banks. The friendly village was dubbed by early canallers as a "fair port" to stop—and it still is today.

As the Canal approaches Rochester it winds through Pittsford,

Fairport's sloped lift bridge is in "Ripley's Believe It or Not."

Fairport, with its three canal-side parks and ample boater services, is a favorite stopover.

Fairport's Canal Days, held annually during the first weekend in June, draw more than 200,000 visitors.

(Left) Fairport restaurants offer a full range of culinary treats in contemporary cafés and historic taverns.

(Below) Bushnell's Basin, accessible from the Canalway Trail, offers fine dining and accommodations in an historic and tranquil canal-side setting.

one of the city's suburbs. This is another community where the canal is center-stage with excellent tie-ups and a short walk to everything travelers could need, including a new luxury canal-side hotel. Pittsford is proud of its nineteenth century charm, evident in its well-maintained businesses and homes. Schoen Place, an historic business district, features several shops that rent bikes, kayaks, skates, and canoes.

Just west of Pittsford is Lock E-32 (there's no E-31), which has a pleasant state canal park. It's only a six-minute journey to Lock E-33, the closest lock to Rochester. New York State's third largest city, Rochester is actually north of the Erie Canal but can be reached with a turn to starboard onto the Genesee River. Tie-ups are available at the recently renovated Corn Hill Landing located just above the

This office building, built about 1812, was a hotel for more than 125 years.

Daniel Barnes, the Town of Pittsford's Building Maintenance Supervisor, also oversees the flowers adorning Town Hall.

(Right) One of the shops in Pittsford's canal-side Schoen Place . . . a must-visit for Cruising America's Waterways' canal-loving dog, Pearle.

(Above) People of all ages enjoy watching passing boats and a year-round population of ducks along the Canal in Pittsford.

Court Street Dam. From here it is an easy walk into this city, known as America's friendliest.

From Rochester west the canal follows much of the Old Erie, giving boaters a sense of what travel was like in the 1800s. After leaving Rochester there is a succession of small canal towns, many of them with lift bridges. The first is Spencerport, with its waterfront gazebo and docking space not far from Main Street's services.

Two lift bridges, just 900 feet apart, signal arrival in Brockport. It was here in 1846 that the first 100 McCormick reapers were manufactured, bolstering the start of the Agricultural Revolution. Home

(Near right) Large crowds turned out for the 2000 World Canals Conference held in Rochester. Lifeguards were stationed along the Corn Hill Landing Wall to watch over the thousands who came to enjoy the conference's grand opening festivities, which included a flotilla of boats of all sizes.

(Far right) The Erie Canal made Rochester America's first boomtown. Originally known as Flour City for its flour-milling industry, today Rochester, home to such Fortune 500 companies as Kodak, Xerox, and Bausch and Lomb, is nicknamed the World's Imaging Center.

(Right) Rochester's Strong Museum bills itself as "The Fun History Place for Kids of All Ages." One of its most popular permanent exhibits is "Can You Tell Me How to Get to Sesame Street?" created in conjunction with the Children's Television Workshop.

(Below) This millstone is from the Moseley and Motley Milling Company, which produced flour from the 1850s to the 1920s in Rochester's High Falls Historic District. This area is the center of the city's nightlife, including laser light/fireworks shows over the 96-foot-tall High Falls.

The George Eastman House, the former 50-room Rochester mansion of Kodak founder, George Eastman, has been restored to its early 1900s appearance.

The George Eastman House is home to the International Museum of Photography and Film, containing one of the largest collections of photographs, motion pictures, and photographic equipment in the world.

One of Rochester's famous citizens was Susan B. Anthony, who spent most of her life fighting for women's rights. The home where she spent her last 40 years is now a National Historic Landmark open to the public.

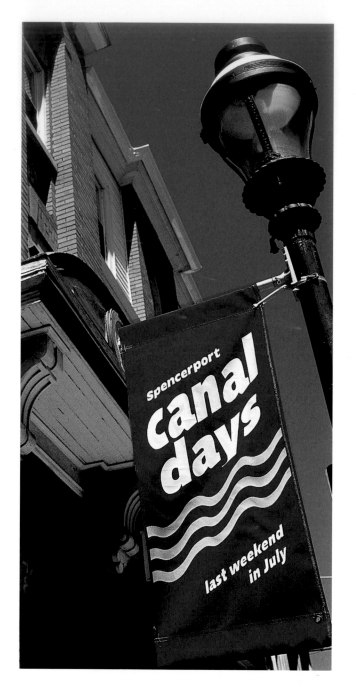

to the State of New York's College at Brockport, the Victorian-like village offers plenty of modern-day amenities.

Quiet countryside dotted with fruit orchards is interrupted by the small villages of Holley, Albion, Medina, and Middleport. The communities, with a distinctly nineteenth century charm, have been investing money to improve their waterfronts and boater services. All have restored historic buildings, canal parks, and dockage.

Holley was named for Myron Holley, an Erie Canal proponent and one of the first canal commissioners. Albion was home to George Pullman. It is said that the inspiration for his invention of the railroad sleeping car—the Pullman—were the sleeping quarters he saw on packet boats. Medina's sandstone was used in some of its own buildings as well as in structures all over the world, including Buckingham Palace. Middleport, in addition to a well-maintained terminal wall, provides boaters with access to showers.

The city of Lockport, with about 22,000 residents, is named for the innovative five pairs of locks that took the Erie up and down the rocky Niagara Escarpment. There are several canal-side parks, a fitness trail, and a small museum in a former powerhouse at Locks E-34 and E-35. These locks, one right after the other, are the only double set on the Erie.

E-35 is unique. It has two upper lock gates—an insurance policy against water from Lake Erie rushing through a damaged lock. Also, as boaters exit the lock they pass under a short 425-foot-wide bridge, one of the widest in the world.

The Lockport Cave and Underground Boat Ride combines a walking tour with an underground boat ride through a 2,430-foot tunnel, built in 1859 to supply water to area mills. Visits to local museums, narrated boat rides on the Erie, and a host of amenities including ample dockage, make Lockport a favorite canal stop.

Spencerport, like many canal communities, has an annual festival to celebrate its canal heritage.

For those who don't have their own watercraft, there are boats offering canal cruises, including this one, tied up in Holley for a summer celebration.

Members of Holley's Garden Club participated in the annual Canal Days here.

The Niagara Escarp-ment is the same wall of rock responsible for the creation of Niagara Falls.

The twin cities of Tonawanda and North Tonawanda, about 21 miles from Lockport, represent the western terminus of today's Erie Canal. There was just one small village here in 1826, but the Erie Canal and a lumber shipping industry that spurred the growth of manufacturing enterprises caused the sprawling village to become two separate cities by 1897. The two cities are united today, however, in their efforts to provide boaters with the services and information they need to enjoy a visit to the area. A week-long annual canal festival held here is the largest on the Erie.

Among the area's attractions is the Herschell Carrousel Factory Museum, which tells the story of the Herschell-Spillman Company. After Allan Herschell invented the first steam-driven "riding gallery," the company grew to become the world's largest producer of carousels.

Buffalo was a much smaller town when the Erie Canal opened in 1825. Today the Greater Buffalo area encompasses suburbs that are small cities in their own right. It is no surprise that the Tonawandas are often considered part of Buffalo.

To reach Buffalo from the Tonawandas, boaters may use the Niagara River or a combination of the Niagara River and the Black Rock Canal. This short canal offers a respite from the challenge of strong river currents. There is one lock on the canal, which is overseen by the U.S. Army Corps of Engineers.

Plans are being made to make Buffalo's Inner Harbor as busy with tour boats, attractions, restaurants, and shops as its commercial counterpart is with barges and grain elevators. The original Erie's commercial dock was recently discovered here during waterfront excavations. After heated debate, it was decided that rather than reburying the old dock, believed to have been destroyed when this part of the waterfront was filled in during the 1920s, it would be

Canal tour boats offer excursions that introduce visitors to both the past and present canal.

A stretch of the Erie near Lockport viewed from an "upside-down" railroad bridge. It is said that the bridge, with all its supporting structure facing the water rather than the sky, was built this way to prevent taller cargo items from being shipped by canal, favoring rail service.

Many boaters stop in the Tonawandas before venturing on to Buffalo, New York's second largest city.

(Facing page) Taking a ride on this 1918 Herschell Carousel, made in North Tonawanda, is a favorite activity for visitors of all ages at Rochester's Strong Museum.

Buffalo earned worldwide fame with the creation of tangy-tasting Buffalo Chicken Wings in 1964. At the Anchor Bar and Restaurant, where the snacks were first served, more than 36,000 pounds of wings are dished up every month.

restored. It was from this spot that Governor DeWitt Clinton, as part of the Erie's grand opening in 1825, departed on his Wedding of the Waters voyage from Buffalo to New York City.

The Buffalo and Erie County Historical Society's exhibits on area industries feature more than 700 Buffalo-made products including Cheerios. Sports are big in Buffalo, home to the NFL's Buffalo Bills. Tour boats offer cruises on the Niagara River, and the spectacular Niagara Falls are only a short drive away.

That first boat to travel from Buffalo to New York City via the Erie Canal and the Hudson River did so in nine days—from October 26 to November 4, 1825. The same trip would take less time today, but rushing is a mistake. Canal towns, those like Rochester and Syracuse that grew into major cities as well as places like Fairport and Lyons that have remained villages, offer a diversity of experiences for those who take the time to enjoy them. The Erie is more than a highway of water; it's an opportunity to experience and celebrate the past with all the comforts and insights of the present.

One of the newest canal harbors on the system is here in the Tonawandas, as the two cities are often called.

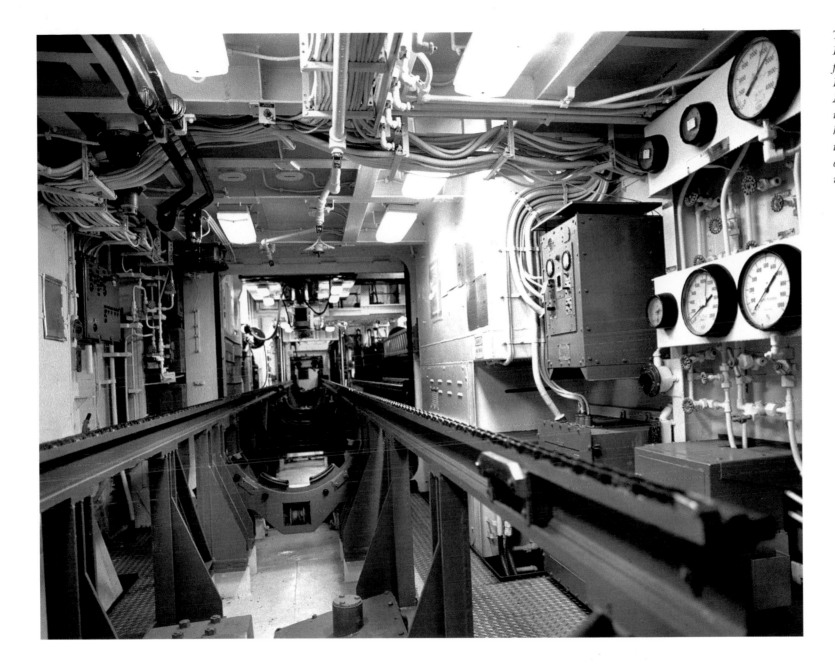

The ongoing Buffalo Inner Harbor Project features the Buffalo and Erie County Naval and Military Park, the largest inland naval park of its kind in the nation. This is the missile launching area on one of the naval vessels moored there.

Buffalo's Albright-Knox Art Gallery is home to one of the greatest collections of modern art in the world.

TRAVELING THE OSWEGO CANAL

T HE "OLD" Oswego Canal, opened in 1828, is often termed the world's second most successful canal—after the Erie, of course. For many years the primary cargo carried on the Oswego was salt, produced in Syracuse and shipped to eager Great Lakes and Midwest markets. The Oswego Canal's original route ran from Syracuse, where it joined the Erie at the Syracuse Weighlock Building, (now the Erie Canal Museum) to Oswego, on Lake Ontario. Once north of Syracuse, the canal, with its 18 locks, followed the route of the Oswego River.

Today's Oswego Canal is, with few exceptions, the canalized Oswego River. The Oswego, one of the few rivers in the world that flows north, begins at the Erie Canal's Three Rivers junction and is about 24 miles long, with just seven locks.

The Oswego Canal is dotted with small islands, from Treasure Island with its tale of gold left behind by fleeing Frenchmen and never found, to Battle Island and its popular 18-hole golf course. Hydropower plants are a common sight.

Phoenix, the first of several communities that hug the river's edge, is barely two miles from Three Rivers. A white building on the

A dam, adjacent to one of the locks on the Oswego Canal.

One of the oldest of the hydropower plants is housed in a former mill located near Lock O-2.

canal's east side comes into view just before the first lock. The building consists of two sections. The smaller one-story section, known as the Buoy House, was built in 1939 to store buoys in the winter. The taller three-story portion is the Bridge House, built in 1917 to house the controls needed to operate a drawbridge over the canal. The bridge was removed in 1989 and replaced with a newer one to the north. The old bridge controls remain in the Bridge House, which is now a small informal museum maintained and staffed by the Bridge House Brats, who also oversee the adjacent community park.

The story of this group of nearly 50 young people, ages eight to twenty-one, is one of the most unusual examples of entrepreneurship on the canal system today. Throughout the summer months, once school is over, the Brats work nearly 12 hours a day, six days a week, welcoming boaters to Phoenix. They help them tie up and cast off the Phoenix wall, provide visitor information, handle sewage pump-outs, clean and baby-sit boats, and give tours of the museum.

In addition, the Brats run a café food operation out of the Buoy House, now nicknamed The Brats' Shack. Boaters and visitors to the park review a menu that consists of breakfast, lunch, and dinner selections available from area restaurants. Once orders are placed, Brat "runners" go pick up the food, tray it in the Brats' Shack, and then serve it to their customers. The Brats also offer ice cream sundaes for $1 that they prepare themselves, and remind visitors that coffee, iced tea, and lemonade are always available free of charge.

And that's not all. The Brats plan a calendar of park special events, including weekly concerts and an annual fireworks display; clean and paint all park equipment as well as the Bridge House; and plant and water flowers and shrubs throughout the area. The Brats write a column in the weekly newspaper about the boaters they meet; maintain a website—www.bridgehouse.freehosting.net; and monitor VHF

Catherine Lee, the Brats' adult advisor, with three of Phoenix's Bridge House Brats—Ben Patterson, Billy Hall, and seven-year-old "Brat-in-Training" Cody Hall.

channel 13 (call sign: Bridge House Brats, of course). They do all of this on an annual budget of $500 that they raise themselves with a walk-a-thon. They solicit the support of area businesses to cover the cost of the fireworks. Clearly, these young people are anything but brats.

Phoenix is worth a stop, not only for the Bridge House Brats but also for the other waterfront amenities that are among the most convenient on the entire canal system. A grocery store, laundromat, bank, and bakery are just steps away from the Phoenix wall.

After locking through O-1 at Phoenix, boaters pass under a lift bridge and enter a very scenic area. There are glimpses of the old canal towpath as well as the remains of old locks. The roar of engines can sometimes be heard from the nearby Fulton Speedway that overlooks the river.

The smokestack of the Nestlé Company factory, just visible through the trees, signals arrival in Fulton, a city of 13,000. The factory originally made baby food, condensed milk, and cheese before converting to chocolate manufacturing in 1907. Today all of America's Nestlé Crunch bars are made right here. The city's chocolate heritage is celebrated each year with a Chocolate Festival.

Fulton is proud of its relationship to the canal and has worked hard to provide a welcome for today's canallers. This is especially true at Lock O-3. The city maintains a canal park and marina adjacent to the lock. Several restaurants, banks, a drug store, and shops are within a short walk.

There are four hydropower plants located near Locks O-2 and O-3 in Fulton. The use of water to turn wheels to provide energy is a centuries-old technique that powered America's earliest mills, including those along the Oswego River. Hydropower is considered a "clean" form of electric production.

Water from the Oswego River is funneled through large pipes to turbines, which are large wheels with blades. The force of the water on the blades turns a connected shaft providing mechanical energy. The turbines are connected to generators, where the mechanical energy is converted into electricity. This power is sent through transmission lines to transformers that supply voltages appropriate for home and business use.

There are eight hydropower plants located along the river—more than the number of locks on the canal. For those keeping track of lock numbers, the Oswego Canal has no Lock 4. Just like the Champlain's missing Lock 10 and the Erie's omitted Lock 31, the Oswego's Lock 4 was in the original Barge Canal plans but later deemed unnecessary.

Fishermen are a familiar sight on the canal. The Oswego River offers a wealth of fishing opportunities. Steelhead, perch, bass, trout, and walleye can be found in the river. Smallmouth bass, in particular, like the water near dams and locks. In the fall, the area is a magnet for those trying to catch salmon that move into the river from Lake Ontario.

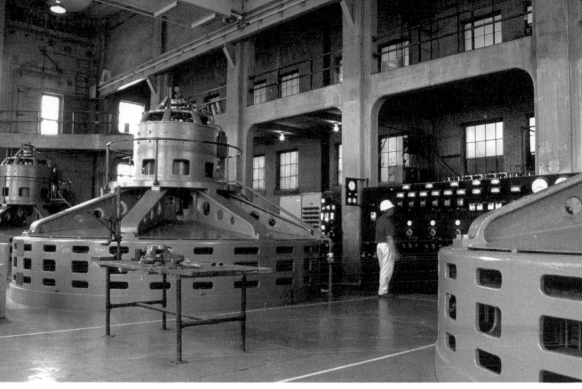

Large generators in the Oswego Falls East Side Plant near Fulton.

Speaking of Lake Ontario, after Lock O-5 near Minetto, there are three locks (O-6, 7, and 8) over a two-mile stretch that brings the canal to its end at Lake Ontario and the Port of Oswego. Oswego is a Great Lakes port of call; it is also the oldest freshwater port in North America.

The center of attention in Oswego is the water. The name Oswego is based on the Native American term meaning "pouring out place." Oswego is where the Oswego River pours out into Lake Ontario. There are restaurants, museums, shops, and marinas all located

*Boats preparing to exit
Lock O-3 after locking
through.*

Fishermen enjoy the challenge of reeling in salmon on the Oswego River.

(Left) This woman traveled from Atlanta, Georgia, in hopes of catching Chinook or Coho salmon.

(Above) A former powerhouse at Lock O-5 near Minetto.

along the water. Oswego has an active sport-fishing charter fleet with captains assuring a good day's catch. Boats of all sizes can be found in Oswego Harbor, including small cruise ships, pleasure craft, and even naval vessels.

Lake Ontario, the smallest of the Great Lakes, has had a U.S. Coast Guard installation since the early 1800s. A short distance away is the Oswego Lighthouse, built in 1934. Before it was automated in 1968, the light was maintained by the Coast Guardsmen.

Many Oswegonians believe the lighthouse is haunted, the result of a tragic accident that occurred in 1942. Eight Coast Guardsmen

Coleman's Restaurant is located in the oldest commercial building in Oswego. Built in 1828, the waterfront building once housed canal stores as well as the Cahill Fish Market.

One of the benefits of charter fishing: someone else cleans your catch.

A Civil War encampment at Fort Ontario.

The National Historic Landmark Tug LT-5 *is part of Oswego's H. Lee White Marine Museum's collection. It is the last remaining large tug used in the 1944 Normandy landings on D-Day.*

boarded their boat to relieve the lighthouse keeper, who had been on duty several days due to a winter storm. After safely delivering a new keeper to the lighthouse, the crew headed back to shore. Rolling seas smashed the boat into the lighthouse's foundation. Six men drowned. Since then it has been said that the lighthouse emits mysterious lights, voices, and even the sound of footsteps.

Echoes of the past are alive at Fort Ontario, which overlooks the lake. The fort and its soldiers saw action in the French and Indian War, American Revolution, and the War of 1812. The fort also housed the only American camp for Holocaust survivors. It is being restored to its Civil War-era appearance.

The Oswego Canal is both a recreational and working waterway. Although today's canals, including the Oswego, were designed in the early 1900s specifically for shipping, clearly they do much more. The canals are part of the state's flood-control system and provide water to generate electricity. Canal-side communities like Phoenix and Fulton are generating an energy of their own as small but friendly canal ports. The port city of Oswego is an exciting destination for those traveling northward, and serves as a gateway to the canal system for Great Lakes and Canadian boaters headed south.

U.S. Coast Guard Executive Petty Officer Jeff Egelston aboard a Coast Guard search and rescue vessel.

Trim your feeble lamp my brother
Some poor sailor, tempest-tost
Trying now to make the harbor
In the darkness, may be lost.

OSWEGO INNER HARBOR LIGHTHOUSE 1890

One of a series of murals painted on Oswego buildings celebrating the port's heritage.

One of the 26 bridges that cross the Champlain Canal.

TRAVELING THE
CHAMPLAIN CANAL

STARTED IN THE SAME YEAR as the Erie Canal—1817—the Champlain Canal was completed more than two years before the Erie's 1825 opening. It was built to create an efficient shipping route between the Erie Canal-Hudson junction and points north all the way into Canada.

Unlike its sister canals, there are no cities on the Champlain Canal. Instead, the Champlain passes near small communities, many of them former mill towns, which welcome visitors. It is this small-town America feeling, coupled with the pastoral beauty of the region, that gives the Champlain its unique charm. Many of these communities have been hard at work increasing the amenities available to boaters. Major new harbor facilities have been constructed in Waterford and Whitehall. Mechanicville has a long wall with free dockage for boaters, Schuylerville has a new canal park, and Fort Edward has created its yacht basin, all just steps away from local businesses.

The Champlain Canal runs through a part of New York State that is steeped in hundreds of years of military history. Native Americans waged war here over territory; key battles of the American Revolution were fought here; and such towns as Fort Ann, Fort Edward, and Fort Miller draw their names from former army posts in the region.

Lock C-4 near Stillwater.

A popular fishing spot at the base of Waterford's flight of locks.

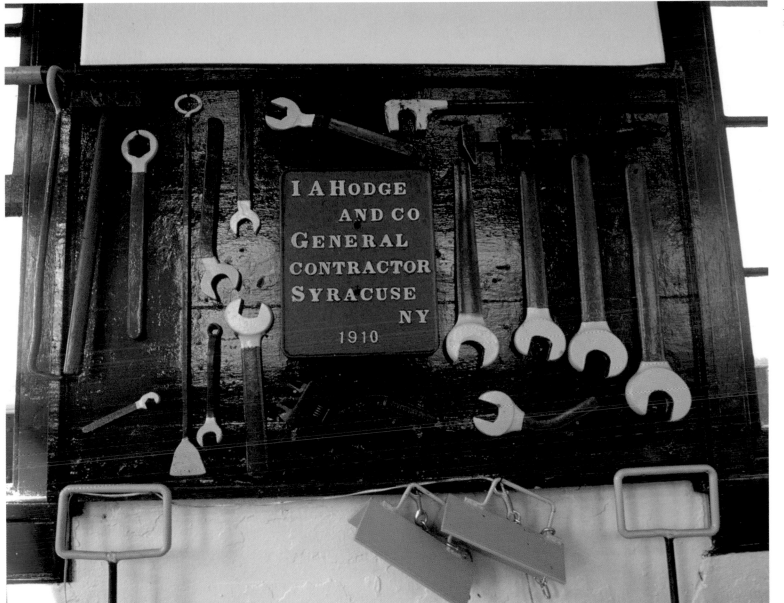

Lock C-2's powerhouse's original tools are still in use today.

These cannon are reproductions of the originals (found in the park's museum) surrendered by the British during the Battle of Saratoga in 1777. The cannon bear the insignia of Kings George II and George III.

The Champlain's southern terminus is where it meets the Erie—at Waterford. The Champlain Canal runs about 60 miles north to Whitehall, where it meets Lake Champlain. For those traveling the Hudson River, the Champlain Canal is less than five miles from the Federal Lock in Troy. From Troy to Fort Edward, the Champlain Canal is actually a 39-mile stretch of canalized Hudson River.

The Champlain has 11 locks which are numbered 1 to 12 since the lock identification system wasn't altered to reflect the fact that Lock C-10 was never built. The first lock is located just outside the village of Waterford. Although there are no ocean tides in the Hudson River north of Troy, there is a current that's noticeable up to Fort Edward, where the canal and river diverge, with the canal flowing north through a man-made channel.

Henry Hudson, aboard his ship, the *Half Moon,* ventured up the Hudson River as far as where Lock C-1 stands today. A few miles north is Lock C-2, one of only three locks on the entire canal system that still has an original (dating from the opening of the 1918 Barge Canal) working generator in its powerhouse. This lock is often referred to as the most attractive one on the system because of its rugged, rocky scenery reminiscent of New England. Lock operators recommend a visit here in the fall, when migrating geese are so plentiful around the lock that it's hard to see the water.

An attractive park is located at Lock C-4, near Stillwater. Between the villages of Stillwater and Schuylerville, four cannon are visible from the water. They are on the grounds of the Saratoga Battlefield, also known as Saratoga National Historical Park. The park also includes the Schuyler House and Saratoga Battle Monument, both located near Schuylerville. The Battle of Saratoga, considered the turning point of the American Revolution, was fought here. The battle helped convince the French to support the colonists, leading to the eventual withdrawal of the British from American soil.

In the town of Schuylerville, one and a half miles south of Lock C-5, is the Schuyler Canal Park Visitor Center, whose friendly staff is ready with good advice and helpful brochures. Just steps from the visitor's center is the Surrender Tree marker. This plaque marks the

Docking at the Schuyler Yacht Basin, operated by Judy and Phil Dean, just two blocks from the center of Schuylerville.

location of a large elm tree under which British General Burgoyne signed the Convention of Saratoga, formally surrendering his troops to American General Gates. The park features a self-guided walking tour along the towpath of the old Champlain Canal.

The Schuyler House was the summer residence of General Philip Schuyler and is actually the third Schuyler residence on the property; the other two were burned to the ground during the French and Indian War and the American Revolution. The town of Schuylerville was once known as Old Saratoga before the town was renamed, in 1831, in honor of the Schuyler family. Saratoga Springs, once famous for its mineral springs but today popular for its racetrack and performing arts center, is ten miles west. Saratoga Springs is also where potato chips, originally called Saratoga chips, were first produced in 1853.

A short walk from Schuylerville's main street is the Saratoga Battle Monument. It was completed in 1883 to memorialize the famous battle and its heroes. Three of the four sides of the monument feature sculptures of the American generals. The fourth side should have sheltered a sculpture of Benedict Arnold, who, although instrumental to the success of the Battle of Saratoga, earned America's scorn as a traitor to the cause of liberty. The niche without a statue is his memorial.

Once past Lock C-5, New York's famed Adirondack Mountains are visible to the west and Vermont's Green Mountains to the east. At Fort Edward the Hudson River turns westward, while the Champlain Canal continues north via a 23-mile dug channel. A cut to the west side of Lock C-7 leads boaters to the Fort Edward Yacht Basin where there is dockage and easy access to the village.

Fort Edward was an important military outpost during the eighteenth century, with both British and American troops passing through the area. The Old Fort House was built as a private resi-

Restoration work at the Saratoga Battle Monument, a 155-foot-tall granite obelisk patterned after the Washington Monument in the nation's Capitol.

(Left) The organ on exhibit in the Old Fort House Museum was shipped here in 1840 via canal boat.

(Above) Different rooms in the Old Fort House Museum reflect varying periods in the house's history, including this kitchen dating from the 1930s.

Captain Robert Foster and the M/V Sadie, *a turn-of-the-century-style launch, which offers canal/river tours from Lock C-5. Foster also operates a 60-passenger stern-wheeler from this location.*

dence in 1772 with timbers from the ruins of the fortifications at Fort Edward. It also operated as a tavern and housed both British and American officers (although not at the same time!) during the American Revolution. George Washington dined here during two visits in July 1783. The structure is the centerpiece of the Old Fort House Museum complex. Several other buildings, including a law office, a one-room schoolhouse, and a tollhouse were brought to this site.

Each of the first eight locks on the Champlain Canal raise north-bound traffic to meet the waters ahead. The final three locks on the system, Locks C-9, C-11, and C-12 lower boats to the southern tip of Lake Champlain at Whitehall. Whitehall is a fitting terminus for the Champlain Canal. There is plenty to see and do in this charming community. Downtown boasts early-nineteenth-century buildings, excellent eateries, and shops.

Formerly called Skenesborough, Whitehall is considered the birth-place of the U.S. Navy. The first American fleet was built here in 1776 during the American Revolution, a tale recounted at the Skenes-borough Museum.

The museum, also home to the Whitehall Urban Cultural Park

With Lock C-12 just to the north, Whitehall's harbor features a redeveloped waterfront and beautiful scenery.

These young people are testing the kayaks they built as part of a summer camp program on a journey through the Champlain Canal and Lake Champlain.

On a pedestrian bridge over Lock C-12 is the unique Bridge Theater, which offers theatrical productions during the summer months.

*The all-volunteer
S.O.S. has opened
Skene Manor to the
public, operating a
tea room and gift shop
while it works to restore
the manor to its
original condition.*

The Lock 12 Marina is located adjacent to Lock C-12 at the southernmost tip of Lake Champlain.

The Skenesborough Museum/ Whitehall UCP *Visitor Center explores the important role transportation by water and rail plays in the community's development.*

Visitor Center, is housed in a 1917 canal terminal building located adjacent to the canal on the newly developed waterfront. Whitehall's naval, transportation, and industrial history is the subject of the museum's exhibits, which feature artifacts from a collection of more than 4,000 items. An outdoor exhibit displays the remains of the *Ticonderoga,* the first ship to bear that name and a veteran of the War of 1812.

Overlooking Whitehall's harbor is Skene Mountain, dominated by Skene Manor, which is constructed of stone quarried from the mountain. Built as the private residence of a judge in 1874 but named for the town's founder, the manor has also served as a restaurant.

Threatened with demolition by an out-of-state buyer who wanted to purchase the building so that he could use the stone, it was saved by the nonprofit group Save Our Skene (S.O.S.).

Although only 60 miles long, the Champlain Canal offers visitors a chance to slow down and enjoy the natural beauty and historic attractions of the region. The small towns that border the canal are filled with architectural treasures and residents who are happy to share local folklore, recommend a restaurant, or give directions. The landscape here has changed so little over the years that a cruise on the Champlain Canal is a journey into the past.

Just beyond Lock C-12 lies Lake Champlain, the largest American freshwater lake outside of the Great Lakes. There have been attempts, unsuccessful thus far, to make Lake Champlain the sixth Great Lake.

The Cayuga-Seneca Canal is the waterway of choice for many hire boat captains getting their first canalling experience.

TRAVELING THE CAYUGA-SENECA CANAL

T HE CAYUGA-SENECA CANAL is an intriguing blend of man-made canal and deepwater boating. The dug canal channel is only 12 miles long, but add to it 90 miles of navigable lake waters, specifically the two largest Finger Lakes—the Cayuga and the Seneca—and the result is a varied cruising experience.

There is the rural tranquility and access to small towns typical of the other canals, but on the Cayuga-Seneca there is also the opportunity to enjoy boating on lakes whose shores boast wineries and waterfalls. There is also exceptional fishing and varied cultural life available in several small lakeside cities.

The Montezuma Wildlife Refuge is located near the junction of the Erie and Cayuga-Seneca Canals. It consists of more than 7,000 acres of protected marshland that is a major resting, nesting, and feeding area for migratory birds.

At the southern boundary of the refuge is the first of the canal's four locks. Grilles, picnic tables, restrooms, a boat launch, and tourist information are all available here. Lock CS-1 is also where boaters have a choice to make. They can continue south on Cayuga Lake or head west on the stretch of canal that leads to Seneca Lake.

At 40 miles in length, Cayuga Lake is the longest of New York's Finger Lakes. Its name, translated from the Iroquois, means boat

On warm summer days boaters may be surprised by cows from nearby farms cooling themselves in the canal.

(Right) On or off the water, a variety of wildlife —from bald eagles to wild turkeys—can be seen at the Montezuma National Wildlife Refuge.

(Below) Castelli's Marina on the east shore of Cayuga Lake.

(Below) The headquarters of MacKenzie-Childs, Ltd., dedicated to the art of gracious living.

(Right) Over 300 craftspeople create whimsical pottery, furniture, and decorated wares based on the imaginative designs of company founders Victoria and Richard MacKenzie-Childs.

landing. There are marinas, parks, college towns, and even a winery or two with dockage.

About halfway down the lake, on its east shore, is Aurora, home to Wells College, founded in 1868 by Henry Wells, of Wells Fargo Stagecoach and American Express fame. Nearby is MacKenzie-Childs, Ltd., an innovative home furnishings company. An outlet store, restaurant, and the factory-studio, open for tours, are set amid spectacular gardens, ponds, and even a "chicken palace."

On the southern shore of Cayuga Lake sits Ithaca, nicknamed the City of Gorges, where more than 150 waterfalls can be found within a ten mile radius. Ithaca is the home of Ithaca College and Cornell University, considered one of the most beautiful college campuses in the nation. The Ivy League university has over 19,000 students enrolled in its 13 colleges and schools. Twenty-seven Nobel laureates have been either Cornell students or faculty members. Cornell graduates include Kenneth Blanchard, Ruth Bader Ginsburg, Janet Reno, and Christopher Reeve.

Thanks to the word-of-mouth efforts of Cornell students, the ice-cream sundae, invented in Ithaca in 1891, became a worldwide favorite. And speaking of food, Ithaca is the unofficial "vegan" capital of the United States. The Moosewood Restaurant, whose vegetarian dishes have been featured in a series of best-selling cookbooks, is an Ithaca institution.

Allan H. Treman State Marine Park is a natural place for boaters to dock and then take a taxi or bus into Ithaca to reach many fine museums, restaurants, and Ithaca Commons, the downtown "plaza"

Founded in 1865 to be a place "where any person can find instruction in any study," Cornell has a 700-acre campus featuring more than 260 buildings including the Clock Tower, a Cornell landmark. Its 19 chimes are played daily by student and alumni chimesmasters, who draw from a repertoire of more than 200 songs.

(Left) At Ithaca's Buttermilk Falls State Park, visitors can swim at the base of the falls under the watchful eyes of park lifeguards.

(Below) Allan H. Treman State Marine Park, with 399 boat slips, is one of New York State's largest inland marinas.

Taughannock Falls has the tallest straight drop of any waterfall in the Northeast United States.

shopping area. Within walking distance of the park is the Hangar Theater, located in a former airplane hangar. It offers professional adult and children's theatre productions.

About eight miles north of Ithaca is Taughannock Falls State Park, named for the falls that, at 215 feet, are higher than Niagara's. The park has marina, picnic, swimming, and camping facilities. Hiking on well-marked trails is a great way to stretch "sea" legs and experience the rocky magnificence of the park.

Agriculture is New York State's leading industry, and that's evident throughout the Finger Lakes region, where some of the best lake views are from farm fields and winery vineyards. Ice-age glaciers created the region's deep lakes and neighboring hills, providing ideal conditions for growing grapes. Halfway up Cayuga Lake, on its west shore, is Goose Watch Winery, one of the newer wineries offering excellent dockage. Cayuga Lake's oldest winery, Lucas Vineyards, has a tugboat captain in the family and a unique motto: "wine if by land, tug if by sea."

A short stretch of dug canal links the north end of Cayuga Lake with the north end of Seneca Lake. Heading west the pace becomes slower. An occasional blue heron lazes at the water's edge. The rhythmic buzz of cicadas and the chirping of frogs are punctuated by the occasional splash of a fish jumping. Small camps and cottages serve as reminders that civilization is near. It's a relaxing respite from the speed of lake boating.

The elevation difference between Cayuga and Seneca Lakes is 64 feet. Two locks with 25 feet of lift each form a double lock, CS-2 and CS-3. Boaters move from one lock to the next, with the last gates opening onto Van Cleef Lake in Seneca Falls. The village was named for the waterfalls that existed here before the canal and its locks eclipsed them.

This buoy is near the entrance to the Cayuga Inlet, one of five tributaries in the area that feed Cayuga Lake.

(Right) With more than 70 wineries, the Finger Lakes region is the nation's second largest wine-producing district.

(Below) A view from the east shore of Cayuga Lake.

(Left) It's just a short walk from the dock to Goose Watch Winery and its tasting room in a restored, century-old barn.

(Above) A sampling of Lucas Vineyard's nautical-themed vintages.

Seneca Falls is the birthplace of the women's rights movement and is today the site of the Women's Rights National Historical Park. The first women's rights convention, where Elizabeth Cady Stanton presented the Declaration of Sentiments, modeled on the Declaration of Independence, was held here in 1848. At the time, only men who owned property had the power to elect government leaders who made the laws that affected everyone. A married woman was unable to keep her own earnings, sign contracts, initiate a lawsuit, or have custody of her children.

Stanton's home, a very informative visitor's center, and several other buildings are part of the park. The National Women's Hall of Fame, the nation's first membership organization devoted to the

Seneca Falls has an attractive waterfront with free electric and water hookups for boaters. Attractions, shops, and restaurants are a short walk away.

accomplishments of American women, and several other museums can be found here.

Less than five miles away is Lock CS-4, located in the village of Waterloo. In 1866, Waterloo celebrated the first-ever community observance of Memorial Day, leading to the establishment of the national holiday. Exhibits about holiday observances, war veterans, and nineteenth-century Waterloo life are featured at the Memorial Day Museum.

Marinas and canal-side homes become more plentiful as the Cayuga-Seneca Canal approaches Seneca Lake. From Waterloo, the mouth of the lake is barely five miles away. The Crow's Nest Restaurant, popular with boaters who enjoy its free dockage, is near the entrance to the lake, as is Seneca Lake State Park, which features a large marina.

The park borders Geneva, on the lake's north shore. This city of about 15,000 is also known as the Lake Trout Capital of the World. Home to Hobart and William Smith Colleges, Geneva offers elegant lakeside dining and accommodations. The city's South Main Street Historic District, with its spectacular lake vistas, preserved homes, and century-old trees, has been called one of the most beautiful streets in America.

Heading south from Geneva, on the lake's east shore, is Sampson State Park, offering marina, picnic, camping, and recreational facilities. It is also home to the Navy Memorial Museum, staffed by servicemen that were stationed here. Housed in the original Navy brig (jail), the museum recounts the days when the park was the site of the nation's second largest naval training station, opened in 1942 to prepare recruits for service in World War II.

Seneca Lake is the widest and deepest of the Finger Lakes. In fact, the lake's 632-foot maximum depth makes it the second deepest in

Tours of the Wesleyan Chapel, where the first women's rights convention was held, are offered by the National Park Service.

Food is a social element in small-town life. Church dinners, strawberry festivals, and chicken barbecues offer modern-day canallers a chance to enjoy good, old-fashioned home cooking.

the United States. The lake was named for the Seneca Indian Nation, one of the six nations of the Iroquois Confederacy. "Seneca" means stony place, and with the steepest shoreline in the region, the lake's name fits. The Confederacy was formed to bring peace among the different Native American nations living in upstate New York. The Iroquois Confederacy and its Great Law of Peace are believed to have served as models for America's Constitution.

The village of Watkins Glen anchors the southern tip of Seneca Lake. Essentially, the waterway ends here. But there is a short stretch of what is called the Seneca Canal that takes boaters south of the lake to Montour Falls. This stretch of canal once connected Seneca Lake with the Chemung Canal, which is no longer in operation.

Watkins Glen is synonymous with auto racing and its gorge, both of which draw visitors from around the world. In 1948 the village

Hector Falls is visible from the road and from Seneca Lake, to which its waters cascade.

Watkins Glen has a busy, well-developed waterfront with a wide range of activities for visitors to enjoy.

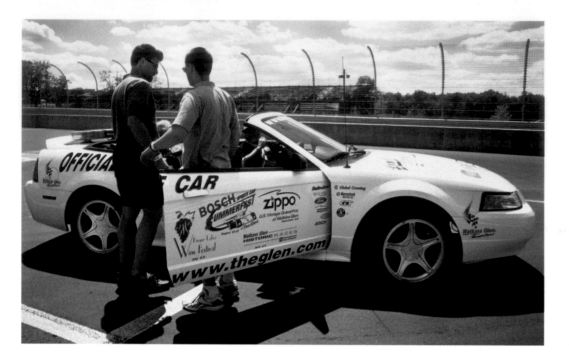

hosted the first post–World War II road race in the United States; today Watkins Glen International offers a full schedule of NASCAR racing events.

Located in the heart of the village is Watkins Glen State Park. The gorge, with nearly two miles of trails and 19 small waterfalls, has been called the eighth wonder of the world. More than 300 campsites and a 50-meter pool are popular park amenities.

Seneca Lake is surrounded by wineries. In fact, the Seneca Lake Wine Trail, which leads visitors from winery to winery, is the largest in the Finger Lakes Region. The area is also popular with hikers and bikers who appreciate its well-marked trails and challenging rolling hills. The Cayuga-Seneca Canal provides entry into this world of striking natural beauty and contrasts, from pastoral countryside and wineries in small towns to the gorges, waterfalls, and amenities of city life found on two of the most pristine lakes in the nation.

A ride in a Watkins Glen pace car is an unforgettable experience.

The best way to view Watkins Glen is by foot. The gorge trail features tunnels, stone bridges, and more than 800 stone steps.

Manhattan Island's name came from a Native American term meaning "island of hills." The island's most noticeable feature today is its skyline of tall buildings, including the Twin Towers of the World Trade Center and the Empire State Building.

TRAVELING THE HUDSON RIVER

THE HUDSON RIVER has a unique relationship with New York's canals. Although not officially acknowledged as a part of the canal system, the Hudson River made it possible for the 1825 Erie Canal to achieve its goal of linking the Great Lakes with the Port of New York and the Atlantic Ocean. That successful connection resulted in the Hudson River becoming one of the nation's most important commercial waterways. The Hudson, as part of the Champlain Canal, is also linked to Lake Champlain, providing access to Canada and the St. Lawrence River.

The Hudson is 325 miles long, from its headwaters at Lake Tear of the Clouds in the Adirondack Mountains to its meeting with the Atlantic Ocean. The river was named for English explorer Henry Hudson, who traveled it in 1609. He wasn't, however, the first European to see the Hudson. That honor goes to Giovanni de Verrazano, who briefly sailed on the river in 1524. The Verrazano Narrows Bridge, which connects New York's Staten Island with Brooklyn, is named for the Italian navigator.

Hudson's "discovery" of the river resulted in an influx of Dutch and English settlers and the establishment of a fur-trading industry. The Hudson was considered a vital commercial and military route, as evidenced by the many Revolutionary War battles fought along and even on it. In addition, as the young nation developed, the Hudson

River Valley became an address of choice for many of America's "rich and famous." Today the Hudson River Valley is a patchwork of charming towns and mansions built with breathtaking views of the river.

New York Harbor, at the mouth of the Hudson River, is one of the world's largest with more than 700 miles of shoreline. A wide variety of craft ply its waters daily—from cruise ships and oceangoing tankers guided by sturdy tugboats to water taxis and ferries transporting tourists to harbor area attractions.

One of the best ways to appreciate the beauty of "the city that never sleeps" is from the water. Dinner cruises that glide by the Statue of Liberty glowing in the moonlight; sightseeing excursions that feature stops at Ellis Island, where over 15 million immigrants were welcomed to America; and harbor cruises aboard historic schooners departing from the South Street Seaport Museum are just a few of the opportunities to get on the water.

From New York City to Troy, about 140 miles north, the Hudson River is just about at sea level, subjecting it to ocean tides. Although considered a freshwater river, the Hudson gets saltier as it approaches the ocean.

Some of the most spectacular natural scenery on the Hudson River can be found just north of New York City. The river narrows

New York's skyline seen from a Circle Line cruise boat.

At the northern edge of the Hudson Highlands sits Storm King Mountain.

It was at West Point, from 1778 to 1782, that the 500-yard-long Great Chain of iron links, floated on logs across the river, was used to keep British ships from sailing northward. It was here that America's first continuously staffed Army post was established in 1778. Four years later the United States Military Academy at West Point was signed into being by President Thomas Jefferson. It is the nation's oldest service academy.

Nearly three million visitors tour the academy and its grounds annually. West Point graduates include Generals Ulysses S. Grant, Robert E. Lee, George Patton, Dwight D. Eisenhower, and Norman Schwarzkopf. In 1998, President Clinton, speaking at West Point, officially declared the Hudson an American Heritage River—one of 14 rivers awarded this designation based on its important role in the development of the nation.

The historic *M/V Commander* offers cruises in the Hudson Highlands with departures from West Point's docks. Just a short distance from here is Storm King Mountain, whose beauty was marred by extensive quarrying in the 1800s, making it a landmark battleground in the environmental protection movement. A 1960s proposal to build a huge electric power plant on Storm King Mountain triggered protests that led to its defeat. The environment, including the river and more than 250 species of fish found in it, continues to be an important issue in the Hudson River Valley. Legendary folksinger Pete Seeger has lent his support to local environmental efforts with concerts and several trips on the Hudson aboard the *Clearwater*.

Travel on the Hudson River reveals towns, mansions, and even monasteries that have been built along its banks. Nowhere is this

and passes through the Palisades. With cliffs as high as 550 feet looming above the water, it's clear why the river is also a fjord. The river widens before passing through an 11-mile curving stretch known as the Hudson Highlands. Here the river reaches its greatest depth, over 200 feet, as it narrows amid mountains that extend down to its banks. Ruggedly beautiful, this area has attracted artists as well as those skilled in the practice of war.

During the American Revolution, defense of the Hudson River was considered key to the colonies' war efforts against the British. The strategic military heart of the river was the Hudson Highlands, particularly in the area known as West Point.

West Point commissions nearly 900 new officers every year. Each serves a minimum five years of active duty.

(Left) Built in 1917, the M/V Commander is the last operating vessel that served in the U.S. Navy during World War I.

(Below) Cold Spring, less than two miles north of West Point, is a charming community of Victorian buildings.

more obvious than in the mid-Hudson area, especially north of Poughkeepsie. The curves and bends of the Highlands are replaced by a wider, straighter river. Near Hyde Park on the river's east shore stands a large brick complex—the Culinary Institute of America.

The Hudson River Valley offers many opportunities to sample foods reflective of the diverse groups who have called this region home. But at the CIA, as the institute is known, food preparation is taken to new heights. Housed in a former turn-of-the-century Jesuit seminary, the CIA, founded in 1946, is the oldest culinary college in the United States. The 150-acre campus features four restaurants, each serving a different cuisine: French, Italian, American regional, and nutritional/vegetarian fare. The restaurants are open to the more

than 400,000 travelers who visit each year. All food is prepared and served by the college's students, under the watchful eyes of more than 125 chefs and instructors from nearly 20 countries.

Hyde Park was the hometown of Franklin Delano Roosevelt, the 32nd president of the United States. It was to the Roosevelts' Hudson River Valley mansion, Springwood, that Franklin brought his wife, Eleanor, following their 1905 marriage. In 1943, President Roosevelt donated Springwood to the American people. Today it is a National Historic Site of 290 acres adjacent to the FDR Library and Museum. Eleanor's retreat, Val-Kill, is nearby.

Two miles north of Springwood is the Vanderbilt Mansion and Historic Site. The Beaux-Arts-style house was completed in 1899 and

A glassed-in bakery/classroom allows visitors to watch CIA students at work.

The Roosevelt family bought Springwood in 1867. Through a series of additions to the former farmhouse, built in 1800, it evolved into a mansion.

(Above) Europe's ancestral homes provided the inspiration for the Vanderbilt Mansion, the smallest of the family's estates.

(Left) The main-floor bathroom in the 50-room mansion displays extraordinary artistic detail and craftsmanship.

used by Frederick and Louise Vanderbilt as their country retreat. Frederick was the grandson of Commodore Cornelius Vanderbilt, of railroad fame, who began his career developing a successful Hudson River shipping business. Virtually unchanged since the Vanderbilts lived here, the fully furnished mansion is considered one of the best examples of the grand estates built by nineteenth-century American industrialists.

Continuing north, at the junction of the Hudson River and Rondout Creek, near Kingston, is the Rondout Lighthouse, one of four lighthouses on the Hudson River. Although there has been a light

The captain and members of the crew aboard the Rip Van Winkle, *a 300-passenger motor vessel that offers narrated river and lighthouse cruises.*

here since 1837, the current structure was built in 1915. The lighthouse was automated in 1954 by the U.S. Coast Guard, which leases it to Kingston's Hudson River Maritime Museum. The museum ferries visitors to the lighthouse from its dock on Rondout Creek.

Founded in 1653, Kingston became the first capital of New York State in 1777. The Rondout Creek waterfront area is a destination for small cruise ships and a departure point for Hudson River boat tours.

Located just minutes from the Rip Van Winkle Bridge in Hudson is Olana, the hilltop home of nineteenth-century landscape artist Frederic Edwin Church. Designed by Church in a decidedly Moorish style, the house, now a state historic site, features a 360-degree view of the Hudson Valley. Church wanted each window of his home to "frame" views of nature, which he felt were far superior to his paintings.

Church was a member of the Hudson River School, considered the first group of American landscape painters. Many of the artists, including Church, lived and painted in the Hudson River Valley. The Hudson River School style, popular from 1820 to 1880, is characterized by painstaking detail combined with a romantic love of nature. Paintings by artists like Church uniquely showcased dramatic American landscapes.

Albany is the second largest city on the Hudson. It was here that the 1825 Erie Canal and the Hudson met. Celebrations marking the official opening of the canal included a rather unique cannon salute. Cannons were stationed along the entire length of the Erie and the Hudson River. The first cannon was fired in Buffalo. Each succeeding cannon was fired when the prior cannon's blast was heard. It took 3 hours and 20 minutes for the cannon salute to travel from Buffalo to New York City and back.

Kingston's historic Rondout waterfront features shops and eateries housed in buildings from the mid-nineteenth century.

Construction began on Olana in 1870, with the family moving into the house's second floor in 1872. Church lived at Olana until his death in 1900.

Catskill Mountains from the Home of the Artist, *1871. Courtesy: NYS Office of Parks, Recreation and Historic Preservation, Olana State Historic Site.*

Today's Erie Canal meets the Hudson River a few miles north of Albany. But the capital city of New York State, which the Erie Canal helped build, retains a strong waterfront presence on the Hudson River. Albany's chief business is government, evident in the eye-catching blend of historic landmarks and daring modern architecture that convey New York's status as the Empire State.

Barely six miles north of Albany is Troy. The city, which earlier utilized its water resources to power industries and ship commercial goods, has redeveloped its waterfront with quality restaurants and shops, renewing this area as a focal point for the community and transient boaters. Nicknamed Collar City after its many shirt collar factories in the 1800s, Troy was the home of Samuel Wilson, the meat packer who served as the inspiration for America's famed Uncle Sam.

EMPIRE STATE PLAZA
DEDICATED TO
THE PEOPLE OF NEW YORK
NOVEMBER 21, 1973
NELSON A. ROCKEFELLER
GOVERNOR

The Empire State Plaza is a government center encompassing the state capitol, the New York State Museum (and an archive that includes a collection of canal documents and images), a convention center, a performing arts center, the Plaza Art Collection, and an outdoor plaza with reflecting pools, sculpture, and free public events during the summer months.

Troy's Town Dock and Marina is at the eastern gateway to the New York State Canal System and is the home port of the Mallory Line Collar City Charters.

The Troy Dam was built to ensure adequate water depth on the Hudson for safe navigation between Troy and the New York State Canal System.

When the Erie Canal opened in the Troy area, the city sent the first boat, loaded with 25 tons of merchandise, to travel the canal westward. Today, Troy serves as the jumping off point for boaters heading upriver for either the Erie or Champlain Canals. Once past Troy's Federal Lock and Dam, built in 1915, boaters can bear to port to the Erie Canal, or continue north on the Hudson to the Champlain Canal.

As a link to the canals of New York State, the Hudson River's importance to both the state and the nation grew. Today, that link provides those traveling the canals with an opportunity to explore one of America's great rivers and the communities that grew up along it. As it was for Henry Hudson so long ago, the journey is one of challenge, discovery, and beauty.

The Weighlock Building and its award-winning Locktender's Garden.

9

CANAL MUSEUMS:
REMEMBERING THE PAST

MUSEUMS FOCUSED on canal history can be found in a number of Canal Corridor communities across New York State. They are committed to preserving and interpreting the canals' past, adding to our understanding of the continuing evolution of these waterways. What's especially fascinating about the New York State Canal System is how little the equipment used to make it operational has changed since the opening of the Barge Canal in 1918. So it is no surprise to discover that the majority of the museums' collections consist of artifacts from the nineteenth and early twentieth centuries.

Visitors to these museums, even international visitors, have heard of the Erie Canal and want to learn more about its history. Many are amazed to find out that the Erie Canal, along with three lateral canals, is still an active waterway. Several of the museums offer exhibits and programs that try to link the past with the present, encouraging visitors to apply their interest in the historical with first-hand explorations—field trips and canal cruises—of the contemporary canal system.

The central New York area has the largest grouping of canal museums in the state. This is due, in part, to the presence of Old Erie Canal State Historic Park. Operated by the New York State Office of Parks, Recreation and Historic Preservation, the park encompasses 36 miles of the Enlarged Erie Canal between DeWitt (just east of Syracuse) and New London (just west of Rome). Museums in Canastota and Chittenango are located alongside stretches of the canal within the park.

The nation's leading museum dedicated to Erie Canal history is in Syracuse. The Erie Canal Museum is housed in the 1850 Weighlock Building, the only structure of its kind in the world and the sole survivor of seven Erie Canal weighlocks.

The Weighlock Building itself is the museum's most important artifact. It was the busiest weighlock on the canal system, in part because it sat at the juncture of two canals—the Erie and the Oswego—that met in downtown Syracuse. The Greek Revival–style building was built to weigh canal boats so that tolls could be determined. When tolls were abolished in the 1880s the Syracuse Weighlock Building continued to serve as an emergency dry dock and housed canal administration offices. Much of the 1918 Barge Canal was designed in the building's second-floor offices.

The museum, which opened in 1962, has restored the Weighlock Building to its appearance in the 1800s. Exhibits include a reconstruction of a line boat, built using plans in the museum's archives drawn by a family of canal boat builders. The boat, which could carry both cargo and passengers, sits in the weighlock chamber. Visitors

The Syracuse Weighlock Building, 1907. Courtesy: Erie Canal Museum, Syracuse, N.Y.

can marvel at the chamber's original stonework and board the boat to learn what it was like to live, work, and travel on New York's canals.

The museum also serves as Syracuse's Urban Cultural Park Visitor Center, so there are exhibits about the relationship between Syracuse and the canal system as well as an audio-visual orientation program narrated by the late E. G. Marshall. The Weighmaster's Office features a presentation telling how boats were weighed, and a second-floor gallery features changing exhibits that draw upon the museum's nationally significant collections.

Just west of Syracuse is the Camillus Erie Canal Park and Mu-

seum. Within the park's 300 acres are seven miles of navigable canal dating from the first enlargement period, a replica of a lock tender's house, and a trail system popular with hikers and cross-country skiers. The Sims Store Museum serves as the park's headquarters.

The museum is actually a reproduction of the 1856 Sims Canal Store, which was located about two miles from the park. The original Sims building was both a general store and a departure point for canal travel. It was destroyed by fire in 1963. The new "store" was built in 1976 and serves as a visitor center and a departure point for the park's seasonal narrated boat tours and dinner cruises. The building features exhibits about the Erie Canal, utilizing early photos,

Sims Store Museum.

local artifacts, and several models of locks, aqueducts, and canal boats. On the main floor is a re-creation of a general store, where books, postcards, and other souvenirs can be purchased.

This facility is an excellent example of volunteerism in action. The park, including the museum, was built and is operated by the Camillus Canal Society. The town of Camillus provides funding for materials and equipment, but it is the volunteers who cleared the canal bed and trails and built bridges, boats, and boathouses as well as the Sims Store Museum. And their work isn't over. Volunteers continue to maintain the park, staff the boat cruises, and restore the 1844 Nine Mile Creek Aqueduct, a project estimated to cost more than $1 million to complete.

East of Syracuse are several other museums. In Chittenango (the birthplace of L. Frank Baum, the author of *The Wizard of Oz*) stands the Chittenango Landing Canal Boat Museum. The museum, now a New York State historic site, also has a strong history of volunteerism. It recounts the history of the Chittenango Landing dry dock, constructed in 1855. Boats were built and repaired here. Today

(Left) The gates on the dry dock chamber at Chittenango Landing Canal Boat Museum.

(Below) The interior of the dry dock chamber.

an excavated, three-bay dry dock, remains of a sunken canal boat, and reconstructed miter and drop gates bring an earlier period into view. An interpretive center houses exhibits, a library, and a store.

The nearby canal towpath leads visitors to an 1855 aqueduct. The site also includes a reconstructed sawmill, mule barn, and woodworking and blacksmith shops. Chittenango Landing offers archaeology digs where visitors, by appointment, can participate in unearthing canal history first-hand.

East of Chittenango, is the Canastota Canal Town Museum. The building sits along the canal, in Old Erie Canal State Historic Park, which is directed into culverts running under Peterboro Street in the center of the town. The museum is housed in a canal-era building that earlier served as a private residence and bakery.

The museum is operated by the Canastota Canal Town Corporation, whose mission is to foster continued development of the Erie Canal as an historical and recreational resource as well as to promote

Canastota Canal Town Museum employee Margaret Stange.

The General Store at Rome's Erie Canal Village.

the preservation and restoration of buildings in Canastota's Canal District. Every room in the small but interesting museum is filled with exhibits about canal history and early town industries.

Erie Canal Village, in Rome, is a recreation of a nineteenth-century canal-era community. It is located near the site where the first shovel of dirt was turned to initiate construction of the Erie Canal on July 4, 1817. Most of the village's 15 buildings, including a blacksmith shop, church, tavern, and general store, have been brought to the area from locations within a 50-mile radius.

There are three different museums in the village. The Clarence C. Harden Museum boasts a collection of horse-drawn carriages and farm equipment, the Canal Museum familiarizes visitors with basic canal history, and the New York Museum of Cheese features a re-creation of a cheese factory and an exhibit on the development of New York's dairy industry.

The star attraction at the Erie Canal Village is the packet boat. The *Chief Engineer of Rome* is a replica of the passenger-carrying boats that were popular on the Erie. Visitors can enjoy a leisurely ride on the boat, ably towed by a team of two mules.

Heading east, the next canal museum—Schoharie Crossing State Historic Site—can be found in Fort Hunter. Within sight of the Schoharie Crossing Visitor Center are the remains of the 624 foot Schoharie Aqueduct, which carried the Enlarged Erie Canal over Schoharie Creek. Also part of the 250-acre site are the East Guard Lock and Lock 20, from the Old Erie, as well as a one-half-mile stretch of "Clinton's Ditch." There's also a set of lift locks from the Enlarged Erie, and a former canal store building with an exhibit about canal stores. For those who enjoy walking, Lock E-12 on the current Erie Canal is only five minutes away.

On the western end of the Erie Canal is the Lockport Erie Canal Museum. The museum is housed in a Barge Canal–era powerhouse

One of the mules used to pull the packet boat at Erie Canal Village.

The tour boat ride at Erie Canal Village offers visitors a chance to experience nineteenth-century canal travel.

Six of the original fourteen arches of the 1841 Schoharie Creek Aqueduct.

found at the base of Lockport's famous flight of locks. The power-house, used to produce hydropower for the locks and nearby bridges, became a museum in 1986. The New York State Canal Corporation owns and maintains the building, with the city of Lockport providing staffing during the canal season. The museum features photographs of canal construction and operation, early canal navigation lights, hand tools, and a model of the original generator.

Also in Lockport is the Erie Canal Heritage Interpretive Center run by Lockport Locks and Erie Canal Cruises. The center is part of a re-created canal town complex made up of a four-story 1840s stone building and the remains of a nineteenth-century factory that now houses dining facilities and a gift shop. Exhibits cover basic canal history and recount the engineering challenge of constructing Lockport's locks.

(Above) The Lockport Erie Canal Museum is located at Locks E-34/35.

(Right) The Erie Canal Heritage Interpretive Center also serves as a departure point for narrated canal cruises.

The Urger, *the New York State Canal Corporation's "teaching tugboat," on a visit to Brewerton.*

Probably the most unusual canal museum can be found on the Oswego Canal near Phoenix. The informal museum is known as the Bridge House, which is described in Chapter 5.

The New York State Canal Corporation operates the tugboat *Urger* as a kind of "floating museum." Built in 1901, the *Urger* is one of America's oldest working boats still afloat. Originally a fishing boat in Michigan, the *Urger* eventually served more than 60 years hauling machinery, maintenance equipment, and other boats on the Erie and Champlain Canals.

Today the *Urger* carries information about the history of the canals and how their construction helped New York grow. The *Urger* is a popular attraction at summer canal festivals with adults and children alike touring the tug and taking part in canal-side education programs. During the spring and fall the *Urger* is a field trip destination for fourth grade students, for whom canal history is a required part of the curriculum.

Although all of these museums specifically focus on the canals of New York State, there are other museums, historical societies, and interpretive centers in the Canal Corridor that include canal information in their exhibits. And with the redevelopment of the canal system, more canal museums are sure to be established as communities work to preserve and share their canal heritage.

Canal-side construction of the harbor at Whitehall, the northern terminus of the Champlain Canal, took place during the summer of 2000.

10

NEW YORK'S CANALS:
LOOKING TO THE FUTURE

THE ONLY THING THAT IS
PERMANENT IS CHANGE

New York's Canal System, anchored by the legendary Erie Canal, is and always will be a work in progress. The attention directed towards the canals and the rate of change vary with the times. As commercial shipping diminished, it looked as though the canal system's glory days were ending. The truth is, they were only changing and the best may lie ahead. The canal system will never again shape the growth of a nation, but the future economy of New York State may again be bolstered by this truly incredible resource as it assumes its rightful position as a major tourist attraction for people worldwide. The Erie Canal is a national treasure, and debate continues regarding the role that the National Park Service should have in its development and preservation. Various organizations have been custodians of New York's canals, but they really belong to the people

Waterford, at the eastern terminus of the Erie Canal, has redeveloped its waterfront to include overnight amenities for boaters including power, showers, water hookups, and this visitor's center.

This amphitheater in Baldwinsville's waterfront held its first concert late in 2000. Lock E-24 and the Lock 24 Restaurant can be seen just to the right of the structure. A powerhouse and taintor dam are located to the left. The site is easily accessible to boat and land-based travelers.

Fairport has long offered boaters "in town" dockage, with all needed amenities nearby, as well as sight-seeing cruises.

This is the redeveloped western terminus of the Erie Canal at Tonawanda, providing easy dockage with water and electric service.

who supported and paid for their construction, and have continued their relationship on the water and along their banks. The canal system's meaning is derived from the people who use it for flood control and irrigation, for power generation and recreation. And no one knows precisely what the future will bring.

In 1991, New York State's Constitution was amended establishing the New York State Canal Corporation and the Canal Recreationway Commission, a 24-member body, to advise the corporation regarding canal-related activities. Members of the commission were appointed to represent the range of interests associated with the canal system's future. In 1995 the commission, working with the Canal Corporation, completed the *Canal Revitalization Program,* a $32 million, five-year program, to preserve and rehabilitate canal infrastructure so that it is safe, accessible, and available for future use; to enhance recreational opportunities for water-based and land-side users; and to promote and foster economic development throughout the corridor.

The *Canal Revitalization Program* focuses on four major elements: canal harbors, canal service port and lock projects, the Canalway Trail, and canal system marketing. Required funds will come from a mix of state and federal sources including public-private partnerships. Seven *Canal Harbor* locations have been identified along the system: Tonawanda/North Tonawanda, Rochester, Seneca Falls, Oswego, Little Falls, Waterford, and Whitehall. And in the center of the canal system, the Syracuse Inner Harbor is undergoing an extraordinary redevelopment that will make it the eighth, and perhaps grandest stopover of all. Each harbor will typically include wall improvements to facilitate boater access, docking, boat-launches, and

(Right) Even the smallest villages along the canals offer attractive new resources, including docks, shady gazebos, and restroom and shower facilities.

(Facing page) The Syracuse Inner Harbor is a redevelopment of an Erie Canal Barge terminal that facilitated the transport and storage of fuel for the metropolitan area.

essential boater services such as potable water, electricity, and sewage pump-out. It is hoped that the infrastructure improvements will encourage the private development of marinas, charter and tour boat operations, restaurants, hotels, and other related services.

Canal service port and lock projects are designed to improve canal frontage at locks and towns along the canal system that are between the designated canal harbor locations, so that, for example, fuel service will always be within reach. And the *Canalway Trail* will connect and develop hundreds of miles of trail along the waterway, providing long, well-maintained land segments for hikers and bikers. A *marketing program* will focus on two very different markets: first, the tourists who will be attracted to the system; and second, the entre-

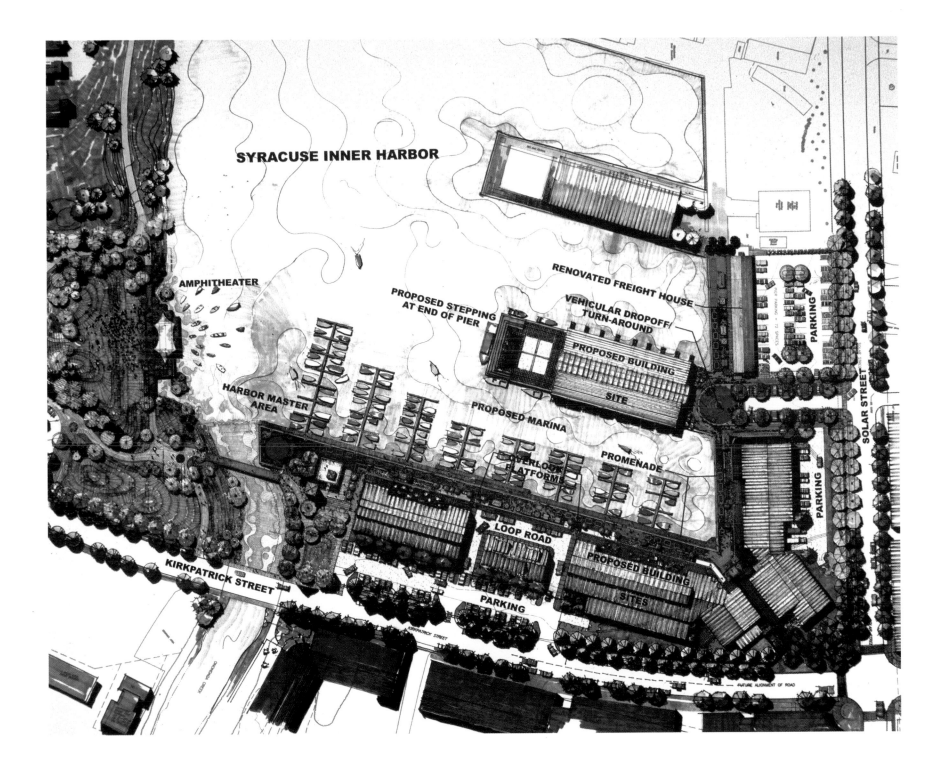

SYRACUSE INNER HARBOR

AMPHITHEATER

RENOVATED FREIGHT HOUSE

PROPOSED STEPPING AT END OF PIER

VEHICULAR DROPOFF/ TURN-AROUND

PROPOSED BUILDING SITE

PARKING

HARBOR MASTER AREA

PROPOSED MARINA

PROMENADE

OVERLOOK PLATFORMS

PARKING

SOLAR STREET

LOOP ROAD

PROPOSED BUILDING SITES

KIRKPATRICK STREET

PARKING

KIRKPATRICK STREET

FUTURE ALIGNMENT OF ROAD

(Left) Portions of the Syracuse Inner Harbor will be operational in 2001, as it develops into a major attraction including one of the largest shopping malls in the country located within walking distance of marina slips.

(Below) This historic freight house that served commercial traffic on the Erie will be converted into a multipurpose visitor's center.

preneurs who will be drawn to the system to build additional water and trail-based resources to support the growing popularity of this premiere travel destination.

The development of such a vast and dynamic resource carries its own Catch 22. People are attracted to the canals by the increasingly available amenities, but investors want an assurance that there will be enough people attracted to the canal system to support their investment *before* their start-up, a sort of "Which comes first, the chicken or the egg?" challenge. The simple truth is that the canals are totally user-friendly today, just as they have been for many years. But they're also rapidly changing, going "upscale" to compete in a world of elevated expectations, thus providing more options for the boater or trail user. Large and small communities all along the route are embracing New York's canals as they did more than 100 years ago, developing their waterfronts anew to again benefit from their canal-side locations and the parade of people passing through.

This is a wonderful time for the canals as they emerge as an important element in New York State's second largest industry, tourism. And it's a wonderful time for each of us who can experience an adventure that is both old and new, fun and illuminating. There's no theme park this large, this old, this diverse, or this memorable. There is only one Erie Canal. It's ours, it's now, and it's a gift from the past that continues to reveal the American spirit.

An interpreter of DeWitt Clinton welcomes people to an international meeting that pays homage to those who built the canals, while exploring their best use in a very different age. Mr. Clinton would, no doubt, be truly proud of America's accomplishments.

The Genesee River allows a short northward excursion to visit Rochester's new waterfront, here filled with people celebrating the World Canal Conference 2000.

INDEX